WHAT PEOPLE ARE SAYING ABOUT

A DESTINY BETWEEN TWO WORLDS

There is a dearth of literature on Okinawa in the Pacific War years, and this book goes a long way toward filling that void. By situating history in a cultural context, it fills a particular need as a resource for educators who teach about Japan and the Pacific War. In my work as an East Asia outreach programming director, I would place this book on my recommended reading list for Japanese history. It should also be of great interest to US military and civilian personnel who live and wo
Dr. Anne Prescott, Director, Five Colle
Studies, Smith College

T0159451

Mr. Fuqua's *A Destiny between Two Worl*
the history and culture of Okinawa as seen through the eyes of one family who lived through the tumultuous events that besieged the region as the Second World War came to a close. This novel is highly recommended for all those who not only are interested in Japanese history but also love great storytelling.
Dr. Randy Green, Asst. Professor, Gyeongnam National University of Science and Technology

Not unlike its title, Fuqua's *A Destiny between Two Worlds* engages the reader with both powerful, emotive narrative and accurate historical context. While many stories portray the lives of those central to the outcome of World War II, the effects on others caught up in events beyond their control remain concealed in the shadows of history. Jacques Fuqua brings these effects to light through the accounts of Koreans and Okinawans living under the yoke of Japanese colonial rule. Their struggles, failures and triumphs during the most trying of times remind us of our common human desire to not just survive but to reach for a better state of existence than what came before. This is a most compelling read that will enlighten and entertain anyone interested in the human condition.

Dr. Derrick Frazier, Political Science, University of Alabama (Tuscaloosa)

A Destiny Between Two Worlds

A Novel about Okinawa

A Destiny Between Two Worlds

A Novel about Okinawa

Jacques L. Fuqua, Jr.

Illustrated by Yoshimi C. Fuqua

Winchester, UK
Washington, USA

First published by Top Hat Books, 2015
Top Hat Books is an imprint of John Hunt Publishing Ltd., Laurel House, Station Approach,
Alresford, Hants, SO24 9JH, UK
office1@jhpbooks.net
www.johnhuntpublishing.com

For distributor details and how to order please visit the 'Ordering' section on our website.

Text copyright: Jacques L. Fuqua, Jr., 2014

ISBN: 978 1 78279 892 7

All rights reserved. Except for brief quotations in critical articles or reviews, no part of this book may be reproduced in any manner without prior written permission from the publishers.

The rights of Jacques L. Fuqua, Jr., as author have been asserted in accordance with the Copyright, Designs and Patents Act 1988.

A CIP catalogue record for this book is available from the British Library.

Design: Stuart Davies

Printed and bound by CPI Group (UK) Ltd, Croydon, CR0 4YY, UK

We operate a distinctive and ethical publishing philosophy in all areas of our business, from our global network of authors to production and worldwide distribution.

Dedication

This work stands as testament to and in gratitude of those Okinawan citizens who have proved to be enduring influences in my life over many years, but most importantly to my late mother-in-law, Chinen Hideko. It was through her love, patience and sincere commitment to teaching me about the long-term plight of Okinawans from which this novel finds its genesis. Indeed, it was her personal experience surviving unexploded ordnance from a US combat aircraft while out picking sweet potatoes that served as the centrifugal force for this work. I will always hold Chinen-様 (sama) in the highest regard and will forever treat her memory with the utmost respect. I again felt her loving hand guiding me as I developed this narrative, especially those areas particularly difficult to articulate.

To Professor Nancy Abelmann (University of Illinois, Urbana-Champaign), a dear friend and mentor, whose wise counsel, boundless energy and laudable record of scholarship have served as beacons for me as I have made my way through academia. It is her example I will continue to strive to emulate.

Finally, special thanks to my life partner, Yoshimi, who has righted my course over thirty years of marriage more times than I can count and who again willingly and unfailingly lent an indispensable hand in the creation of this manuscript. And to my two daughters, Sakura and Miyako, who reinforce for me daily the life lesson I tried to teach them—that nothing is beyond your grasp provided you have commitment and passion.

Yagaji Island
Motobu Peninsula
Nago
East China Sea
Yomitan
Kadena
Hagushi Bay
Pacific Ocean
Naha
Chinen Peninsula
Itoman

List of Major Characters

Alphabetical Order

Arashiro Chiyoko	Close friend of Yoshiko
Atsuko	Munekazu's older sister; married to Isamu
Isamu	Atsuko's husband
Jiro (Kuniyoshi)	Munekazu's best friend and teacher at Naha National School
Kamadū	Munekazu's mother
Kaori	Munekazu's youngest sister; student
Kazuo	Kiyoko's husband
Kido Family	Megumi's family
Kiyoko	Munekazu's younger sister; married to Kazuo
Megumi	Seiho's wife
Munekazu	Protagonist
Nakagusuku Fumiko	Proprietress of the Matsuda-ya
Nakamura (Sergeant)	Close patron of Ushī at comfort station
Seiho	Munekazu's older brother
Tomiko	Yoshiko's older sister
Ushī	Juri at the Matsuda-ya; Munekazu's love interest; and jugun ianfu
Yamashita (Colonel)	Japan Imperial Army officer
Yoshiko	Munekazu's wife

Pronunciation Guide

Vowel pronunciation in both the Japanese and Ryukyuan language is generally similar. Following is a simple guide to assist with properly pronouncing words in either language.

Vowel	**Japanese**	**Ryukyuan**
a	"a" as in ah	"a" as in ah
i	"ē" as in meet	"ē" as in meet
u	"oo" as in soon	"oo" as in soon
e	"e" as in set	"e" as in set
o	"ō" as in only	"ō" as in only
ai	"ī" as in idle	"ī" as in idle

Throughout this work words delineated by (O) are of Okinawan derivation; those marked with (J) are Japanese.

始めに

(In the beginning)

The greatest tragedy of war is time. Time allows us to sculpt with the hand of revisionism memories for future generations, thus rendering the thousands of lives lost and the millions laid asunder, less poignant while in the same instant paving a road that will allow similar mistakes to be repeated.

Chapter I

Of Those Things Yet to Come

Yoshiko ran blindly, almost mindlessly, across the *sūhama* (O: salt fields) near their family home in Takahashi-chō, arms and legs propelling her body forward while her heart raced wildly and her head throbbed with a strange sense of detached awareness. Inexplicably, she felt nothing, almost as if she existed outside her own body and had become a spectator to her own life. She had long since shed her straw sandals and was running barefoot through the outskirts of Naha, Okinawa's capital city. She could hear sounds all around her, but they were muffled, their various sources almost indistinguishable in her current state of frenzy. She dared not look around to survey the scene that now enveloped her for fear of slowing her pace, but she knew she was not the only one running for her life. The other passengers with whom she had been sharing a quiet and uneventful bus ride had also hastily disembarked soon after the vehicle lurched to a sudden and unexpected stop as the first bombs began to fall, shattering the serenity of the island's morning calm.

Yoshiko and the others ran in nearly all directions of the compass, most with little thought to where they were going. Some, like Yoshiko, sought to return to their homes to make sure loved ones were safe—while not consciously aware of it at the time, Yoshiko's primordial instincts were taking her back home to ensure the safety of her two children, Muneyasu and Hideko, left in the care of her mother-in-law, Kamadū. Others in a state of abject panic, simply trying to escape the portending doom from above, ran for their lives in whatever direction appeared to afford the most immediate safety. A good number would come to regret their choices, particularly those who ran in the direction of the city's downtown area, as the storm of steel now raining down from the sky would select its victims with the cold and indiscriminate calculation of a death reaper, one whose icy touch would be felt across the whole of Naha.

It was the tenth day of the tenth month of Showa 19 (Tuesday, October 10, 1944), and the Pacific War had finally reached the Japanese home islands via the shores of Okinawa. But what Yoshiko and the island's other residents would come to realize painfully late was that the events of this day that shattered the routine of their daily lives would only be the beginning—the tip of the American military spear of what would be known as Operation Iceberg: the assault of Okinawa in preparation for the invasion of Japan's main islands. Despite Naha's near complete destruction that day, none of the island's residents could begin to fathom the death, destruction and almost complete obliteration of the island's culture and way of life that would ensue less than seven months later.

Until today, the sight of planes around Okinawa had not been a particularly menacing one; indeed it had become a rather routine occurrence. After all, since Japan's 32nd Army was constituted in March 1944 and garrisoned on Okinawa, the Japanese military had energetically undertaken construction of several airfields on the main island of Okinawa and throughout the Ryukyu island chain. Achieving and maintaining air supremacy against the American enemy was considered the backbone of the Ryukyu defense. The airfields being constructed on Okinawa, Tokunoshima, Yaeyama, Miyako-jima and Ishigaki-jima were considered a mutually supportive air defense network. These, in turn, were considered the outer defensive perimeter of Japan's main islands. So Yoshiko, along with the island's other roughly 450,000 residents, had grown accustomed to aircraft overflying the island on a regular basis. In fact, young Muneyasu sometimes pointed skyward with glee when a passing aircraft flew low enough to catch his attention. But today, of course, was different. These weren't planes of Japan's imperial forces—they were US aircraft launched from aircraft carriers assigned to Admiral William F. Halsey's Third Fleet and under the immediate command of Vice Admiral Marc A. Mitscher as part of his Fast Carrier Task Force. Their mission that day was to prevent Japan's air forces from disrupting US military landings on the island of Leyte in the Philippines. Consequently, Japan's military air bases on Taiwan, China and the Ryukyu island chain were attacked. The city of Naha, however, would also become a major military objective.

In all, two hundred planes took part in the attack, coming in five separate waves. The primary targets were military, particularly the Naha harbor area, where important port facilities and significant supplies of munitions were destroyed, including 5,000,000 rounds of machine gun ammunition. Military airfields, where some eighty aircraft were destroyed on the ground and another twenty-three shot down, were also important targets. (The Japanese Imperial Army's airfields at Kadena, Ie Shima, Naha and Sobe on Okinawa were specifically targeted.) Reportedly, twenty cargo ships, forty-five smaller vessels, four midget submarines, a destroyer escort, minesweeper and submarine tender were also destroyed, along with 300,000 sacks of rice.

Naha's civilian population, however, was not spared either as about 1,000 men, women and children were killed. Property damage throughout the Ryukyus was extensive—11,451 buildings were destroyed, to include large numbers of civilian homes—but the preponderant weight was shouldered by Naha residents as seventy-five percent of Naha's 533 acres were razed during the attack. This scenario would be replicated in April of the following year, only on a much grander scale. As the US military undertook operations to tighten the noose around Japan's imperial military forces in the coming months, the civilians of Okinawa would come to pay a heavy price.

2

Yoshiko, along with a small group of three other bus passengers, quickly realized that the aircraft were targeting the city's center; some planes made strafing runs, the spray of bullets from their mounted machine guns tearing into the ground, buildings, and—she conjectured—people, while others delivered their payloads of bombs. To her reckoning, scores of planes were flying overhead—harbingers of doom—like so many gnats flying about on a sultry summer evening. She briefly thought of her husband, Munekazu, a teacher at the Naha National School, and prayed for his safety. The bus had stopped at a point near Maejima-chō where they were surrounded by the familiar sūhama local fishermen and their families used to produce salt for the city's residents from the waters of the East China Sea. Yoshiko had been heading into downtown Naha to visit with her older sister, Tomiko, who lived in Kume-chō not far from the bus line. They had planned to make a day of it, going to the pottery market together to buy another cistern for Yoshiko's family to catch and store additional rain water. While she enjoyed spending time with her sister, Tomiko's children were a bit rambunctious and quite a handful to manage. She was not looking forward to trying to keep her two young nephews in tow as they tore about the market. They usually settled down if Tomiko bribed them with a treat, one of their favorites being *bukubukucha,* a popular local beverage, which while called tea, was made from unpolished rice whipped into foam and sometimes flavored with ground peanuts. Although a drink enjoyed primarily by women, her nephews, Seitaro and Ichiro, savored it and would set out to find the merchant who sold the tasty treat at a mere hint that they would be rewarded if they behaved.

But Yoshiko now reversed course and traversed on foot back over the ground covered during her bus ride. Her destination was Takahashi-chō, located on the northern perimeter of Naha, where she and her family lived. She thought momentarily about taking cover in one of the several salt making huts that dotted the landscape of the sūhama, but quickly thought better of it, fearing it would not afford any real protection from the attack. Yoshiko wasn't quite sure what she would do once she arrived home—she certainly couldn't stop the strafing bullets or exploding bombs, but she was driven by the need to make sure her family was safe. Yoshiko and the others ran through the sūhama toward the streets of Maejima-chō where the second of three bridges crossing a canal and connecting the northern outskirts of Naha to the city's main downtown area, would take her home. As they emerged from the eastern edge of the sūhama two low flying aircraft sped toward them from the direction of downtown Naha, one dropping its payload about fifty meters away from Yoshiko and the others. Quickly hitting the ground facing away from the bomb while instinctively covering her head and neck, Yoshiko's thoughts were suddenly filled with memories of her relatively short twenty-three-year life—her husband, Munekazu; children—son, Muneyasu and daughter Hideko—her parents, now both deceased; Tomiko and their girlhood experiences together; all these images coalesced in her mind yet remained distinctly clear, feeling as though each had carved out a special place within her head. Curiously, Yoshiko also recounted a conversation she had had with her father when she was about seven years old as he explained that when people were about to die, their lives flashed quickly before their eyes. Strangely, she thought, her life events weren't playing out chronologically as she had always imagined. Rather, they were exploding random and disparate remembrances, seemingly unconnected, yet vividly portrayed in her mind's eye.

Waiting for what she knew would be the end felt like an eternity, but was in reality only a few seconds, after which she felt a dull thud vibrate across the ground and through her body. Lying face down and hugging the ground ever closer, she awaited the inevitable—a strong blast of manmade death breaking free of the steel shell that encased it. Strangely, there was nothing. After waiting a few seconds, her heart nearly bursting through her kimono, she mustered her courage, raised her head and looked around. What she saw was nearly inexplicable intellectually, but instinctively she understood. The bomb meant for her and the others had somehow failed to detonate. Instead, it had buried itself into the ground about one-quarter of its length.

She immediately rose to her feet and began running even harder than she had before. At this point her actions were not the result of any conscious thought or reasoning, rather she moved forward on pure instinct to survive. She quickly glanced over her shoulder to see two of the three passengers also running toward the road leading to the bridge, but the third man was nowhere in sight. Yoshiko stopped and turned, wiping the sweat from her brow while cupping her hands over her eyes in an effort to see further. She could see the third man still lying on the ground. Had he been injured? Was he dead? How could he be if Yoshiko and the others were still alive? She quickly concluded that this man, whom she had never met, was no concern of hers and that she needed to fend for herself and her family. She turned and took a few steps more toward the bridge and stopped again, this time surveying the sky. There were no aircraft in the immediate vicinity although one could very clearly hear the roar of their engines in the distance as they continued the attack on the main downtown area. She also glimpsed the bus she and the others had been riding, which now appeared to be riddled with bullet holes and left a smoldering heap of metal. If anyone had sought refuge within it, they had certainly perished. She had no way of knowing, but that is precisely what the young bus driver had done, unwilling to leave his post. He would be among the many islanders to perish that day.

While scolding herself for doing so, Yoshiko ran back toward the man still lying on the ground. He still hadn't moved although he was clearly alive. Pulling on his arm and trying to drag him across the ground a short distance, Yoshiko yelled at him, "C'mon, let's go. They'll be coming back," referring to the US aircraft that now fully besieged the downtown area. Although small in stature she somehow managed to drag him a few feet.

Still the man would not stand. This time she shrieked at him, "Get on your feet you idiot! Do you want to die out here?" Indeed, she yelled at him with such force that she was not certain the voice she heard was actually her own. She now realized that the man had been frightened so badly that he was simply unable to move. She also realized that the growing anxiety she was directing toward him was a reflection of her own fears. Yoshiko was no hero and was herself scared, a fear unlike any other she had ever experienced. In fact, that she had even returned to render assistance to this stranger went against every survival instinct she was presently feeling, but she was also not without compassion; she simply could not bring herself to leave the man behind as a human target for the planes flying overhead. And this stranger's inability to help himself strangely reminded Yoshiko of her own father during the final months of his life—unable to take care of himself and inexplicably detached from everything and everyone around him—he had not even recognized members of his own family.

Realizing that she lacked the strength to drag him any great distance, Yoshiko stood over the stranger and hoisted him up from beneath his armpits with what seemed her last bit of strength. She was surprised that an old man who appeared so frail could be so difficult to lift. Now standing, Yoshiko pulled his arm to hurry him along and she noticed that the front of the man's kimono was soaked and darkened with the stain of urine, now mixed with the dirt of the road on which he had been laying and through which she had dragged him. Yoshiko was overwhelmed with a sense of pity for him. She also noticed that the man's gaze appeared fixed on some undetermined and distant object, unable to focus on anything within his close field of vision, making him inaccessible to anything in the way of reason. She wasn't even certain that the man could hear her. In the distance she was barely able to make out tiny nondescript figures of Naha residents running panicked throughout the city's streets. She put her arm around the man's waist and hurried him off toward the relative safety of Takahashi-chō.

3

Yoshiko burst through the entry way of her home, breathless and struggling, calling out to her children and mother-in-law, "Muneyasu! Hideko! Anmā!" (O: mother) Her son and daughter answered almost immediately, but the familiar glee in their voices had been replaced with obvious tentativeness. Her mother-in-law, however, did not immediately answer, giving rise to a new fear. She tore through the front of the home toward the back where the kitchen was located and from where her children had answered her call. To Yoshiko's relief, there was her mother-in-law with the children. She sat quietly without movement and fixed her eyes on Yoshiko, widened in disbelief at the events occurring outside their home and trying to comprehend the incomprehensible. Yoshiko, spreading her arms as widely as she could, made an effort to embrace all three simultaneously.

Unsure of what might happen next, she looked directly at Kamadū and said, "Anmā, it's not safe to stay here. We've got to leave. We can return after the bombing is over."

Her mother-in-law nodded slowly without saying a word. With some measure of rationale thought having returned, Yoshiko had the presence of mind to quickly grab a few cooked *umu* (O: sweet potato) and stuff them inside her *basājin* (O: kimono made of banana fiber cloth). Quickly picking up the youngest child, Hideko, and holding her in her right arm and grabbing her son's hand with her left, she nudged Kamadū through the house and out the front door. As soon as the family emerged into the front courtyard Yoshiko recalled she had yet another problem to resolve—Tachikawa-san, the man she had helped escape. Tachikawa was not his real name, indeed she had no idea who this stranger was, but Yoshiko found it somehow easier to give him a name; it helped not only to humanize the situation, but strangely made it easier to extend some measure of compassion and assistance to him.

Tachikawa-san's condition had not improved much. Yoshiko was no medical doctor so could conjure no diagnosis, but in layman's terms she suspected he had simply been scared out of his wits—there was certainly nothing physically wrong with him. Indeed, her diagnosis was not far off. The man was suffering from situational trauma, a result of the sudden and unexpected attack on Naha and his own proximity to it. Most Okinawans intellectually accepted the idea that because Japan was involved in a war against its enemy, America and its allies, there existed a remote possibility that the island could become a military target. But recent fortification of the island with troops and aircraft, along with years of propagandistic bloviating about the superiority of the Japanese soldier, and by extension the invincibility of Japan, like the sound and rhythm of an endless drumbeat, led most to conclude the possibility of an attack was so remote as to be unworthy of serious consideration. After all, the newspapers had for years chronicled Japan's military victories on land and sea in the Pacific. The day's events, however, foretold a different truth.

Unable to render any medical assistance, Yoshiko decided upon the only medicinal remedy she could think of—a shot of *awamori*, a locally produced rice-derived alcohol. With a renewed fear overtaking her, she quickly ran back into the house, returning to the room containing the *tukunuma* (O: decorative alcove) and where the house kami, or god, was thought to reside, located in the first room on the right of the house as one entered, as it was in many Okinawan homes. Grabbing the *dachibin* (O: ceramic awamori hip flask, Illustration 1) containing the awamori from the top of the chest of drawers, along with a small brown envelope containing 200 yen hidden in one of the bottom drawers behind some smoking utensils, Yoshiko quickly ran back out into the courtyard. Slinging the rope affixed to the dachibin over her shoulder and across her chest for ease of carrying, she quickly picked up Hideko, turned and looked squarely, but pleadingly into her mother-in-law's eyes and said, "I need your help. We have to get the children to the caves on the edge of town. You lead Muneyasu toward the caves while I tend to the stranger." She had seen some of their neighbors running for the relative safety of the caves as she returned home. Her persona had again taken on an air of franticness as tears welled up in her eyes.

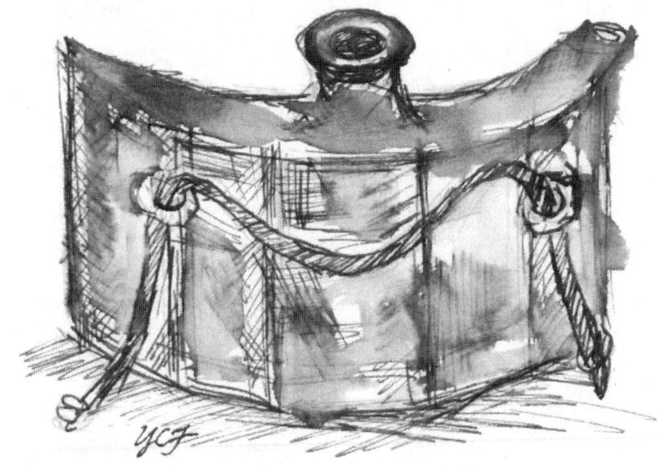

Kamadū, whose condition up to this point could best be described as having been in a walking comatose state, was suddenly jolted back to reality by the explosion of a not too distant bomb. She returned Yoshiko's gaze, and without saying a word, vigorously nodded her head in agreement. Kamadū quickly grabbed her grandson by the arm and moved past the makeshift garden patches in their front yard and toward the crumbling and decrepit old outer coral gate surrounding their home (Illustration 2).

Yoshiko grabbed Tachikawa by the arm and the five of them quickly ran north of the city toward the cliffs honeycombed with caves, the stranger more in tow than running of his own accord. The irony of their current situation had not escaped Yoshiko—she was desperately trying to get her family to the safety of the caves that she had so often scolded Muneyasu to stay away from because of the hidden danger they presented. The caves offered a haven for the highly venomous *habu* snake, which sought their refuge in order to escape the heat of Okinawa's climate (Illustration 3). There were common stories of habu dropping down on the unsuspecting upon entering the caves, leading to grave consequences.

Having reached the cliffs directly behind the Takahashi-chō neighborhood, Yoshiko began to worry that any cave they occupied in this area would be in the direct line of sight of low-flying pilots who might be able to see them hiding inside,

Habu Snake
Illustration 2

making them a potential target. She quickly ushered their small group along the southeast expanse of cliffs, guiding it left as the cliffs turned toward the north. For the first time since the attack began Yoshiko felt a slight sense of relief—while she could still hear the attacking aircraft, they were no longer in sight. Having settled on a cave, Yoshiko signaled Kamadū to have the children crouch as close as possible to the contours of the cliff so they wouldn't stand out. She quickly searched for a long stick that she could use to poke around the cave's entrance and into its labyrinth of crevices that ran its length to locate and remove any hidden habu—yet one more test of courage on a day that had already stretched the core of her being. Truth be known, she not only detested habu, she quite disliked any reptiles, even the island's ubiquitous gecko lizard. She finally broke a branch of sufficient length for the task from a nearby tree. The cave itself was not that large, perhaps extending to a depth of ten feet and about eight feet in width at its widest point, but it would afford the necessary shelter and keep the five of them adequately hidden. Luckily, her cursory inspection uncovered no reptilian occupants. She quickly emerged from the cave and ushered the others in, finally breathing that sigh of relief one does when the fear and adrenalin rush brought about by trying circumstances finally begins to subside. With this, however, also came an almost overwhelming fatigue.

Fighting the urge to close her eyes, she moved the family toward the back of the cave, although tentatively as she was still not certain her quick inspection would have uncovered any habu hidden further back in the darkness afforded by the cave's shadows. Yoshiko moved closer to the front of the cave, bringing Takahashi along with her. As she sat looking out of the cave toward the east, she could see the railroad tracks that ran between Naha and Kadena. There was no train in sight. Suddenly remembering the dachibin hanging from her shoulder, which was about half full, Yoshiko took a short sip of the awamori it contained, half hoping to redouble her fortitude and forget the ordeal in which they presently found themselves. *This stuff tastes awful,* she thought to herself. *How on earth can Munekazu drink this with such enjoyment?* She seldom drank any alcohol. Yoshiko then put the mouth of the dachibin to Tachikawa's mouth, which at first remained closed, sending the liquor trickling down his chin and onto his bare chest exposed by his half-open kimono. Yoshiko then parted his lips with her index finger and poured just a little; this time Tachikawa swallowed a bit of liquor. Yoshiko repeated this action again. By the fourth time Tachikawa quite willingly put the dachibin to his mouth; Yoshiko stopped him on his next attempt as he had begun gulping the vessel's contents—she was not inclined to minister a drunken stranger.

Suddenly, Yoshiko heard the roar of aircraft engines nearby, but she dared not stick her head outside the cave to investigate. She saw one aircraft drop a bomb not too far from the cave entrance—the enemy was bombing the rail line located about seventy-five meters away from their present location. Several pieces of hot metal bomb fragments peppered the outside of the cave, ricocheting about the entrance. She quickly grabbed Tachikawa by the arm, who by now was responding more normally, and joined her family toward the back of the cave. As she sat, she was overcome by her thoughts. *What had led to such a turn of events? What had brought death to their doorstep? How and when would it end?*

And why would the Empire of Japan permit one of its own prefectures and loyal citizens to endure such an attack?

4

Historically, Okinawa had been a peaceful island nation, guided more by the art of diplomacy than the skill of war in its relations with foreign nations. Thus, it had been, and would remain, susceptible to the vagaries of military might, much as the Satsuma domain of southern Kyushu had displayed against the island in February 1609 when it launched a punitive expedition in response to the kingdom's monarch, Sho Nei's, unwillingness to pay formal respects to Japan's new shogun, Tokugawa Ieyasu. And even as the Okinawan royal court continued its voluntary tributary relationship with China during Japan's Edo period (1603-1868), alongside compulsory subjugation to the Shimazu clan of Satsuma, nothing like the events of October 10 had ever been experienced.

Sixty-five years had passed since Okinawa was first absorbed into Japan's administrative structure as a prefecture in 1879. Administratively, Okinawa's assimilation had proved much easier to accomplish than the cultural and social assimilation of its residents into broader Japanese society. There were promises of a better life and prosperity at the beginning; these expectations now left largely unfulfilled owing to the low regard in which Japanese held the islanders, more akin to "colonial natives" than citizens of the Japanese empire. As Yoshiko saw it, many of her fellow islanders had proven themselves as patriotic as other Japanese citizens. Indeed, nearly 25,000 had been pressed into service by the Imperial Army, armed only with rudimentary tools, to build military airstrips on the main island of Okinawa alone. Many others labored digging fortifications for 32nd Army soldiers. The empire's clarion call for a *Greater East Asia Co-prosperity Sphere* in 1940 had given rise to renewed hope among many Okinawans that the discrimination and second-class citizen status the islanders suffered under Japanese rule would abate and that they would take their rightful place among Japan's citizenry. None of this had happened, leaving Yoshiko, and others like her, disillusioned.

She and Munekazu differed quite significantly in their respective assessments of Japanese rule and its effect on Okinawa. Munekazu fervently believed that Okinawans needed to discard the old island traditions and Ryukyuan language in order to fully assimilate into Japanese culture and only then would Okinawa's true potential within the Japanese empire be realized. "Okinawa for Japan, Japan for Okinawa," Yoshiko now recalled was one of his sayings. He foresaw economic, political and social benefits for islanders accruing from such a course. He considered the "old ways" to be shackles to the past; Okinawa's future laid with Japan. One of their worst disagreements on this topic occurred when Munekazu overheard a discussion Yoshiko and Kamadū were having about the loss Okinawan womanhood suffered in 1899 when Japan's Meiji government outlawed their practice of *hajichi* (O: women tattooing the backs of their hands in the old Ryukyuan style) that most would have done when a young girl came of age or was married. (Hajichi designs differed by locale. Illustration 4) He became so furious that it surprised even Yoshiko. The gist of his argument centered on the bad influence discussions like this might have on their children, his standing as an educator, and the broader deleterious impact such acts would have on Okinawa vis à vis Japan. (During this argument, Kamadū remained silent. Having been born in 1874, not long after the Meiji Restoration [1868] and before Okinawa's formal assimilation into Japan's administrative structure, her own hands were tattooed in the hajichi style.) Never fully certain why he reacted as strongly as he had, Yoshiko decided it was best to avoid such sensitive topics in the future.

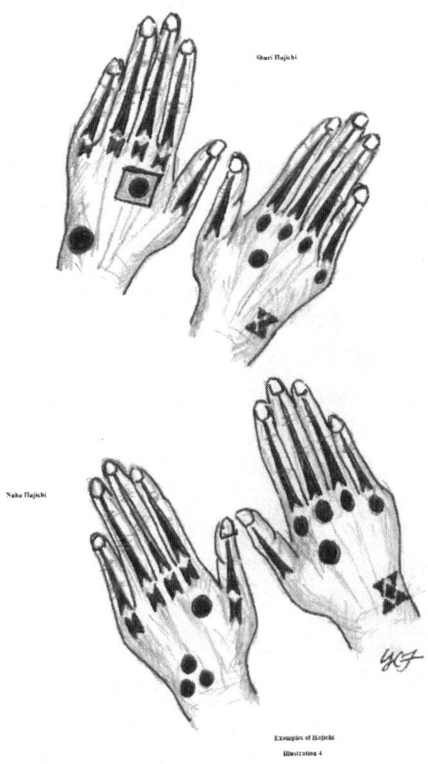

Examples of Hajichi

Illustration 4

Yoshiko's attitude toward Japanese rule, on the other hand, was one of ambivalence—she did not see her life necessarily benefiting as a citizen of Japan. While she was resigned to the islanders' second-class status within Japan's social hierarchy, she sometimes chafed at the thought of it. What she had grown to resent most was the subjugation, and in some cases, eradication of Okinawan culture in favor of the larger Japanese culture. Under the euphemistically derived term of *dōka* (J: assimilation) the Japanese government sought to transform Okinawans into imperial subjects by replacing indigenous language, culture, clothing and general behavior with those aligning more closely with the sensibilities of the Japanese. To her way of thinking, the entire concept of dōka was manifested in the statue of the Meiji emperor erected at Naminoue in which he is described as *kokka,* or the nation, and the price for Japan's recognition of Okinawa was full assimilation—cultural, political, and social. She, on the other hand, regarded the island's traditions and culture as the sum total of who their ancestors were, and in turn, who they now were. *One can't simply ignore his own spirit,* she thought. Munekazu considered Yoshiko's attitude symptomatic of the problems Okinawans confronted and often became quite exasperated with her when this topic came up; they learned to avoid discussion of it as much as possible, more so for Munekazu's sake than for Yoshiko's. She briefly wondered how the day's events might affect his thinking.

After months of reading about Imperial Army and Navy military victories over their enemy throughout the Pacific, war was now on the shores of their home. How could this happen if Japan was defeating the enemy? Where was the might of the Imperial Navy that would drive off these attackers? Where were the aircraft that now defended the island? These were the thoughts that filled Yoshiko's mind. Despite any feelings of ambivalence in the abstract, she fully understood that Japanese and Okinawans alike shared a common fate in this war. And the anger and growing resentment she was now feeling was directed at their common enemy—America. Yoshiko had no way of knowing, but the bulk of the Imperial Japanese Navy's strength had been destroyed months earlier in the battle of the Philippine Sea (June 19-20, 1944) against US naval forces. In that engagement, the Japanese Navy lost three aircraft carriers and approximately 600 aircraft—it ceased to function as an effective fighting force. Nor did she realize at the time that the day's attack had caught the island's defenders completely off guard, thus no credible defense had been or could be mounted.

She sat in the dark cave huddled with her family, at once feeling fatigued, numb and plagued by a strange yet growing sense of betrayal. There had been rumors several weeks earlier that US aircraft may have flown over Okinawa's airspace, but she and Munekazu chose not to give those rumors any credence. They had simply dismissed the talk as idle gossip. "Why would US aircraft risk the might of the imperial military forces of Japan if the enemy was being defeated throughout the Pacific?" Besides, there had been no attack and the absence of any at the time confirmed for them the emptiness of the rumors. Unschooled in military tactics, it never occurred to them that US bombers had indeed flown over Okinawa on September 29 to conduct reconnaissance of Okinawa and its outer lying islands in preparation for this and subsequent attacks.

Absorbed with such thoughts, Yoshiko had completely forgotten the umu she brought along for the children that remained tucked away inside her basājin.

"Muneyasu," she called. He quickly ran to her side. "Here are two umu. One is for Anmā." Then breaking the other in half, she said, "And these are for you and Hideko." She then returned to the thoughts that preoccupied her, hardly noticing her own hunger pangs or her mother-in-law singing softly to Hideko to help keep her calm.

5

The attacks had begun at 8:00am and stopped just as suddenly by about 4:00pm, returning the skies over Naha to an uncomfortable silence; its residents had endured a full eight hours of nerve-wracking uncertainty. With the tentativeness of one walking across an unsteady rope bridge, the five members of Yoshiko's party slowly emerged from the cave looking skyward to ensure the aircraft had in fact departed the area. With the immediate danger gone, Yoshiko and Kamadū now had both children in tow as they quickly moved back toward their neighborhood, apprehensive at what sights might await them.

Tachikawa followed slowly, but now at least under his own power. Had their home been completely destroyed? How many of their neighbors might have perished in the attack? As they rounded the bend in the coral cliffs, Yoshiko was relieved to see others emerging from the southern facing caves that provided a line of sight to distant downtown Naha. In the background she could hear the tormented wailing of others—she assumed it was the result of fear, relief or expressions of grief for those who might not have survived the attack, but she did not stop to check on them. As they and others moved away from the caves and toward their homes she heard someone yell, "*tanmē, tanmē*" (O: grandfather, grandfather) and saw a young girl who couldn't have been more than nine years old come running in their direction. She was soon followed by the rest of what appeared to be her family—two younger boys, a woman and man. The woman was older than Yoshiko, but who even in her disheveled state she could tell was from a well-to-do family—it was "Tachikawa's" family. Now reunited and freed from the burden of uncertainty that accompanied the day's events, they spent several minutes in tearful embraces. She learned that the man she had helped was actually Hanashiro Tetsuya, a retired petty prefectural government bureaucrat who lived with the family of his son in Sougenji-chō, the neighboring hamlet.

By this time, Yoshiko was nearly overwhelmed as waves of conflicting emotion engulfed her, but she was suddenly grateful that she had returned to help Hanashiro. She could not imagine the sadness her own family would have suffered had their father and husband been found dead in the sūhama through which they had initially fled to safety or worse yet, had never been found at all. Then the remaining gravity of their situation hit with full force—she had not yet heard from Munekazu. Had he survived? Was he safe? The Naha National School was located in downtown Naha and much closer to the area the enemy had targeted.

Anxious to return home, Yoshiko and Kamadū thanked Hanashiro's son and wife for their kindness as they both entreated them to come to their home for tea and cakes. *Tea and cakes?* Kamadū thought rather quizzically. *Really, at a time like this?* She supposed people responded to disaster in different ways. Unlike the elder Hanashiro, who had shut down emotionally when confronted by danger, the husband and wife appeared to take comfort in adhering to social conventions—Yoshiko had helped the elder Hanashiro, thus they must in some way extend a reciprocal kindness recognizing what she had done for their family. When considered from that perspective their behavior seemed less odd to her, but still both Yoshiko and Kamadū were anxious to return to their own home to find out what fate had befallen Munekazu and assess any damage that might have occurred. They bowed deeply to the Hanashiro family promising to be in touch once things had settled down and quickly left them to return home.

The scene that greeted Yoshiko, Kamadū and the children when they finally reached their home was entirely unexpected—their house had survived the morning attack unscathed. Indeed, most of the neighborhood appeared to have survived largely intact. Despite the day's good fortune, Yoshiko again was struck by the realization of how their home had become a monument to the times and decades of impoverishment that beleaguered the island and its people. It once stood as a structure that, while not grandiose, was a symbol of earlier affluence enjoyed among some Okinawans—before the onset of Japan's war in the Pacific in 1937 or even before the great 1923 Kanto earthquake, a contributing factor to the Showa period depression that adversely impacted Okinawa as well. Their home had fallen into a state of disrepair, as indeed had many of the homes in the area, although to a lesser degree. The specially crafted red roof tiles were now noticeably chipped and cracked—there was no extra money to see to such mundane tasks anymore. Even if there had been, neighbors would have considered these efforts a meaningless exercise in putting on airs and wartime rationing had long ago curtailed such activities in any case. The times demanded a departure from such extravagance and greater vigilance toward austerity.

Munekazu and Yoshiko were luckier than some of their neighbors—the disrepair into which their roof had fallen remained by all measures superficial, primarily due to the past diligence with which Munekazu's father and grandfather had kept up the old place even during the most trying of times—Munekazu, however, was unskilled in such tasks. Some neighbors, like the Miyazato family, were forced to put wooden buckets throughout their homes during heavy rains to catch the sometimes cascading water falling from the roof. The single benefit to this was that the water could be used for other purposes if collected in cisterns. Both Yoshiko and Munekazu realized that it was only a matter of time before their home too suffered a fate similar to those surrounding it—still, it remained their home and that of their ancestors; with good fortune it would next pass to Muneyasu. Some of the tatami mats had also become worn and tattered, although their general state was not too objectionable. Kamadū was prepared to suffer a few indignities for the Japanese war effort, but she strangely drew the line at the home's tatami mats, looking after them assiduously. She considered tatami in good repair the last vestige of civilized living and thus demanded that the family expend the effort necessary to keep them in useable condition.

The grounds surrounding the home had long before been transformed into a patchwork of vegetable gardens and animal pens to help sustain the family—their former beauty reduced to mere functionality. Now instead of the various flora that had once adorned the grounds, Chinese bitter melon, umu and magwood patches formed a strange hodgepodge around their home's exterior. The backyard had undergone similar modification long ago, albeit for purposes of accommodating the family's pigs, the meat, extremities and lard of which would be used in various ways. The meat and extremities (ears and feet) would be shared among family and neighbors during celebrations of Obon and the New Year. The lard was indispensable to daily life and used for cooking the family's meals. Nothing could afford to be wasted; even umu leaves were used in soups. In short, their home was, by any measure, a farm, but they were quite fortunate when compared to the destitute conditions in which many other Okinawans lived.

As Yoshiko looked toward the direction of downtown Naha, however, multiple columns of billowing black smoke and a heavy haze hovering above the city's horizon evidenced an entirely different narrative. The downtown and surrounding areas had clearly borne the brunt of the day's attack.

"Munekazu, where are you?" she repeatedly asked, her thoughts becoming more frantic as time passed. Fatigued, but remaining slightly agitated awaiting word from Munekazu, Yoshiko found solace in making preparations for her ritual ceremony.

Yoshiko was a very traditional wife, adhering to centuries-old Ryukyuan customs and practices. One of these customs called for giving prayers of thanks to the god of the hearth for any good fortune the family enjoyed, in this case for emerging safely from the attacks. After completing her prayers at the hearth, she moved to the tukunuma to continue the ritual. Having completed this task, she then moved on to the gate outside their home to pray. All this was done to show proper reverence and thanks to the kami for their blessings. As senior female of their household, a role passed on to her after her father-in-law's death and her assumption of the position as head female of the household, undertaking these rituals had become solely her responsibility. She feared failure to show proper thanks and reverence would bring *ugwanbusuku* (O: divine calamity) on the household. These were precisely the traditions Munekazu regarded as outmoded, yet had grown up with, only it was Kamadū, his mother, who had performed them.

As Yoshiko was undertaking the ritual in the front courtyard area, she let out an uncontrollable shriek—she saw Munekazu walk into the courtyard. Stopping in the middle of her chant, she called to her children and mother-in-law, all while hugging Munekazu. He was still visibly shaken by the day's events, but unharmed.

Chapter II

A Darker Side of Paradise

Munekazu and the children sat around the dinner table, he consumed in thought about the day's events and barely noticing the simple evening meal of umu, radishes and soup with boiled umu leaves Yoshiko had served. Muneyasu and Hideko, on the other hand, having eaten only a small bit of umu earlier in the day while in the cave, ravenously tore into the evening's repast. Kamadū and Yoshiko, now in the kitchen, chatted animatedly with neighborhood friends who had dropped by to check on the family and share their thoughts on the earlier attack and what it might portend for the future. Yoshiko's kitchen often served as their meeting place. After all, Kamadū was considered the senior member of their informal group and propriety demanded such displays of filial piety.

Munekazu, sitting at the table with his chin resting in the palm of one hand while mindlessly tapping the end of a chopstick on the tabletop with the other, had long since tried to tune out the women, having regarded their talk as mere banality.

What meaning would the gossip of women bring to greater understanding about the enemy's attack? he thought. *This is nothing more than idle chatter to help pass their time.* Besides, in his estimation, Yoshiko and most of her friends were of similar opinion—they were distrustful of the Japanese government and in little ways sought to protect the traditions of Ryukyuan culture, much like Yoshiko's efforts to pay homage to the god of the hearth after returning from the caves, which he regarded as counterproductive.

Our duty is to support our emperor and country at this important time so Okinawa plays a meaningful role in Japan's war victory and we reap the benefit of our present sacrifices after the war. Munekazu simply could not envisage any scenario under which Japan would not emerge victorious over its enemies. *The only uncertainty is how quickly Japan can bring about victory,* he thought. *What other reasonable conclusion could there be, when all news of the war reports victory after victory for the Imperial Army and Navy.* But because his own mind was so closed to the possibility that Yoshiko and her friends might offer important insights into what could actually be happening with Japan's war effort against the United States and its allies, indeed closed to anyone who did not share his belief in the infallibility of Japan's empire, he missed tantalizing clues the women suggested during their discussion.

Arashiro Chiyoko chimed in quite forcefully and defiantly as their discussion continued. "What about the Tsushima-maru?"

Offered in part as a rhetorical question and in part challenging the others to provide a logical alternative response, she keenly searched the eyes of the other women with her in Yoshiko's kitchen. They merely looked at each other while nodding in assent.

Feeling that her argument was gathering momentum among the group's members, she continued. "How can Japan be winning the war when a ship filled with Okinawan school children was sunk on its way to Kagoshima? It wasn't sunk by the Japanese navy, was it?"

"Maybe it was—it might have been aiming at an enemy ship and missed completely," quipped Takashiro Hiromi, known for her wit and sharp tongue throughout the neighborhood.

While Yoshiko and the others laughed haltingly, she was uncomfortable joking about such a matter. Death hardly seemed a topic of levity to her. Kamadū offered that the fate of the Tsushima-maru was only rumor; there was no evidence or confirmation that it had been sunk.

Chiyoko, undeterred, continued. "Why then haven't the parents of Nanbu National School students heard from their children? Or from students of other schools for that matter? The ship sailed in late August and still not a word from any of them? *Masakā*!" (O: nonsense) she exclaimed. "No one knows for sure how many Okinawans might have died when that ship was attacked, but I'll bet it was a few thousand. And if Japanese ships are being sunk in our home waters there's no telling what might come next."

Try as he might to ignore them, Munekazu had by this time tuned back in to the women's conversation. Feeling a growing sense of exasperation, he prepared to leave the house for a walk, despite the lateness of the hour. Encouraging the children to quickly finish their meal so they could go to bed, he stood and moved toward the home's entrance at which point he overheard one of the women ask with a sense of foreboding, "What does this mean for us? Is this a sign that things have turned badly?"

Unable to contain his growing frustration, he turned on his heels and headed back toward the kitchen. "Why do you say these things? What's the use of empty speculation? Government officials keep us informed of the war's progress—victory is being reported throughout the Pacific and still you doubt the outcome of our efforts. Share in the burden of Japan's fight to ensure Okinawa's future," he said, almost pleadingly. And with that, he turned and left the house.

The women, dumbfounded by Munekazu's sudden appearance and outburst, but not by the persuasiveness of his argument, sat quietly looking at one another and cautiously eyeing Yoshiko, who had cast her gaze downward and continued sipping her tea without saying a word. Chiyoko herself managed only to utter a meaningless "hmpf," clicking her tongue against the roof of her mouth and turning away from the direction of Munekazu, intent on continuing their discussion.

She had never been his favorite among Yoshiko's friends. Munekazu's impression of Chiyoko was that she tended to be a bit opinionated and headstrong, ironically characteristics he was readily able to discern in her, but not in himself. His dislike of

Chiyoko was further fuelled by what he regarded as her somewhat objectionable facial features, a point over which he sometimes chided himself for its superficiality, but he could not help himself. At times he even found himself secretly studying her face intently. None of the individual components were in and of themselves distasteful—chin, nose, mouth, eyes, or forehead. But he somehow found their sum total unusual. Each had sharp angular cuts to them: her chin jutting out from the bottom of her head; the nose small and pointed; high angular cheekbones and a rather large forehead, which together made her an unpalatable sight to Munekazu. All this was set atop a lanky and unusually tall frame for an Okinawan woman. He recognized his feelings as irrational, perhaps even childish, but dismissed them as part of the human condition—there are those people in life one is destined to dislike no matter what the circumstances.

Arashiro Chiyoko was not too far afield in her assessment of circumstances surrounding the Tsushima-maru. The ship was part of a larger effort undertaken by Imperial General Headquarters to evacuate Okinawan civilians to the island of Kyushu, roughly 80,000 of whom were so relocated. The ill-fated Tsushima-maru set sail from Naha port as part of Convoy Namo 103 on August 21 (Showa 19, 1944) en route to Kagoshima, located on the southwestern tip of Kyushu, Japan's southernmost of its four main islands. The convoy, however, changed course after departure and headed toward Nagasaki. The ship was sunk on August 22 just after 10:00pm by the US Navy submarine *Bowfin* near the island of Akusekijima. Of the Tsushima-maru's estimated 1,788 passengers, 1,476 perished on that stormy August night, nearly 800 of whom were school children. The Japanese government did not officially divulge the ship's fate, indeed government and police officials took active measures to maintain the secrecy of the Tsushima-maru's sinking to include threatening survivors into silence, but rumors among Okinawa's residents took root nonetheless, not through direct knowledge, but rather through a dearth of information.

Tragic as the Tsushima-maru incident had been, it was only a single contributing factor to the overall growing sense of foreboding enveloping the island. Rumors had engulfed Naha several months earlier surrounding the fate of a troop transport ship, Toyama-maru, which never arrived on the island as scheduled, but about which no additional information had been forthcoming—and not without good reason. Carrying 6,000 troops of the 44th Independent Mixed Brigade, it was sunk on its voyage to Okinawa on June 29, 1944 by the US Navy submarine *Sturgeon*. With only 600 soldiers surviving the attack, it remains among the top ten maritime disasters of all time.

Having left Kamadū, Yoshiko and the other women behind, Munekazu was now alone with his thoughts and could no longer hide behind the protective veil of his patriotic fervor for comfort or solace. While annoyed with the women's discussion on purely philosophical grounds, his real irritation was with what he was coming to realize was his own fear—not of Japan's defeat, but personal loss. As a teacher at the Naha National School, he had been notified several weeks earlier that he, along with other teachers at the school, would be required to lead their students to mainland Japan as well, perhaps as early as December. The initial indication was that their destination would be Miyazaki prefecture on Kyushu island. His first reaction, ignoring the ramifications of such circumstances, was one of pride—he was being asked to make a measurable contribution to the war effort. However, as the full implications of what he was being asked to do set in, he began to feel a certain inexplicable emptiness. Part of it, of course, was the necessity of leaving behind the family he loved so dearly. But that didn't account for the entirety of what he was experiencing. Still, he was unable to form his feelings into anything concrete that would offer greater insight—and that amorphous sense of unease that had begun to envelop him would continue leaving him unnerved.

He had not yet broken the news to Yoshiko, his mother or the children—he could not bring himself to say the words that would lead to significant disruption in their lives. As a teacher at a national school, he could not refuse a prefectural order to evacuate. He remained hopeful, however, that his family too would somehow be able to accompany him. *What if,* he thought uncomfortably, *he and his family had been selected for the Tsushima-maru and it had indeed been sunk? What would have become of them?* Conceptually, he understood that sacrifice for the sake of Japan's victory was a wartime necessity, but even mere discussion of this rumor began to disquiet him a bit. What he had not divulged to anyone, even Kuniyoshi Jiro, one of his closest colleagues at Naha National School who too was a teacher of first year advanced students, was that he had slipped away during the day on August 21 to witness the departure of Nanbu National School students and teachers, along with other islanders. The scene that greeted him was a dismal one, quickly washing away any initial feelings of pride he had felt, replaced by a slow but steady, nearly overpowering presentiment, not unlike a cauldron slowly bubbling over with too much cooking rice. A throng of people gathered at the port that day, many for boarding, but also those who had come to see off loved ones. In fact, there were so many people that he was unable to identify anyone he knew in the mass of humanity. The crowd was so large that what he saw no longer resembled a group of individual human beings. Rather they had coalesced into a single entity resembling an amoeba—expanding here, contracting there, as this now-living organism moved about the port area.

Passengers, family members and friends alike had begun gathering before sunrise—he arrived about three o'clock in the afternoon and still no one had been permitted to board. It wasn't until after four o'clock that he recalled having heard the first call to board. Subjected to the unrelenting August sun, oppressively humid and breezeless Okinawan summer, and the fetid air generated by such a large confined crowd, he witnessed several people getting sick from the heat and lack of water. He watched while friends and family scurried about trying to assist the ill. What resonated most with him, however, were the many parents seeing off their children. Mothers tearfully hugged their young children and tucked away *furoshiki* (J: traditional Japanese cloth used to wrap and carry various things) laden with home-cooked foods for the voyage to the mainland. Fathers patted the shoulders of their young sons in encouragement letting them know everything would be alright. It was at once touching and gut-wrenching—there was glee among most children at the prospect of experiencing the unknown—large cities, spring cherry blossoms and other unfamiliar things of mainland Japan—and trepidation among the many parents for the same reason. The scene was, in a word, surreal.

The ship was a large vessel, so large in fact that it could not dock in port. In the distance it looked to him to be the equivalent of a four-story building, maybe five. Several small fishing vessels were pressed into service and used to ferry passengers out to the Tsushima-maru and he recalled watching passengers climb up rope ladders to reach the ship's deck—men, women and children. The scene that greeted him that day—the reality of the evacuation—remained indelibly imprinted in his mind's eye.

His thoughts then returned to the chaos that had earlier enveloped Naha National School and the scenes of destruction that confronted him in downtown Naha. As far as he knew at the time, none of the children nor any school staff had been lost in that attack because most of the bombs targeted other areas of the city, but primarily Naha port. Still, the school had suffered some structural damage, mostly shattered windows and destruction of smaller unoccupied buildings. Several students and teachers had been wounded by shrapnel and flying glass, but nothing too serious. The school medical staff had quickly tended to the injured. Unknown to anyone at the time, two students had indeed become victims of the attack, the result of their fateful decision to dally on the way to school.

By this time schools no longer resembled that for which Munekazu had studied and trained; they had been transformed into paramilitary organizations. Imperial Army personnel were now assigned to organize students and teachers in support the war effort and fortify the island's defenses. Girls and boys alike at Naha National School now labored carrying tiles at Oroku airfield where barracks were being newly constructed. He had always considered this a point of pride—Okinawans doing their part to ensure Japan's victory, but there now crept into his consciousness a certain hollowness of purpose, which he quickly put out of his mind. "Where was the Tsushima-maru?"

Once the attack was under way the scene inside the school turned into one of bedlam with students scrambling to reach the relative safety of classrooms under the direction of Army personnel; the principal trying to retrieve the portraits of Emperor Hirohito and Empress Nagako as he was the designated school official responsible for ensuring their safety; and teachers trying to curb students' youthful curiosity and keep them away from windows for fear of possible flying glass. Anxious to ensure his family's safety, he left the school grounds once all students and fellow teachers were accounted for and an inspection of the school revealed no substantive damage. It was only then that school officials realized two of their students were missing and someone dispatched to their homes to make appropriate inquiries.

Staff and students alike were dismissed and urged to return home. Munekazu was, however, unprepared for the scene of carnage and destruction that greeted him. Large plumes of billowing black and grey smoke dotted downtown Naha like long cords of thick twisted rope and fires visible as far as the eye could see. He was beset by the smoldering ruins of once vibrant shops and his nostrils assailed by the strong choking stench of charred bodies and burning wood that permeated the air; and the dead littered the streets while the wounded were ministered by military and medical personnel. Even rats, now dislodged from their usual hiding places, scurried about looking for safety. Although he saw all the destruction and carnage, strangely he was unable to grasp its full meaning or impact. One recollection had, however, registered and particularly troubled him. The sight of a family—mother, daughter, and father—their bodies lying mangled on the roadside. The young girl was perhaps Hideko's age, no more than three or four years old. She was in the arms of her mother who was simply unable to protect her daughter or herself from the attack. The father, barely alive tried to call out for help but managed nothing more than a barely audible whisper. Munekazu was moved to the point that he looked for assistance for the dying man, but suspected government personnel, busily trying to tend to others, had given him up for dead. He came across two Army soldiers surveying the area, one with a cigarette in his mouth, and approached them for help. The soldier with the cigarette looked at the other momentarily and then followed Munekazu back to the area where the injured man lay on the sidewalk. The soldier looked at him for a few seconds, inhaled deeply from his cigarette and while exhaling nonchalantly shook his head, and said, "He is already dead or will be in a few minutes. There's nothing we can do for him. We need to help those who can be helped," and with that returned to his comrade to look for others to assist.

Munekazu was as much struck by the soldier's casual assessment of the situation as he had been overwhelmed when he first came upon the family. *Is life so cheap?* he thought to himself. *Surely this man is worth some effort at saving, or at least comforting. The sum total of his life is strewn across the road in front of us and we walk over him like so much trash?*

Munekazu knelt down, taking hold of one of the stranger's bloodied hands, and struggled to find words of comfort as the man called out the names of his wife and daughter, or at least he presumed it was his family for whom he was calling. It was then Munekazu realized that the stranger had been blinded during the attack. He was unable to see their bodies lying next to him. As Munekazu began speaking to him, he noticed what little life had been left in the man was now gone. *What a pitiful ending,* he thought. He stayed with the stranger for a few minutes in an attempt to add some measure of dignity to the otherwise ignominious finality he and his family had suffered. He then rushed home to see to his own family.

Ensconced in these thoughts as he continued walking through Takahashi-chō and the adjacent neighborhood of Sougenji-chō, Munekazu suddenly stopped in his tracks and was overcome by a sudden foreboding tinged with a sense of guilt. He recalled the figure of whom he had grown so fond over the past year and one whose name now filled his consciousness—Ushī. In his haste to return home and ensure his family's safety, he had forgotten all about the welfare of his favorite *juri* (J: geisha) at the Matsuda-ya, or Matsuda House. Indeed, he had not even thought to check on how the Tsuji district, which served as Naha's entertainment center, had fared during the attack. For less noble reasons he hoped the Matsuda had not sustained too much damage: it was the one place where he could see Ushī. Adding to his trepidation was recollection of the stories his father told him as a child of the great Naha fire in October of Taisho 8 (1919) that resulted in 600 homes being burned down completely along with theaters and the entertainment district. Of course, all that had been rebuilt, but most of the buildings were still constructed of wood and thus easily destroyed.

Yoshiko of course, and many of their friends, would never condone his relationship with Ushī, if it could even be called such, so they could never be seen in public together. The occasional male dalliance was considered a normal part of life, but their relationship had blossomed into more than a meaningless interlude and the Matsuda offered a quiet haven for their continued trysts, although it still maintained a certain air of "business." Even Jiro, who he trusted a good deal, did not know the full extent of Munekazu's feelings for Ushī. The need to maintain such secrecy, however, did not diminish the intensity of his feelings for her nor his willingness to go to great lengths to arrange his schedule and salary to see her once or twice a month. He suspected that Yoshiko had some inkling of the relationship although she did not know of Ushī in particular. Provided his affairs with her were handled with discretion, Yoshiko was content not to pry. He never had, however, nor would he ever consider Ushī in the same regard as he did Yoshiko. The life he had with his wife was sacrosanct, in fact he considered Yoshiko irreplaceable. He loved her dearly. Nonetheless, Munekazu had become smitten with Ushī that balmy September evening a year ago when Jiro first introduced him to the Matsuda-ya. And the intensity of his feelings for her since that time had only strengthened, yet it was not the love he felt for Yoshiko. He had long since given up trying to understand his feelings for Ushī—they were simply too complicated to make sense of. It was easier for him to reductively rationalize his incongruence to human frailty.

Ushī was special in Munekazu's eyes—different from the other juri at the Matsuda-ya who struck him as both coarse and crude in their obvious coquettishness. She, on the other hand, was an amalgam of intriguing contradiction. Ushī, who was only seventeen years old, was at once disarming with her youthful innocence, yet graced with wisdom and maturity that belied her years. Engaging, yet aloof; accessible, yet unattainable; feminine, yet with an air of indestructibility—these were the dichotomies that drew Munekazu to Ushī despite being five years her senior. There was also an inexplicable sadness about her that touched him. Beyond her physical attractiveness—soft olive-colored skin that was without blemish, almond-shaped eyes, a gently featured face atop her long slender neck and jet-black hair—there existed in Ushī an inner beauty. She reminded him of the women in the reproduction of the Kiyomitsu II triptych ukiyoe print of the happy, sad and angry drinkers that hung in the main hallway of the Matsuda-ya. He wasn't much of an ukiyoe aficionado, but this was by far his favorite woodblock print. Specifically, it was the angry drinker Ushī most resembled, who the artist had imbued with an air of obvious self-assurance while still exuding traditional Japanese femininity and beauty.

The evening was warm and quiet with a soft breeze blowing across a starlit sky from the direction of the East China Sea. It was a stark contrast to the day's beginning. As he continued walking, his desire to check on Ushī's well-being was nearly overpowering, but propriety simply would not permit him to head down to the Tsuji district on a night like this. As there was little he could do about it at the moment, he quietly prayed that she was safe and then did his best to push her out of his mind.

2

Dazed, unable to breathe and in a total state of consternation, Ushī slowly opened her eyes. She looked about trying to make sense of the scene laid out before her, but the usual points of reference no longer existed. The dust and debris surrounding her not only lent an air of surrealism to what was wholly incomprehensible, it choked her as she gasped for air. The front of the building in which the Matsuda-ya had been housed no longer existed—the coral gate surrounding the establishment, wooden shoji-like sliding doors and windows, indeed the entire edifice having been completely destroyed only moments before. Adding to her confusion was the fact that she could look straight up and see the rain-laden clouds billowing above—where had the second floor of the Matsuda-ya gone? Just as she was trying desperately to gather her thoughts, she caught the acrid scent of burning wood nearby. Having the presence of mind to begin looking for a way out of the jumbled mass of debris that had only moments before represented the sum total of her life, she picked herself up off the floor and looked around. There seemed no way out, but she realized that the stench and crackle of burning wood was closer than she first suspected. It was, however, difficult to see through the haze caused by settling dust and smoke.

Purposefully but without panic, she tried several different directions to make her escape, but to no avail. She found her way blocked by piles of lumber and remnants of tanshi and other furniture. As she tried to move toward what she thought had been the rear of the establishment she stopped in her tracks, greeted by a ghastly sight—the mangled, bloodied and lifeless body of Tsurū, the friend with whom she had been tidying up the Matsuda-ya. Tsurū had been on the second floor, Ushī on the ground floor. She gasped in silent horror, her hands instinctively raised to cover her mouth as tears welled in her eyes, wanting desperately to turn away from the scene of horror confronting her, but somehow unable to do so. Finally, after several minutes, as if the momentum had been building up inside like cascading water fills a hole, she let out a loud shriek. Ironically, it was her screams at the death of her friend that alerted rescue workers outside there was a survivor in the rubble of the Matsuda-ya; they had already passed by the remains assuming no one had survived.

Finally, she heard someone shout, "Is there anyone in there?" and "Are you alright?"

Still choking from the dust and smoke, she tried to respond, but couldn't replicate her earlier feat to make herself heard for lack of breath. Looking around, her eyes caught sight of the small brass bell that hung on the inside of what had been the Matsuda-ya's front entrance and that once announced the arrival of guests. Hurriedly she moved across the room, draping a piece of cloth over her nose and mouth as she went trying to keep the dust at bay, and began ringing the bell to alert those outside of her whereabouts. *Strange,* she thought, *the bell always seemed loud enough to hear wherever one was when inside the Matsuda-ya.* It had not been a particularly large establishment, in fact it only employed five girls including herself, but somehow today the bell seemed inconsequential to performing the task of alerting others. She continued with as much strength as she could muster in her arm, for what seemed like an interminably long time.

Finally, someone called out, "We can hear you, but we can't see you. Keep ringing."

She did as instructed and after some time several voices arrived outside her location in the Matsuda-ya. "Listen, there's a fire out here so we can't get to you right now. We need to get water from the well up the street to put this out."

The men outside the Matsuda-ya then began running back and forth with buckets of water as they fought the flames that licked at the establishment's remains. Luckily, it was not a major conflagration that required large numbers of people to fight—city officials were busy battling fires near Naha Port and other parts of the city; citizens were pretty much left to fend for themselves.

After some time, Ushī became alarmed as she saw what she thought was a greater amount of smoke entering the Matsuda-ya.

She yelled out, "What's going on out there? Is the fire spreading? The room is filling with smoke."

A reassuring voice responded, "Don't worry. It's not smoke, it's steam from the water. We'll have you out in no time."

Soon thereafter, she could see large pieces of lumber being removed from the front of the building and finally a uniformed figure emerged before her. She did not know who he was but the Japanese soldier carefully extended a helping hand and led her over fallen timber and, to the extent possible, around broken shards of glass and out into the open. The destruction that greeted her made little sense and seemed without logical basis. Her usual frames of reference had disappeared—she was surrounded by complete devastation. It appeared nothing had been left unscathed.

"Are you okay?" asked a seemingly disembodied voice. "Are you hurt? Was anyone else in there with you?"

Still dazed she responded simply with, "My friend... she's inside....dead."

The soldier and other rescue workers looked at each other briefly with knowing glances and moved up the street.

Most of the girls had in fact left the Matsuda-ya with the establishment's proprietress, Nakagusuku Fumiko, to do some of the daily shopping at Higashi-machi (Naha's Eastern Market) for the day's meals and snacks for the evening's anticipated guests. Ushī and Tsurū had been left behind to help with the cleaning. But just at that moment she remembered Kenjiro, the Matsuda-ya's handyman and general custodian and Nakagusuku-san's younger simpleton cousin. As best she could recall, he had been puttering about the kitchen area at the time of the attack, an area now completely destroyed by the flames that had engulfed it. She would learn later that Kenjiro had not survived.

The Matsuda-ya had been located in the Tsuji area of Naha, its red-light district, made up of three streets: *mae michi* (J: front street); *naka michi* (J: middle street) and *ushiro michi* (J: back street) on which numerous drinking establishments and houses of prostitution were operated. The Tsuji area was first established in 1672, along with the Watanji and Nakashima districts, all comprising Naha's pleasure quarters. Both the Nakashima and Watanji districts were closed in 1908 while Tsuji was expanded in the same year to accommodate the displaced residents of the other two. The October 10 attack saw the near complete destruction of the Tsuji district.

Ushī was what was known locally as a *juri nu kūga* (O), a girl sold into prostitution before the age of ten. She had been just shy of her tenth birthday when she came to the Matsuda-ya. She had three older brothers, none of whom she had seen in years. Shimabukuro was her family name, or at least it was before she came to the Matsuda-ya. Juri really had no need for family names. Most customers came and went and cared for a girl for about as long as it took to be sufficiently entertained and satisfied. Her family lived in the southern city of Itoman, and still did as far as she knew. They had been extremely poor, barely surviving on a hand-to-mouth subsistence. The family had at one time owned a small sugar cane farm that they lost in the early 1920s when world sugar prices dropped precipitously leaving them in ruins, a turn of events from which they never recovered.

She had not enjoyed the warmth of her mother's hug or her father's reassuring smile since they sold her to an Itoman broker of prostitutes in 1937, who ultimately sold her to the Matsuda-ya in Naha. She could vividly recall the days when she and her brothers would go into the countryside in search of *sotetsu* (J: cycad), a local plant Okinawans relied upon for food during times of acute famine, much as they had during the major drought of 1904. Sotetsu, a toxic member of the palm family, served as an important source of food during famine because of the starch it provided. While the plant could be eaten if properly prepared, it required careful boiling to draw out all of its poison in order to avoid the possibility of accidental death. Ushī's father sometimes told the family of a time called sotetsu hell in the years following the great 1923 Kanto earthquake, the economic repercussions of which hit Okinawa particularly hard, leaving many Okinawans on the brink of starvation and leading to widespread dependence on sotetsu as the primary source of nourishment.

Ushī, now safely outside the debris field of the Matsuda-ya, sat alone quietly on the roadside wrapping her feet with strips of cloth torn from the bottom of her kimono—they were bleeding from having stepped on shards of pottery, bits of broken glass and sharp ends of broken lumber as she was led to safety. There she sat absorbed in solitude and weeping, oblivious to all the activity going on around her, filled with thoughts of her childhood and of what the future might bring. Despite her best efforts, she found herself calling out softly, "mother, father."

Chapter III

Before the Dawn

Sleep continued to evade Munekazu. As soon as he began drifting off something inside jolted him back to consciousness, suddenly and indelicately. He tossed and turned for hours. Even the long walk he had taken had not helped. The house was quiet, cocooned in a deep stillness. The children, Yoshiko and his mother, all fatigued to their limits of endurance by the day's events, slept heavily. From what Yoshiko had described to him, it was certainly a rest well deserved. Because of that he decided to sleep in the room with the tukunuma when he had returned so as not to disturb her sleep. Yoshiko, Kamadū and the children slept peacefully in the room that served double duty as the dining area. He still marveled at Yoshiko's presence of mind through the whole ordeal as she explained her experience in the sūhama, assisting old man Hanashiro, and leading the family to safety. Would he have exhibited such strength of character? He hoped he would have, although he remained unsure whether, in the face of such calamity, he would have gone back to render assistance to a stranger.

Still too agitated to sleep, he finally sat up, and crossing his legs with his back resting against the wall, smoked a cigarette. In the end, he decided somewhat impulsively, that he might drop in on Jiro. The old German-made Aristo mantle clock tucked away in the far corner of the room softly chimed three times; it was only then he realized how early it was. Still, he wondered if his friend might not be up and about. Unmarried, Jiro led a somewhat unconventional lifestyle, at times enjoying Naha's nightlife into the early morning hours while at others voraciously reading books and writing essays for days at a time cognizant of nothing or anyone around him. His current project had something to do with the economic impact on Okinawa of Japan's annexation of Formosa (Taiwan) in 1895 following the defeat of China in the first Sino-Japanese War (1894-1895).

A study in contrasts, Jiro was at once cultured with a keen intellect while still being quite an affable fellow. Munekazu admired that most about his friend. He had an ease about his personality that seemed to draw people in—he was equally at home with a scholar as he might have been with a street peddler. There was a Western term for such a man, but it now escaped Munekazu because of a "thickness" in his head that usually accompanied lack of sleep. He lit another cigarette. Inhaling deeply, he watched the various patterns the smoke formed as the cigarette burned. As his mind wandered to other things, "Renaissance man," popped easily into his head. Yes, this was the term that best described Jiro—an Okinawan Renaissance man.

Jiro's background was somewhat unusual. Born on Okinawa, his family moved to Tokyo in pursuit of a better life at the end of the Taisho period (1912-1926). Jiro's father had gone to work for a sugar exporting business with operations on Taiwan and had done reasonably well. By Okinawan standards his family had flourished. After completing his education, Jiro was assigned to the Naha National School as a teacher where he and Munekazu struck up their friendship several years earlier. He had always considered Jiro's background a bit reminiscent of the circumstances described in author Kushi Fusako's article, *Memoirs of a Declining Ryukyuan Woman,* that appeared in the June 1932 issue of *fujin koron* magazine (J: Women's Forum) that caused all the controversy among Okinawans. Kushi's story portrayed an Okinawan man who moved to Tokyo and prospered in business. He ultimately married a Japanese mainlander and had children, but kept his Okinawan heritage a secret from all—employer, co-workers, even his wife and children, trying desperately to pass as a mainlander. He severed all ties with his family on Okinawa although he did occasionally provide them with money. The story caused such an uproar, particularly among Okinawans living in the Tokyo area, that the planned series of articles for the monthly magazine was abruptly cancelled after the first article was published. Munekazu still thought about this story on occasion, impressed by how the author had so skillfully captured the bleakness of the times. He wondered how she would have ended her story had the series continued. In any case, while his family had moved to Tokyo and prospered, Jiro never made any pretense about his own Okinawan heritage. And, according to him, neither did his family. While fully assimilated into Japanese life and culture, they also never tried hiding their island roots. Still, Munekazu wondered at times why Jiro had such little contact with them, but never pressed the issue.

Striking a match for light, Munekazu again glanced at the clock and realized only ten short minutes had passed since he last checked the time. He thought briefly about lighting the oil lamp for more light, but quickly dismissed the idea—they had to conserve their small store of oil. He suddenly began feeling famished and regretted not having eaten dinner earlier. While he sometimes tired of the ubiquitous umu that made its appearance at nearly every meal, he also reminded himself that he should be grateful for them because they offered an important source of nutrition and, in the end, helped stave off famine. As his mind wandered aimlessly, he tried recalling what he knew of its history to help pass the time.

The first plants were brought to the Ryukyu Kingdom in 1605 to the Noguni district of Kadena village from Fuzhou, China (Fujian Province) by Noguni Sōkan, he thought to himself. *And with the assistance of a well-placed benefactor, Gima Shinjo of Kaki-no-Hana (location of present-day Futenma Marine Corps Air Station), cultivation of the umu flourished on the islands. By 1675 the plant was introduced into Japan via Yamakawa village in the Satsuma domain (southern Kyushu).* Munekazu also briefly recalled learning that it was the same Gima Shinjo who in 1623 sent lower ranking officials to China to learn methods of cultivating sugar cane. There was more, of course, but given his growing restlessness and the increasing intensity of the grumbling emanating from his stomach, he gave up trying to recall any more details.

Unable to restrain himself any longer, he checked on the family, all of whom were still sound asleep, and left the house heading toward Jiro's small home in Matsuyama-chō. That there were no taxis or busses running this time of morning was not surprising; nor were there any rickshaws about. In any case, none would have been able to navigate the debris-strewn streets. Thus, Munekazu decided to make the trip by foot, which would only take about 15-20 minutes. About 10 minutes into the walk he was coming to regret his decision as he began to tire from his lack of sleep, but he decided to press ahead. When Munekazu reached Jiro's home he found it to be dark and lifeless; honestly, pretty much what he had expected. He crossed into the small courtyard and knocked on the door several times. He finally heard the wooden door slide open and was greeted by a weary voice.

"Who is it?" he heard his friend ask in a clearly sleep-filled and slightly annoyed way.

"Jiro-san, it's Munekazu. I'm sorry, but I couldn't sleep."

"What on earth?.....keep your voice down," instructed Jiro. "*Jōshichā* (O: maid) is still sleeping. We only got to sleep a couple of hours ago."

Munekazu noticed that while Jiro used the word jōshichā when referring to his maid, Kiyomi, in the third person, their relationship hardly mirrored that of employer-employee. They were more like family to each other, perhaps akin to an aunt and her nephew. Kiyomi was a kindly older woman, perhaps in her late fifties or early sixties, who doted over Jiro. He, in turn, extended kindnesses to her quite unusual as an employer. Several years ago when Kiyomi's sister, who lived further north in Chatan village, came down with tuberculosis Jiro allowed her to go visit for two weeks so she could help nurse her back to health.

Jiro took his meals at restaurants or had them brought in, quite willing to bear the added expense. When Kiyomi sent word that she might need to stay on another week, Jiro quite readily agreed. Because of additional complications, Kiyomi's sister did not survive, but the incident clearly brought the two much closer together. That neither had any family in the immediate area upon whom to rely only served to further strengthen the bond between them. So Munekazu was now not surprised at the concern expressed in Jiro's voice for Kiyomi to ensure she slept undisturbed.

Running his hand through his hair as he tried to regain a sense of waking consciousness, Jiro invited Munekazu into his room. Their relationship had evolved to a point where the social protocol of inviting him into a formal sitting room was hardly necessary, and in any case, the tiny room that might have been used to receive guests had long since been subsumed by Jiro's mountains of papers and books.

Yes, a Renaissance man, thought Munekazu to himself.

Slowly awakening, Jiro looked intently at Munekazu and asked, "What's the matter? Has something happened?"

Munkazu responded, "No, nothing like that. I'm just worked up over yesterday's attack and can't sleep."

Jiro, shaking his head in assent, reached for the last of his Golden Bat cigarettes, lit it and sat back against the wall with his face toward the ceiling slowly exhaling smoke. (One of the immediate benefits of Japan's colonization of the Korean peninsula was its access to that country's tobacco crop, a benefit Munekazu, Jiro and other islanders also enjoyed.) "There are still a good many unanswered questions about yesterday. Hopefully they will come in time. Fretting about those things we can't control seems a useless exercise though, wouldn't you agree?"

Munekazu just looked at his friend without responding. Jiro continued, "Jōshichā was quite unnerved by the whole ordeal, but who can blame her? Quite a frightening experience after all.

I looked for you at school after we were dismissed, but they told me you'd already left." Jiro then asked, "Is everyone alright at your place?"

Munekazu nodded his response.

Jiro thought it was a bit curious for Munekazu to be out this time of the morning after yesterday's events and to leave his family at home, but did not want to make his friend feel uncomfortable by asking too many questions, so he decided not to press. He waited for Munekazu to continue, which he did by recounting the tale of the family he had encountered by the roadside as he returned home. Jiro took a final drag of his cigarette, ground its stub into the bottom of the ashtray and shared what information he had learned about the fate of Naha. Of course the port area had suffered tremendous loss, although Jiro was short on the specifics. Naminoue had been destroyed he heard, the busy shrine area along the beach on the East China Sea, although strangely the torii gate remained standing, which some regarded as auspicious. (Naminoue had a centuries-long history on the island, but had most recently gained popularity as a place for women to pray for their sons and husbands to be deemed unfit for military service by the Japanese government, particularly during the Sino-Japanese War [1894-5] and the Russo-Japanese War [1904-5].)

As he hurriedly made his escape from the downtown area, he joined up with a small group of people—two women and three men—also fleeing to safety. Although the attacks had apparently stopped, no one was prepared to leave that to chance. During their escape, Jiro learned that the group worked at a local restaurant where only the night before during a banquet, Lieutenant General Cho Isamu, the 32nd Army's chief of staff, confidently told his audience that Japan's Imperial 32nd Army would emerge victorious against the enemy in any battle for Okinawa—the workers had barely escaped with their lives and the restaurant was now no more than a smoldering heap. Jiro noted the irony of the situation without speculating on what it might portend. Despite the day's tragic events, Jiro was able to identify some gallows humor. Munekazu continued listening intently as his friend provided more insights. Busy streets like Tenpichō-dōri lay in ruins and Higashi-machi, a heavily-trafficked shopping area, suffered heavy damage as well. Still Munekazu listened with growing anxiety as he awaited Jiro's description of the fate that had befallen the Tsuji district and the Matsuda, an anxiousness visible enough for Jiro to detect.

Suddenly, much like a bolt of lightning appears from nowhere, Jiro understood why Munekazu had made the trek to his home—Ushī. Despite his efforts to conceal the purpose of his visit or feelings for the juri, Jiro had long suspected Munekazu's feelings ran deeper for Ushī than he was comfortable letting on or that propriety would permit him to share. Jiro was not prepared to sit in judgment of his friend—what an onerous burden to bear. He fully understood the complexities of human relationships—he was not without his own with his family back in Tokyo—and thus felt a sense of empathy for Munekazu's plight.

He thought about this for a moment or two, then slapping his hand on his knee, turned to Munekazu and said, "Let's head downtown and see for ourselves what sort of damage the city suffered. Come to think of it, it's been a while since I last visited the Matsuda; I wonder how it fared?" Looking at Munekazu, he chuckled slightly and continued, "Maybe if I go by and pay proper respects to Nakagusuku-san, she'll take pity on me during my next visit and won't run up the prices on me too much." He concluded by giving Munekazu a wink and proceeded to change into a kimono, which he found more comfortable than his western-style clothes. Munekazu's expression now had about it a certain air of relief, a fact not lost on Jiro.

Munekazu pointed out, "We should be careful. There are

bound to be police and army personnel throughout the downtown area trying to keep curiosity-seekers off the streets."

Jiro responded with a simple "umm" to signify his agreement, and with that, they left the house.

2

As Munekazu and Jiro walked toward the heart of the downtown area, neither could fully absorb what the morning twilight revealed. Many homes were destroyed, if not by the bombs then by the many fires that followed. The first major structure they happened upon was Naha's girls' high school—one half remained intact while the other had been completely obliterated. The pair was struck by the randomness of the destruction. Munekazu thought that but for a split second decision of a lifetime, there were those who likely survived and those who did not; he was touched by the pain families throughout Naha were likely experiencing. His eye caught sight of something softly flapping back and forth in the gentle breeze of approaching morning. Nailed to a pole in front of the school was one of the all too familiar propaganda pictures used by the government to tout the importance of achieving moral purity by eschewing Western thought. This one entitled, "Purging One's Head of Anglo-Americanism," pictured a young woman kneeling and bent at the waist using a comb as if to clean her scalp. Instead of ridding herself of dandruff, however, she was clearing her head of moral impurities depicted by the words *hedonism, materialism, individualism, Anglo-American ideas,* and others. As Munekazu looked around, he saw other pictures posted, most of which were either torn or burned. He assumed they chronicled similar messages.

To their left, remnants of the prefectural hospital fell victim to the licking flames that continued to devour what little was left. The closer Munekazu and Jiro moved toward the port area, the worse the destruction appeared to be. Through Kume-chō they pressed and Munekazu stopped to try and locate Tomiko's home, but the destruction, coupled with the low light of the early morning, was such that he was unable to identify any meaningful frames of reference to determine where Tomiko's house had once stood. This sent a shock through him like nothing else had that day. The notion that his in-laws and Yoshiko's sister might have fallen victim to the day's attack shook him to his core—the full gravity of what had happened was finally sinking in.

Drenched in perspiration and visibly shaken, he dropped to his knees and pounded the dirt road with his fists, repeating to himself, "How could this be? How could this be?"

Jiro, at first unaware that Munekazu had stopped, ran back to where his friend sat in the road and asked, "Kaze-kun, what is it?"

Learning the source of Munekazu's angst, he could do little more than provide a reassuring hand on his friend's shoulder and mutter, "I'm sure they are alright." Even Jiro understood the emptiness of his words, but could offer little else in the way of solace.

Jiro asked Munekazu if he wanted to turn back, to which he flatly replied, "No, I want to see what other carnage and destruction the day has brought." And with that, Munekazu mustered both strength and courage to stand again and the two continued on, albeit Munekazu with a bit more tentativeness. Any sense of fatigue Munekazu felt earlier had been washed away by the adrenalin rush he was experiencing as a result of the sights he encountered in Kume-chō. But he continued to wonder about the fate of his in-laws.

No matter where they went in the downtown area, nearly complete annihilation greeted them at every turn. Daimonmae and Tenpi-cho streets, among Naha's busiest commercial districts lined with various shops, restaurants and residences—obliterated. Yamagata-ya, Okinawa's first department store—

vanished. The city office in Nishihon-chō—gone. The restaurant Munekazu and the family sometimes frequented on their occasional visits to Naminoue, the Café Tengu—reduced to a memory. The fish and pottery markets of the Higashi-machi area now only so much rubble. And as if in silent testament to the scourge the city had suffered, a dead ox lay by the side of the road, its load of black sugar that was being driven to market overturned, but still largely intact.

As they passed the mangled remains of what had once been the meat market, Munekazu had a morbidly nauseating thought: *how could anyone distinguish between the flesh of pigs and humans in this mess?* Severed human limbs and grotesquely contorted bodies still dotted the landscape throughout their trip in the downtown area, but one could at least distinguish between man and swine. What affected him more than anything was knowing that most of the dead in Naha's market areas would have been women; they in effect operated Naha's markets and handled most of the commercial activity that took place within them. Dismayed by the thought, he now vividly recalled images of small groups of women heading to market each morning with their small pigs, strapped down inside straw baskets, balanced on their heads and chatting away with one another—*what had the morning been like for them,* he wondered. Munekazu had always admired these women—their strength of character, business savvy and nonchalant approach to life—they were the consummate entrepreneurs of Okinawan commerce. *What did they experience at the onset of the attack?* he continued thinking. He shuddered as a strange chill overtook him. He hurried along, averting his eyes from the scene around him.

The two friends had other disturbing, if less gruesome, encounters, *munukūyā* (O: Okinawa's pre-war homeless itinerants) being chief among them. They were at once bedraggled, destitute and barely subsisted on a hand-to-mouth existence—islanders upon whom fate had frowned with discernible vengeance. Munukūyā typically made daily rounds to households asking residents for a handout of food to sustain yet another day of life despite the hopelessness that confronted them. Locals were, as a rule, generally tolerant of the munukūyā, sparing what little they could to help those less fortunate than themselves. Munekazu was always touched when he considered how poor Okinawans extended themselves to the even more impoverished among them. Yoshiko often pointed to such magnanimity as a defining cultural trait of the island's inhabitants; he chose rather to see it as a small cultural manifestation of Okinawa's contribution to Japan's broader efforts under its Greater East Asia Co-prosperity Sphere. In any case, this morning the munukūyā were a particularly pitiful sight—some injured; all homeless; and now nowhere to turn for even the most meager of handouts. Munekazu had no idea what would become of them, but secretly believed their numbers would swell as many Naha residents would now be left penniless with no home to call their own.

The clean-up and process of recovering human remains appeared to be proceeding at an agonizingly slow pace. While many remains had been recovered, the work was arduous, made more difficult by all the debris. Workers were overwhelmed at the sheer volume of the task at hand, which may have accounted for the fact that no one even appeared to notice them or the other curious residents of the city who were also out and about.

They were permitted to go no further south than central Higashi-machi. Beyond that the bombing had been even more intense since it was closer to the port areas and Oroku airfield. They were told it would be a waste of time in any case as the North Meiji Bridge and South Meiji Bridge leading to Yamashita-chō and Kakinohana-chō had both been destroyed. Jiro suggested they back-track and head toward the Tsuji district. The scenes were the same everywhere they went—death and devastation. It resembled nothing of the city Munekazu had come to love.

As they approached Tsuji both stopped in their tracks and gaped in awe at the sight that greeted them—virtually nothing remained standing and much of what did stood as little more than charred monuments to what was now the past. What the bombs had not initially destroyed was devoured in the ensuing fires. The scene laid out before them exuded an "other worldliness" as an acrid smoky haze amplified by a soft pre-dawn sunlight cast a dream-like pall on everything in sight. Trying to distinguish among the streets of the Tsuji district, much less where the Matsuda-ya had once stood, was nearly impossible. The two friends stood there for what seemed like a very long time trying to take in what they saw. *Was this their home? Their life? How does one move forward from this?* These were their thoughts as they silently stood looking at each other. And then, almost as a dancer receives a cue to enter onto stage, a light cascading breeze blew in front of them a small poster advertising Sakura beer, one which had likely been hanging in one of the houses of Tsuji. Such a simple thing about which neither would have given a second thought on another day, impacted the two profoundly. It was almost as if the poster was a divine harbinger warning of life's impermanence and ephemerality.

Finally, Munekazu broke their shared silence with one word—"Tragic." Jiro nodded in agreement without saying a word. A group of four workers approached them, one of whom stopped.

He looked at them and, pointing over his shoulder with his thumb, he said, "They're still pulling dead bodies out of that mess. There's no telling how many there are. What a terrible way to die."

Jiro asked about the fate of a few of the establishments he frequented, to include the Matsuda. "There's so much rubble in there, I can't tell one place from the next. But if people were in any of those buildings I don't see how they could have survived." And with that, he trotted off to catch up with the other workers.

Munekazu and Jiro, having listened to that cold and detached assessment, looked at each other in silence, unable to find words to articulate what they saw.

The morning dawned brightly revealing to the two men the full extent of what had remained hidden in darkness. An overwhelming sense of grief and fatigue finally overtook Munekazu, previously held at bay by the sheer rush of adrenalin. But now, confronting the unknown fate of his in-laws and Ushī, he succumbed, falling into a heap onto the dusty road weeping and unable to utter a word.

Chapter IV

Strange Vistas and Paths Unknown

Ushī, still half dazed, wandered about aimlessly throughout downtown Naha, but for how long she did not know. She could not remember the last time she felt any genuine emotion, any real human feelings—she now existed ensconced within a fog, in touch with very little around her. She had neither a destination nor anywhere to return—it had been nearly twenty-four hours since the attack. As she glanced at the ground before her she caught quick glimpses of her bare and bloodied feet. Strangely, she was not cognizant of any pain; her feet and the rest of her body were as numb as her spirit. Having waited for seemingly hours on end at what had once been the Matsuda-ya, neither Nakagusuku Fumiko nor any of the girls who had accompanied her on the morning errands had returned. Were they alive? Had they survived the attack or were they among the many dead? Ushī had finally given up awaiting their return. A combination of mental fatigue and curiosity about all the activity going on around her, she was guided by a youthful inquisitiveness to explore.

She traversed the city, wide-eyed and filled with incredulity, sometimes doubling back over her course, the piles of corpses she encountered along the way growing ever higher with the passage of time. She felt no particular revulsion toward the death surrounding her nor pity for the lost lives they represented. Indeed, she felt nothing; she was merely an empty shell devoid of human compassion or pain moving about a world wholly unfamiliar to her. She stopped once or twice to watch workers pile the dead bodies onto horse-drawn wagons, but had no idea or interest in where they might ultimately be disposed. Only once did she briefly feel anything that might resemble a connection to her life before the morning's attack. As she walked, in the distance she saw two seemingly familiar figures to whom she felt drawn—two men, one of whom looked particularly distraught as he pounded the ground emotively, obviously distressed. But in her present state of mind she was not certain who they were. While she thought briefly of approaching them, she quickly dismissed the idea and continued on her way. But even as she did so, she could not erase the image of the one man pounding the ground while apparently crying—the figure he cut was remarkable both because of the sincerity of his emotion and the growing sense that she had a connection to him, but what that connection was she could not for the life of her fathom.

As she continued along her way, she was spotted by four low-ranking soldiers of the Imperial Army under orders by superiors, as were others like them, to conduct a recovery detail in that particular sector of downtown Naha. Ushī caught their attention and they approached her, at once with a sense of intense curiosity and suspicion, but in any case she was far more interesting than looking for the bodies of dead Imperial Army comrades. She gave them little notice. These, of course, were not the first soldiers she had encountered, but they were the first in whom she had piqued an interest. She looked haggard and disoriented, yet despite her appearance she exuded a distinct sense of beauty.

Private Yoshida, the appointed leader of the group, puffed up his chest and approached her with a haughty air of authority and gruffly said, "Hey, what are you doing out here anyway? Unless you're helping with the clean-up or otherwise authorized, civilians aren't supposed to be on the streets. Don't you Okinawans understand anything?"

Of course, it had been only fewer than two hours earlier that this same group of soldiers encountered Munekazu and Jiro and had completely ignored them as they wandered through these same streets. Had Ushī been aware of her potentially precarious circumstances, Yoshida's furtive looks might have revealed ulterior motives.

Ushī looked at him blankly, not uttering a word. He continued, saying,"Hey, are you simple or something? Can't you understand what I'm saying to you? You can understand Japanese, can't you?"

One of his comrades standing behind him yelled to Yoshida, "Is she a spy?" Groundless rumors had run rampant among the rank and file soldiers all day that Okinawans had somehow assisted the enemy in perpetrating the morning attack on the island. With that, he grabbed her by both shoulders and began shaking her and yelled, "Answer me at once! Are you a spy? Are you working for the enemy?"

As Yoshida continued to shake her ever harder, Ushī regained at least a modicum of her senses. Haltingly, she offered, "I…I…I am Ushī of the Matsuda-ya. Please help me."

Yoshida's eyes immediately brightened as he stared at her. "A girl from the Tsuji district? A juri?" he asked aloud but half to himself. "The gods are with me today." The women of the Tsuji district had always remained unattainable to Imperial Army soldiers, unwilling to discharge their patriotic duties as *jugun ianfu* (J: comfort women) to the Imperial Army; the Army leadership was reluctant to forcibly press them into service. He had heard stories that several non-commissioned officers tried persuading the juri of Tsuji to volunteer their services at Imperial Army comfort stations around the island, but none had heeded the clarion call. *We're here protecting their butts and they can't even do this little bit for us?* he thought. *An absolutely shameful lot, these Okinawans.*

Yoshida thought to himself disdainfully, *Who are these local harlots to refuse us anyway? Ungrateful backwater…* Even as he went through these quiet gestations of his mental tirade a thought occurred to him. If his group brought this one back to their comfort station, he and his comrades might well curry favor with the station's operator and negotiate special privileges. (Many comfort stations were independently owned and operated by Japanese civilians.) And why not? They would be bringing him a gift—a prize of the first order; not like the usual Korean jugun ianfu on Okinawa. *But first,* he thought, *why wait for something you can have immediately? The spoils of war after all. After months of being on this god forsaken island protecting these native islanders, haven't we earned a bit of enjoyment?* Yoshida's thinking continued.

Motioning to his comrades, they came running. "This one's going back to Ishida to work for him at the comfort station, but not before we have a little fun—and I'm first." He chose not to share with them that Ushī was from the Tsuji district.

The leadership of the 32nd Army had expressly ordered that unless the juri voluntarily consented to serving in comfort stations, they should not be pressed into service. This was not out of magnanimousness or compassion—it was a purely pragmatic decision. The Japanese Imperial Army needed the support of the locals in order to conduct necessary defensive operations in protection of mainland Japan—keep the fighting limited to Okinawa rather than the main islands of Japan for as long as possible. If the locals became disaffected, their mission would become that much more difficult to accomplish because they furnished a substantial portion of the labor required to fortify the island. It was simply a matter of keeping the locals assuaged. Indeed, Okinawans had already demonstrated great resourcefulness and solidarity in assisting the women of Tsuji in avoiding service to the Imperial Army—juri had been released from their debt to proprietors so they could flee back to their home towns; fake marriages performed; and forged medical documents produced falsifying their unfitness for duty in comfort stations.

The eyes of Yoshida and his comrades gleamed, not unlike those of a predator circling its prey, approaching ever closer for the final kill. Ushī's eyes widened in disbelief at what was about to happen—while no words were spoken, she instinctively knew and trembled at the thought.

"Now don't give us any trouble," Yoshida offered with a lecherous grin. He looked around and confirmed the immediate area was deserted. He needed to be cautious so other members of their unit who might wander past would not become suspicious about what they were doing. He did not want to be reported; nor did he want to share his personal "treasure." With that, he lunged at Ushī, tackling her around her waist. She opened her mouth to scream for help, but no audible sound came out—in any case, as Yoshida tackled her he simultaneously cupped his left hand over her mouth. As each member of Yoshida's team, in turn, had his way with Ushī—first Yoshida, then Furukawa, then Tanaka, and then again Morioka—the others stood watch.

She closed her eyes and tried to mentally separate herself from her present torment, but by the third time the pain had become searing, like a hot knife cutting her insides. She tried in vain to conjure more pleasant images in her mind's eye—her childhood; her favorite seascapes off Naha; and even of her mother and father, but to no real avail—she could not erase the brutality of her present reality. Having her privacy, indeed her personal being, violated with such indiscriminant violence and disregard of humanity was more than she could ever have imagined. Yet she was totally powerless to stop it. As tears streamed down her face onto the ground, all she was aware of were the animalistic and brutish grunts of her tormentors as they, one after another, satisfied themselves sexually at her expense and then left her there lying on the ground, dirt in her hair and small mud stains on her face where the dirt had mixed with her tears. Instinctively, she sought to curl up in a fetal position as she cried silently, still no audible sounds crossing her lips. Again, she thought of her parents and the warm security of their love; but this was not to be had in such a situation. She was being forced to confront the harsh reality of war on her own no matter how much she yearned to return to her past—there was no escape; there was no solace to be had; there was only the here and now.

When Yoshida and his comrades finished their business, Yoshida ordered Ushī to stand up and fix herself. He was now ready to take her to Ishida, owner of the comfort station that serviced his unit along with several others. Physically disheveled and mentally disoriented, when Ushī did not move quickly enough as she tried to readjust her kimono to cover her exposed breasts and vagina, Morioka grew increasingly impatient, and yanked her by the arm in an effort to get her to stand. In the process of doing so, Ushī felt a snap in her arm where the humerus fit into the scapula and a sharp pain followed. She let out a shriek as the initial sensation gave way to a dull, painful and rhythmic throbbing. Morioka continued pulling on her arm incessantly, Ushī unknowingly uttering guttural pleas for him to stop. The injury she suffered that day, because it was left unattended, would remain with her throughout the rest of her life. While the arm would not become totally useless, it did at times dangle listlessly when she did not remain conscious of how it hung.

Morioka finally eased his grip and allowed Ushī to comply with his demand that she follow the group, which she did as she sought to provide some measure of relief to her shoulder as she gently rubbed it. Morioka, however, unwilling to leave well enough alone, brought up the rear of their small group occasionally pushing Ushī along by placing his hand in the center of her back and shoving her forward, causing her no small amount of pain.

They finally arrived at Ishida's comfort station located not far from 32nd Army headquarters, itself currently housed in an experimental silkworm factory half-way between Naha and Shuri. Yoshida's group was assigned to the 22nd Independent Infantry Battalion, a subordinate unit of the 64th Infantry Brigade, which was charged with fortifying the defenses around Shuri. Although Ushī had neither personal familiarity with the business of comfort stations nor the work of jugun ianfu, she knew enough to piece together what she was seeing and understand where she was—and she was horrified. She had heard stories of women coerced, either by guile or force, into the service of the Imperial Japanese Army as jugun ianfu. She had even seen a few of the Korean women forced to work in this capacity. At no time during her short life, however, could she have ever imagined such a sudden descent into these vile circumstances for herself.

As the Japanese Imperial Army continued its efforts to defensively fortify Okinawa against an impending allied attack, 114 comfort stations were ultimately placed into service, either through constructing new facilities or by commandeering existing structures—hotels, private homes, and public buildings. These comfort stations would ultimately service approximately 80,000 troops. Depending upon the size and number of military units supported, a comfort station could have as few as two or three jugun ianfu assigned to it or many more, although the average number was seven to ten; each woman could expect to service as many as forty to fifty soldiers daily depending on the size of the comfort station, with the average duration of each interlude being approximately 10-15 minutes.

The preponderant number of the 200,000 women forced into service as jugun ianfu was Korean, about eighty percent, to include those on Okinawa. Ten percent were from Vietnam, China, Malaya, Indonesia, the Philippine Islands and the East Indies, which also included Dutch women. The other ten percent comprised Japanese women. The rationale for using foreign women as jugun ianfu was both pragmatic and straightforward. Using Japanese women in such a capacity could have negatively impacted the morale of soldiers—using their sisters or girlfriends as jugun ianfu would have had a deleterious effect on them, and in turn, on the military's ability to carry out its mission. Most women forced into service as jugun ianfu, about eighty percent, were between the ages of fourteen and eighteen.

Ushī was led to a small building resembling an office. Looking around she caught sight of a handwritten sign painted on a small wooden placard just outside the front entrance with the words "administrative services office" on it, beside which was written in smaller writing "Approved by the Japanese Labor Service Corps." (The Japanese Labor Service Corps was responsible for establishing comfort stations for Japanese troops in the Pacific theater of operations.) Ushī had no formal education, so she had trouble reading all the characters, but was able to make some of them out—at least those identifying the hut-like structure as some sort of administrative office; the rest she could not read. What all this meant for her she was not precisely certain yet, but she was astute enough to understand her life was about to take a monumentally drastic turn. There she stood, silently, beads of sweat trickling down what felt like every crevice of her body and the dull throbbing pain in her shoulder a constant reminder of an earlier experience she was trying desperately to put out of her mind.

Looking about and still trying to digest what she saw, Ushī noticed three small, rather dilapidated shacks lined in a row behind the office building; in front of one stood four girls busily washing themselves out of small basins. From what she could tell, they appeared to be about her own age. She did not know what time it was, but they had walked for what seemed like a long distance to get here and the sun was out and burning with an unusual intensity for an October morning. "Jugun ianfu" was the only thought that continuously came to mind. If indeed these girls were who she thought they were, then this is what the military euphemistically considered a "house of relaxation" for military men.

As she stood staring at the girls, the door to the office opened and Yoshida stepped into the sunlight followed by another man who was short and of slight build, exuding a rather unassuming countenance. He sported a mustache, wore round rather thick spectacles, and wore his hair short in a crew-cut style well above his ears. He was donning a white short-sleeved shirt with some folded papers stuck in the pocket along with a pair of gray, somewhat threadbare trousers—on whole, fairly nondescript. He was the type of customer the girls of the Matsuda would surreptitiously mock and bargain with each other to service because they believed he would be easy to please with minimal effort. Ushī, however, had little inkling that Ishida was known locally as the "the samurai from hell" by the girls who worked for him because of the unrelenting way in which he drove jugun ianfu to service the officers and soldiers of the Imperial Army units he supported.

A rabid nationalist, Ishida Atsushi believed there was no sacrifice too great in support of Japan's war effort, least of all the lives of jugun ianfu. He saw them as little more than chattel, to be used and discarded as the situation demanded. It was rumored he had already driven four girls to their deaths; two by their own hands and the others through exhaustion and sickness. Strangely, he exacted such cruelties on his charges while always maintaining an unflappable and composed exterior manner, often sporting a sheepish smile on his face.

Yoshida led Ishida to Ushī as he recounted how his small group had come across her in the downtown area, deftly omitting any mention of their own activities with her—Yoshida had already warned Ushī not to mention anything of the incident. Ishida stood quietly listening.

He then gently took Yoshida by the arm and moved a few steps away from Ushī and said, "Yoshida-san, although she is quite a beauty, I have been forbidden to take in licensed juri. This could bring real trouble."

Yoshida, quickly assessing the situation and Ishida's growing reluctance, preyed upon his greater commercial instincts. "Ishida-san, this is a great opportunity for you. No one knows of this woman's origins and even if she cries about it, we will all be here to call her story a lie. She was all alone so no one will come forward for her—you're in the clear and stand to make a good deal of profit once the officers get a look at her. Don't worry."

Gradually assuaged by Yoshida's words and blinded by the idea of increased profits, Ishida slowly relented. Ushī, standing in the heat and humidity, dripping in perspiration and wracked by the unrelenting pain in her shoulder, grew more and more light-headed and queasy. Not having eaten for over twenty-four hours; trying to bear up under the heat; and having been raped by the likes of Yoshida and his companions, her grip on consciousness grew ever more tenuous. As her head began to spin, she caught bits and pieces of the conversation of which she was not a part but was clearly the subject—"special privileges once a month for Yoshida only…a reduced rate…this would be contingent upon her performance and popularity among the officers"…that was the last she heard. With that, she lost her final grip on the conscious world, and unceremoniously slumped to the ground like a sack of umu being loaded onto a wagon for market.

2

Yoshiko tried in vain to console her older sister, Tomiko, and to silence her endless wailing and thrashing about. She feared Tomiko would cause herself to fall into a state of self-induced fits. Such had been her condition since she learned of her husband Teijiro's death only days earlier. Formerly a fisherman, he had been conscripted by Japan's Imperial Army in May 1944 to assist in offloading cargo from ships that were bringing supplies—rations, ammunition and other matériel—necessary to support the growing number of military personnel on the island. He had been working the dock area the day of the attack and numbered among the many killed.

Now a widow, Tomiko had two children to care for and no means to do so, a reality that only served to exacerbate her angst. Munekazu, never particularly adept at handling such emotional outbursts had absented himself from the house—again. Yoshiko understood that it was not a lack of empathy on his part, but a certain inadequacy Munekazu felt in trying to assist others during such trying times and avoidance was his coping mechanism. She had never really noticed this particular personality flaw until Munekazu's own father passed away; characterizing his attempts to console Kamadū as clumsy was, at best, charitable. He was completely inept. She had come to understand this about her husband. Yet he was perhaps one of the most compassionate people she had ever met. He understood the magnitude of Tomiko's problem long before anyone else had—no husband; her home completely obliterated during the attack; and no means of supporting the family. He had already told Yoshiko it was their duty to assist them and although it would mean greater sacrifice for their family, Tomiko and her children were welcomed into their home.

Understanding all of this, and given Tomiko's condition, Yoshiko quickly concluded that arranging any funeral observances would fall to her and Kamadū, a task with which she now busied herself. Her mind raced as she thought of the many things that needed to be tended to; they were already behind schedule. But Yoshiko's efforts were being hampered by a seemingly insurmountable complication—they could not locate Teijiro's remains. Because of the sheer number of dead and devastation wrought by the attack, military and civil officials were having Naha's downtown area cleaned up as quickly as possible. Munekazu had made several trips to various makeshift government offices in the downtown area inquiring as to how family members might find the remains of loved ones, but was met with a pessimistic response at each turn. Most offices and the officials that staffed them were disorganized and unable to render any meaningful assistance, operating in a state of total consternation.

"Our best guess at this point is that hundreds, maybe thousands, died. You can't expect us keep up with and identify each body. What's the name?"

Munekazu would dutifully, but with decreasing enthusiasm respond, "Agena Teijiro."

Officials would look at lists with various names on them (none appeared to have more than 50-60 names listed) and reply, "Sorry, no one by that name is on the list. You'll need to hold funeral rites without the body."

While dismayed by their lack of success and the seeming lack of empathy of prefectural officials, deep down Munekazu and Yoshiko knew the officials were right, even if their assessments struck them as callous. It was apparent by the somewhat haphazard manner in which victims' names had been recorded that there was not a system in place to cope with current circumstances and accurately keep track of the dead. It was not just the number of bodies that needed to be cleared away. In Okinawa's heat, a body lying around for several days would not only be foul, but likely unidentifiable having become bloated and discolored. Coupled with the destruction of government offices, it only complicated matters further.

This news, of course, only fuelled Tomiko's agitation, but the family felt a symbolic ritual would still need to be performed, which Yoshiko now planned with the assistance of her mother-in-law. Funeral rites were typically planned in the house of the deceased, but as there was little left standing of Tomiko's old neighborhood, Yoshiko's home would have to suffice. Yoshiko and Kamadū lit and burned a large amount of incense at the ancestral shrine in their home and through prayer notified their ancestors of Teijiro's impending arrival, while at the same time asking their forgiveness for offering funeral rites to an outsider. They had done this at Kamadū's insistence, but Yoshiko readily consented. Both also feared the possibility of retribution by

Teijiro's spirit, now a *shini mabui*. Unlike people who had died of natural causes, it was believed the spirits of those who suffered violent deaths would assume malevolent characters and wander the earth as ghosts, causing trouble for the living. Thus, this was their attempt to assuage the spirits of Teijiro and their ancestors.

The next step left Yoshiko and Kamadū both perplexed and at odds with one another. Typically, neighbors in the community were notified of any death so they could extinguish their hearth fires and discard whatever food was being cooked in the belief that the hearths had been polluted. Kamadū felt that propriety demanded they notify the neighbors.

Yoshiko, taking a more pragmatic approach, considered this unnecessary. "There is death all over Naha. Should the entire city to throw away scarce food? And not only that, Teijiro didn't live in Takahashi-cho and died at the docks. Why should the neighbors extinguish their fires and discard precious food for someone they didn't even know?"

Kamadū retorted quite simply, "It's the proper thing to do." She continued, saying, "Besides, if we can say a prayer for an outsider at the family shrine, we have an obligation to tell the neighbors."

It was during this discussion that Munekazu returned home and immediately regretted having done so, although as he listened to his wife and mother argue their respective points of view he became slightly amused that he and Yoshiko had somehow wound up on the same side of an argument the two of them so often found themselves taking polar opposite positions on: tradition versus the pragmatism of the times. To be sure, this was slightly different, but that he and his wife had somehow stumbled into agreement on such a matter was an irony not lost on him. In the end, Yoshiko relented—how can one argue logic with a person clinging solely to tradition? But she left the task of notifying the neighbors to Kamadū. She was struck by a quizzical thought: *was Munekazu's thinking impacting her own regarding*

Okinawan traditions? No, this was simply a matter of showing concern for the welfare of others. This had nothing to do with broader issues of Okinawans abandoning their own cultural roots in favor of Japan. With that, she quickly put the thought out of her mind.

This was about all that could readily be done without Teijiro's remains—there was no body to wash and dress; no need to gather relatives and nothing to take to the family tomb—quite Spartan in comparison to the funerary rites undertaken for Munekazu's father. Yoshiko was secretly relieved. It was one thing to burn incense and offer prayers for Teijiro at their family shrine given current circumstances. It would, however, be quite another to have interred his bones in the family tomb. And trying to arrange Teijiro's funeral through his family would have been nearly impossible and was a situation Yoshiko preferred to steer clear of particularly since Tomiko was in no condition to assist. All of them—Teijiro and Tomiko, Teijiro's elder brother and wife, and his younger sister and husband lived within a stone's throw of each other and had likely suffered as many of the other islanders had. Getting embroiled in Teijiro's family affairs was something she wanted to avoid. And in any case, they had not been particularly close.

She sat trying to steal a quiet moment and gather herself despite all the commotion in the house of the past few days. Yet her mind could not escape drawing the stark contrast between the funeral rites observed at her father-in-law's death and Teijiro's. It was not so much the rites themselves. Rather, it occurred to her that this juxtaposition served as both a symbol and a warning of the new dark reality enveloping the island. It also occurred to Yoshiko that but for the divine intervention of the kami, Tomiko herself and her children would have died as well. Luckily, in order to save time Tomiko had decided to walk to the bus stop, with her two sons, to meet Yoshiko and had sought refuge in a building that was largely unscathed during the attack.

3

Munekazu's father, Muneto, had been well respected throughout the community. Muneto, like his father and his father's father before him, had served as middle-tiered officials in the kingdom's bureaucracy—Munekazu's grandfather in the prefectural government, while his great grandfather remained in government through the closing chapter of the Ryukyu Kingdom and the opening days of Okinawa's history as a prefecture of Japan. His family had been witness to some of Okinawa's most tumultuous times and some of its more memorable ones. They were not historical figures by any means; few would even remember who they were outside the family, but they had watched Okinawa's historical trajectory change over time and had been privy to some of its inner workings. Munekazu's great grandfather had been part of the old Ryukyu government when Commodore Matthew Calbraith Perry visited the island in May 1853 as part of his voyage to compel Japan to open its doors to the West. Munekazu had heard stories of the consternation the visit had caused at the royal court. He could also recall his grandfather's stories of Okinawa's first international baseball game held in 1903 on the Shuri castle grounds played between the American "bluejackets," a team comprised of the crew from a visiting ship, and the Shuri middle-school boys. And, as his grandfather often recounted with some amount of pride, it was in 1906 that the island welcomed its first foreign teacher, Henry Butler Schwartz, who taught at the Shuri Middle School.

The story that most impressed Munekazu, however, was a tale of the strange foreigner Bettelheim (Bernard Jean Bettelheim). Arriving on the British ship *Starling* in May 1846, Bettelheim, an unabashed proselytizer of the Christian faith, over the course of his stay on Okinawa did everything he could to alienate his hosts according to records of the Ryukyuan court. Bettelheim and his family came ashore and, through ruse and deceit, occupied the ancient Buddhist temple at Naminoue, Gokoku-ji, first established in 1367. The Okinawans, skilled at diplomacy but lacking in any temperament for confrontation, ultimately permitted the Bettelheim family to remain, which they did for the next seven years, denying use of Gokoku-ji Temple to locals, which according to Bettelheim was used for the wanton idolatry of Buddhism.

The relationship between the Ryukyuan court and the Bettelheims became increasingly strained, digressing from one of polite acceptance to one of palpable dislike; the greater the resistance to Bettelheim's attempts at proselytizing the Christian gospel, the greater his efforts to convert the island's "heathens." He did, by both Ryukyuan accounts and Bettelheim's own, in the end literally begin breaking into local homes where he felt moved to preach his gospel. By 1849, the Bettelheim problem had become an international affair as the Ryukyu court requested the Chinese to intercede on their behalf with the British government. And by 1854, upon the continued insistence of the Ryukyu court, Bettelheim and his family were removed from Okinawa by Commodore Matthew C. Perry.

His family had also borne witness to the island's turmoil when Okinawa lost its independent sovereignty and formally became a part of Japan in 1879. There had been neither consensus nor clear support at the time for the island's absorption into Japan's administrative structure. But one point was clear. Okinawa had become a regional geopolitical pawn as Japan and China sought to assert their respective supremacy in the region, an unintended consequence of western incursion into East Asia.

His father often lamented the economic decline of Okinawa during the Taisho period due to depressed global sugar markets and the impact that had on Okinawans, particularly sugar cane farmers—this is what led to the sotetsu jigoku period on the island. His family had had ringside seats to history without having any real hand in it, much like watching a Japanese sumo match. Having occupied such a position also helped to buffer at least some of the negative economic impacts of the times for the family that devastated the lives of so many of their friends, neighbors and fellow islanders.

4

Yoshiko learned over time the reason her father-in-law had been so well respected. It was because he treated everyone with dignity. He shared his thoughts, ideas and concerns with community members in measured ways they could understand. Muneto was a teacher, mentor and friend, occupying an almost paterfamilias status in the community—his counsel and advice were sought out by neighbors on just about every imaginable subject. He was patient, easy-going and engaged all with a quiet respect, always making time for everyone. This is why his funeral had been so well attended—his death was seen as a loss not just for the family, but the community as well.

Yoshiko recalled the event quite vividly. At the time of his death, Kamadū had taken complete charge of the funeral arrangements and it was Yoshiko's duty to assist her as needed—with the exception of Kiyoko and Kaori, Kamadū's two youngest daughters who joined them later, none of her children was on the island and thus could not lend a hand. Yoshiko recalled having lit endless sticks of incense and placing them on the family shrine, but it was Kamadū who prayed to the ancestors. It had also been Kamadū who made the rounds within the community to notify neighbors, each then dutifully extinguishing their hearth fires and discarding any food that was being prepared. Munekazu got in touch with local authorities and in short order they came to make an official determination of death; natural causes was their conclusion, a heart attack. It was then the responsibility of Muneto's closest female relatives to wash his body and dress it in his best clothing, a task that fell to Yoshiko, Kamadū, and Kaori.

Kiyoko, traveling from Kadena by train, arrived just after this part of the ritual had been completed. They used a formal kimono Muneto reserved for only the most special of occasions. It was not long thereafter that community members, a representative from each household as she recalled, visited their home bringing small amounts of money to help defray funeral costs, which was tradition. And each burned an incense to pray for Muneto's safe journey into the next life. Most of the visitors had been heads of their respective households in the community and it was Yoshiko's duty to serve them tea and *sātā andagī* (O: a round deep-fried Okinawan doughnut). Yoshiko had been delegated the task of frying the sātā andagī earlier in the day to ensure their freshness for guests. Kamadū spared no expense and had gone so far as to hire a professional wailer whose incessant crying and bellowing struck Yoshiko at once as unnerving and ridiculous—she seemed to have a boundless amount of energy and the lungs of a bull. Yoshiko had never seen a professional wailer, although she had heard of them. And she was particularly bemused by this one. Elderly, sporting a full head of gray hair and small in stature, to the point of appearing frail, her vigor belied the figure she cut. At some level, Yoshiko envied her and hoped she would be similarly energetic at her age. Kamadū had also engaged a chanter who had the job of sitting by the front gate ringing his bell and reciting Buddhist prayers.

She also remembered the long funeral procession to the family tomb. First, the small casket into which Muneto's lifeless body had been fitted, almost doubled over, was placed in a funeral palanquin; the palanquin could not be brought into the yard from the outskirts of the community until ebb tide. It was kept there to safeguard community residents from the pollution of death. Then, after the long line of mourners had been properly assembled, they began the nearly fifteen minute walk to the family tomb, led by a Buddhist priest. (Illustration 5) He was followed by an elderly gentleman carrying a funeral banner with Muneto's name announcing him as the deceased. Yoshiko did not know who this elderly man was. He was followed by four neighborhood men carrying the funeral palanquin who were, in turn, followed by a woman throwing paper flowers about that had been made earlier in the day for the occasion; the flowers were largely the handiwork of Kaori and Kiyoko. Then came the general procession of mourners, men first. Upon reaching the tomb, the priest offered a short prayer and quickly scurried off as if he was fleeing the clutches of something unseen and from the beyond, which had always struck Yoshiko as odd. The priest was the holiest person attending the funeral; if he had reason to fear, what about the rest of those in attendance?

Great amounts of incense were again burned at the tomb and all those present knelt in prayer. With that, the tomb door was opened and the casket pushed inside. The procession, somber until then, was suddenly assailed by the wailing, shrieking and crying of the female mourners, many of them clutching at the casket, Kamadū and Kiyoko among them. Strangely, Kaori was much more restrained and did not give herself up to the emotional outbursts displayed by her mother and older sister. Yoshiko too was crying. She had come to regard Muneto as a father, but her emotions by nature were much more reserved. She felt so uncomfortable by the open display of emotion that she moved aside and allowed the other female mourners, most of them older than she, space to do what they would do. With this concluded, male and female mourners returned home, albeit by different routes in an attempt to confuse the departed spirit and keep him from trying to follow them home. In order to assist the deceased in the next world, various items were left at the tomb door, to include a miniature paper umbrella, sandals, cane, food and drink.

When the family arrived home, Yoshiko and each member of the family was sprinkled with salt before entering the house as a rite of purification. Thereafter, memorial rites were held on specified days after the funeral—7th, 14th, 21st, 28th, 35th, 42nd, and 49th days. On the 49th day, known as *nanka* (J), she and Kamadū returned to the tomb yard to clean up all the items left behind, which they promptly burned. As dictated by tradition, after these memorial rites were held for Muneto, only the 1st, 3rd, 7th, 13th, 25th and 32nd anniversaries of death were recognized by the family. Showa 19 was the fourth anniversary of Muneto's death.

Though Yoshiko had found Muneto's passing personally distressing, with the passage of time and the various memorial rites that had been undertaken in remembrance of him, she grew more inured to the loss. Despite the esteem in which she still held her father-in-law, however, there was one remaining task associated with the burial rites that she found simply abhorrent. The ritual of washing the deceased bones could, in her mind, only be described as a grotesquerie of unique proportion. Sometime between the first and third year after death, the closest relatives of the deceased, which in this case were Munekazu,

Yoshiko, and Kamadū, gathered at the tomb. Of Munekazu's siblings only Kiyoko and Kaori could have come, but Kamadū was insistent they not bother either of them.

The family waited almost a full three years before undertaking this task—no one looked forward to it. Removing the mortar from around the tomb's door, they brought the casket out into the tomb yard. As called for by tradition, and Kamadū remained quite scrupulous about such matters, she had Tomiko hold an umbrella over the casket to keep Muneto's spirit from trying to escape. Next, Kamadū, being judged by the family as having been closest to Muneto during his life, was the first to touch his remains. Then Kamadū, Munekazu and Yoshiko, each using a large set of chopsticks, began stripping away any remaining flesh from the bones. Yoshiko suspected Tomiko was immensely gratified that her job was merely to hold the umbrella. She was, after all, connected to the family only through Yoshiko, but Kamadū had had the foresight to have Tomiko come along because she correctly surmised their unsavory task might be completed more quickly with the three of them cleaning the bones rather than only two. Yoshiko could see Tomiko avert her gaze whenever it got to be too much for her. She too began feeling a bit queasy and tried closing her eyes from time to time but it was nearly impossible to fit the remaining flesh securely between the chopsticks to remove it. In any case, no one was particularly enjoying the task, so she decided that she needed to do her part as well if they were ever to get out of there. It helped a little not to think of these as her father-in-law's remains, but rather just drudgery that needed to be completed.

Having successfully removed most of the remaining flesh, which took the better part of two hours, they next washed Muneto's bones in water several times followed by a final washing in awamori. His bones thus cleansed, they placed them in the urn: first his feet, legs and other bones and concluding with his skull. The urn was then placed on the left side of the tomb with the skull facing toward the structure's back so the deceased would be less tempted to try and leave. All then having said an obligatory prayer of apology to Muneto for having disturbed his bones, the family set out for home. Although all four of them were sprinkled with salt to purify themselves, Yoshiko felt unclean for a long time thereafter and hoped never to have to wash the bones of the dead again in her lifetime.

Chapter V

The Tamashiro Family

Munekazu grew up in the Takahashi-chō area of Naha along with his five siblings. He had two older brothers, Muneyuki, the eldest, and Seiho. Two of his three sisters served as bookends to the story of the Tamashiro offspring, representing the beginning and end of the family line for Muneto and Kamadū. Atsuko was the eldest child and Kaori, the youngest, had been the apple of her father's eye when he was alive; indeed the entire family doted over her. Kiyoko, with whom Munekazu had always been especially close and shared a special bond, was the second youngest. The two siblings traded confidences and dreams they would not dare divulge to other family members. (Illustration 6: Tamashiro Family Tree)

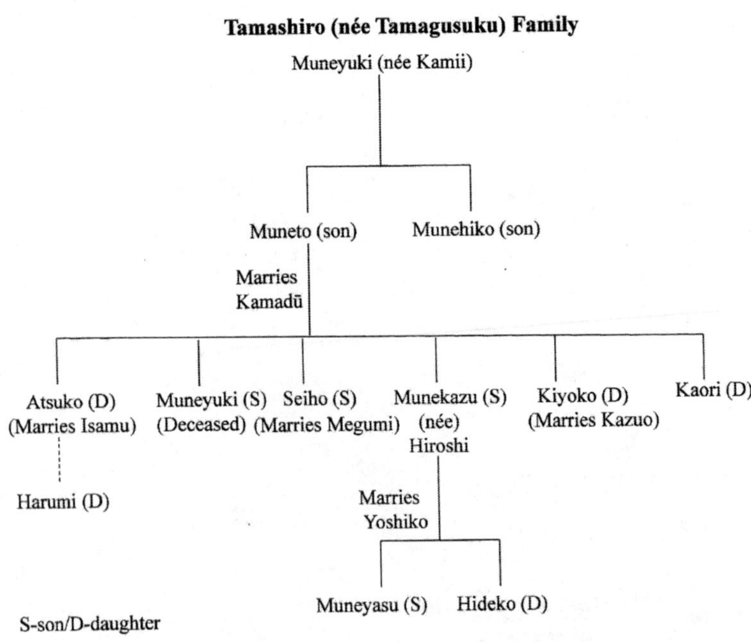

The family was originally from Naha and had been part of the old Ryukyu aristocracy. In those days, society was divided into aristocracy and commoner, the former living almost exclusively in urban areas. Commoners were further subdivided to distinguish between those living in urban areas and their rural cousins. Munekazu's great grandfather and grandfather, just as their forebears had, both held positions in the bureaucracy serving as clerks in the Department of External Affairs within the Board of General Affairs, under an assistant superintendent in charge of relations with Japan, and after its 1609 invasion of the Ryukyu kingdom, more specifically the Satsuma domain of Kagoshima. The Department was located in Naha rather than Shuri, capital of the old Ryukyu kingdom, because the kingdom's foreign relations had always been handled exclusively through Naha, its chief port city.

Each first-born male in the Tamashiro lineage, as decreed by bureaucratic tradition, had inherited this position since the mid-16th century. Younger sons also entered the bureaucracy, but at the next lower level, positions they in turn would pass along to their first-born sons. Keen to protect aristocratic privilege, no member of this class could be reduced in rank to the point that they would become a commoner.

After the forced abdication of Sho Tai, the kingdom's last monarch, on March 27, 1879 and the island's transition to prefectural status in Japan's administrative structure, the old bureaucracy was dissolved and its aristocratic adherents summarily dismissed. The former kingdom was thrown into a state of political flux: it still considered tributary ties to China as remaining extant, but was now officially part of Japan, and its centuries-old administrative structure had been extirpated. Many of the former gentry class left Shuri, abandoning the palace and old mansions, moving to cities to eke out a living while others pursued livelihoods as farmers in more rural areas. Munekazu's great grandfather died in that year, falling victim to the cholera outbreak that ravaged the islands, killing over 6400.

With dissolution of the old court bureaucracy, there was no position for Munekazu's grandfather, Kamii, to inherit. Ever the enterprising type, he presented himself to Japanese authorities as a Japanese-Ryukyuan language interpreter, adopting a distinctly Japanese name for the purpose—Muneyuki. This, coupled with his clerical acumen, made him quite useful to Japanese authorities as the Ryukyuan language was completely unintelligible to them— his family's hereditary position within the bureaucracy gave him the advantage he needed. Understanding the changing tides besetting Okinawa, however, Muneyuki ensured his two sons, now with the adopted Japanese names of Muneto and Munehiko, developed a useful skill. Thus, when they became of age, Muneyuki saw to it that both enrolled in Okinawa's normal school, first established in June 1880—teaching was considered a noble and respected profession. This was the course Munekazu too had chosen to follow and thus transition from government bureaucrat to teacher had been effected for the Tamashiro men. It had also been Muneyuki who decided to build a new family home in the rural area abutting Naha in 1880 to take advantage of farming opportunities. As the population of Naha increased in the ensuing decades, the result of its designation as prefectural capital, so too did the homes in the area, which over time had become Takahashi-chō and other outlying hamlets.

The events and travails of the Tamashiro family over the decades since 1879 were a microcosmic reflection of the monumental social and economic upheaval taking place on the island, for which the year 1895 proved to be a particular watershed. This was the year in which Japan defeated China in the first Sino-Japanese War (1894-5), marking itself as the preeminent power among East Asian nations after centuries of Sinocentrism in the region. In the months that followed victory, many Okinawans, particularly urbanites and the young of Naha and

Shuri, adopted the outward trappings of Japanese culture in order to be en vogue. Families began using Japanese readings of their names—indeed, the Tamashiro family had formerly been known as Tamagusuku (Note: "-gusuku" and "-shiro" can both be translated as castle.) Women adopted Japanese names to include the feminine"-ko" suffix on the end—Akiko, Hiroko, Chiyoko; Kamadū, however, would have none of that, adamantly refusing to adopt a Japanese name for herself. Men too assumed Japanese names and cut their traditional seaweed paste lacquered top-knot in favor of shorter, western-style cuts now sported by Japanese men. But outward appearances are often more easily changed than the human heart and the prejudices resident within them. Discrimination against the Japanese "other" by Japan's administrators, government officials and citizens continued unabated on Okinawa and ultimately throughout Japan's expanding empire. Regarded as benighted, uneducated and backward, and living in an underdeveloped economy, Okinawans became Japan's domestic variant of British author Rudyard Kipling's poem, *The White Man's Burden*.

Passage of time and the hardships of life on Okinawa led the Tamashiro siblings on various paths that were disconnected both spatially and in circumstance. They hardly resembled the family that had for over half a century occupied the land and home in which Yoshiko and Munekazu now raised their own children, Muneyasu and Hideko. His father's quiet ambition had always been to have his children raise their families in Takahashi-chō so he could enjoy his grandchildren in his advancing years. The times, however, would not countenance such easefulness.

Okinawan society was based on Confucian traditions owing in large measure to the centuries the island kingdom had voluntarily submitted to China as a tributary state. In return, Okinawa was permitted to trade with China, dispatch and receive occasional tribute missions, and send promising students to Beijing to study Confucian texts, Chinese classics, techniques of government administration and other important subjects. This knowledge, of course, was brought back to the island where it permeated the royal court and aristocracy. Consequently, Okinawa's traditions of inheritance were also based upon the Confucian precepts of primogeniture—the exclusive right of the eldest son to inherit the family's property; all other sons were expected to leave and establish "branch houses" of the main house. Daughters, of course, married out of the family. As a result, Muneyuki, the Tamashiro's eldest son, was expected to inherit the family's property. In summer 1932, however, at the age of seventeen, he succumbed to the ravages of dengue fever and died. This particular outbreak was, by historical comparison, relatively limited in scope although in its wake it left 524 people dead in the Naha and Shimajiri areas. Such outbreaks were not uncommon during the Meiji, Taishō and Showa periods, and were often quite devastating. An earlier outbreak of the disease in 1905, for example, afflicted over 62,000 people.

Because of Muneyuki's untimely death, tradition dictated that Seiho, now the eldest son, assume the mantle of family heir. But from the very beginning, Seiho proved quite averse to fulfilling the obligations associated with these responsibilities. Things came to a head when Muneto suggested changing Seiho's name to accord more closely with old Ryukyuan tradition. Established practice among the long defunct aristocracy called for using the same first syllable in the given name of each first born male in the family. Muneto's father, however, had adopted the Japanese name of Muneyuki in the late 19th century and had renamed his sons accordingly, all sharing the same first two syllables of "Mune-." Muneto had chosen to name his eldest son after his grandfather because of his deep respect for the elder Muneyuki. Consequently, Muneto suggested Seiho's name be changed to that of his own younger brother, Munehiko.

Seiho, however, was a free spirit and a child of the times, who for years had longed to leave Okinawa to find his fortune elsewhere; adhering to outmoded aristocratic practices simply did not appeal to him. He had always lamented the squalor in which Okinawans were compelled to live and dreamed of a better life, much as the Japanese government exhorted Okinawans to strive for. Such exhortations had induced many islanders to seek work overseas as employees of Japanese companies in areas like Formosa (Taiwan), the Philippines, and Micronesia. Acculturation into Japan's larger society, something ironically Muneto had long advocated, had come to the Tamashiro household, but not in the form he had hoped. It was just after his seventeenth birthday that Seiho left Okinawa on a ship, ultimately winding up in Peru one year later. This broke Muneto's heart, but he remained stoic in the face of his disappointment. In the end, it had been Munekazu who himself suggested to his father that his own name be changed from Hiroshi to Munekazu, who was now by circumstance the family's heir. They very occasionally heard from Seiho, who was in a place called Lima working in a restaurant owned by an Okinawan who himself had left the island years before. His dream was to one day own his own business.

Atsuko too had left Okinawa joining her husband, Isamu, who finally set down roots on the island of Saipan, part of the Mariana Islands, working as a tenant farmer in sugar cane production for the Japanese firm, Nan'yō Kōhatsu. Atsuko found labor in the sugar cane fields onerous, but seemed at least content with her lot in life. She explained in her sporadic letters home that the work was hard and unrelenting, but that they had hired two Korean women to assist with the labor, which made things a bit easier. In any case, they dreamed of entering into some sort of private enterprise in the future once their tenancy was completed although she was never specific as to what kind of business venture that might be.

The couple's original idea had been to travel to Hawaii to begin a new life—they'd heard a great deal about the place, but in the end family members who had emigrated there in 1907, the last year in which such travel was permitted, wrote several dissuading and disheartening letters to them that coming to Hawaii was no longer an option because of the immigration ban against Japanese citizens. They knew of at least two extended family members who had made the trek to Hawaii as contract workers for the sugar cane industry at a relatively young age. Both men, Kenji and Hiroto, who now had to be close to sixty, seemed to be flourishing. They spoke of their families and shared in great detail their early experiences and challenges as they began life in an unfamiliar far-off land. Atsuko's interest was particularly piqued by what could only be described as their unconventional marriages—she read that part of their letters several times with a quizzical expression on her face and repeated, as if asking herself, "Picture brides? Why on earth would anyone do that?" It was Muneto who explained that in those days contract workers, most between the ages of 21 and 35 and unmarried, made the trip to Hawaii. After a few years, they would become lonely and want to get married, but local marriage prospects were scarce. The alternative was to arrange marriages through the exchange of photographs with prospective Okinawan brides. Once marriage was agreed upon, the young soon-to-be bride would hasten down to the village office to register the marriage. This entitled her to travel to Hawaii to be with her husband. He went on to explain that during the period 1908-1924, a result of the "Gentlemen's Agreement of 1908" between the United States and Japan to limit Japanese immigration, this was one of the few ways to get to Hawaii—you had to be a family member—wife, child or close relative of someone already living there. This was commonly known as the *yobiyose* (J), or "summoning" period.

Kiyoko was married and living in Kadena, a small farming village located in the Nakagami administrative district. Her husband, Kazuo, worked as a clerk in the Kadena factory of the

Okinawa Sugar Company, while Kiyoko, along with her mother-in-law and two younger sisters-in-law, tended the small family farm. Munekazu did not get to see much of Kiyoko anymore, whose life now centered on Kazuo's family. He had visited with her only twice in the years since her marriage, once with his mother when they traveled to Kadena and again when she returned to Naha for Muneto's funeral.

Travel to and from Kadena was relatively easy, so inconvenience was not the reason for their sporadic encounters. Kadena was the terminus of the prefectural government-operated train system, Okinawa Prefectural Railways, that ran between it and Itoman in southern Okinawa, stopping along the way in Naha and other towns. Rather, the chasm that had grown to separate the once close siblings found its genesis in the passage of time, distance and differing life circumstances. He wondered if Kiyoko ever experienced the same feelings of lamentation or if she had resigned herself to being moved quietly along life's path, controlled by its ever-changing eddies. This was a question he never asked her.

No matter what her age, Kaori would always remain the "baby" of the family, a position she both eschewed and used to her advantage as circumstances warranted. She was blessed with a disposition that quickly endeared her to most, but also had a strong streak of independence that ran to her core, which served to keep at arm's length those with whom she was not particularly close. She had always been popular among her friends and teachers, but such things did not seem to matter to Kaori; she was quite serious about life and where her journey would ultimately take her. She decided early on that she too would follow in the family's newly founded tradition of entering the teaching profession and was now a first-year student at the women's division of the Okinawa Normal School where students studied to become future teachers.

Yoshiko had also grown up in Naha, but in its bustling

commercial district, and was not of gentry origins. The Kinjō family were craftsmen by trade making basājin, a skill refined over many generations. Although such prohibitions had long since fallen out of practice, during the days of the Ryukyu kingdom Yoshiko and Munekazu's marriage could never have taken place—there was a strict proscription against the intermarriage of classes. Changing residences from one area to another was also proscribed, beginning in 1654. Such moves were undertaken primarily to protect the prerogatives of the aristocracy and safeguard the tax base commoners represented because it was through their toils that the upper class of Ryukyuan society enjoyed its privileges.

The two met serendipitously when Munekazu had gone to Higashi-machi looking for sandals and saw Yoshiko struggling with a particularly large load of basājin piled high above the top of the small cart she was pulling. She was taking the goods to a middleman the family used to help sell their goods; they also sold directly from their storefront, the back of which simultaneously served as their tiny "factory" and home. As she slowly and unsteadily labored with her load, facing the cart as she pulled and walked backward, the basājin piled above the top of the wagon slid off onto the road. The load, now suddenly lightened, no longer needed the extra exertion Yoshiko had been applying and she quickly lost her balance and ended up on her rear end, providing shopkeepers and passersby a moment of levity. Her pride more wounded than her derriere, she picked herself up off the ground and began gathering the clothing that was now lying on the dusty road. It was then that Munekazu had come over to assist her in picking up and cleaning the now dust-laden basājin. After they piled the clothing back onto the cart, he pulled it for her despite her polite protestations. From there the relationship blossomed over time finally ending in marriage. Kamadū, who believed in holding to convention on many things, quite surprisingly took to Yoshiko almost immediately. She liked the fact that she came from a "working" family and was not afraid of getting her hands a little dirty. As time went on and contact with her own daughters became more infrequent, it was Yoshiko who filled the role of surrogate daughter and upon whom Kamadū came to rely more heavily as she advanced in years.

Chapter VI

Prelude to Disaster

Atsuko and her husband, Isamu, were part of an Okinawan diaspora that began at the close of the 19th century and continued through the first three decades of the next, taking islanders to the far-flung reaches of Japan's expanding empire and beyond: the Philippines, Micronesia, Formosa, Hawaii, Brazil, Peru, Bolivia, New Caledonia, Canada, Argentina, Cuba and the United States. The vanguard of the movement emerged in December 1899 when twenty-seven Okinawan men, organized by Toyama Kyuzo of Kin Village (Okinawa), traveled to Hawaii as contract workers aboard the *SS City of China* and went to work at the Ewa Plantation on Oahu. (Twenty-six men actually lived and worked in Hawaii; one was ultimately denied entry and returned to Okinawa.) By 1907 the number of Okinawans in Hawaii had grown to approximately 8,500, and during the yobiyose period, roughly another 8,000 islanders emigrated there.

Japan occupied the islands of Micronesia in October 1914, former holdings of Germany, when it entered the fighting of World War I on the side of the allies, specifically in response to Great Britain's request for assistance in the Pacific against German naval forces. Japan's "prerogatives" in Micronesia, which also included three of the Mariana Islands—Saipan, Tinian and Rota—were officially recognized by a League of Nations mandate in May 1919; by March 1922 it had created the South Seas Government (J: Nan'yō-chō) to administer the islands under civilian authority. During the ensuing years, the Japanese civilian population, to include Okinawans, grew both steadily and quickly as authorities sought to maximize economic benefit from the islands through various commercial enterprises, but cultivation of sugar cane and production of sugar would become and remain the mainstay of economic activity.

By 1935, with over 50,000 Japanese living throughout Micronesia, eighty percent of whom lived on Saipan, Tinian and Rota, the population of Japanese immigrants surpassed that of the Micronesians; and by 1942 more than 96,000 Japanese lived throughout Micronesia, dwarfing the local population. Okinawans represented a substantial percentage of this growth, primarily as laborers in sugar cane fields or some other related aspect of sugar production, and in the end outnumbered even mainland Japanese. This was not by happenstance. Japanese authorities considered the local population of Micronesians unsuitable as laborers because of what they perceived as deficient work habits and being less advanced than other colonial subjects. Conversely, Okinawans were seen as a more reliable work force and thus actively recruited by the *Nan'yō Kōhatsu Company*, heavily invested in sugar production in Micronesia, through the offer of special dispensations to sign on as contract laborers.

Initial patterns of Okinawan migration into Micronesia during the 1920s were similar to those experienced in Hawaii in that most laborers were single males who signed contracts to work for three years. They were recruited to clear vast tracts of jungle along Saipan's coastal plains that would ultimately be put to use growing sugar cane. The government's envisaged colonization of Micronesia, however, proved difficult to undertake with a transient work force; consequently families were also encouraged to go. As the population expanded in size and composition, Japan's logistical footprint also grew on the islands—various shops, bars, schools, factories, and restaurants flourished. This was the Saipan experienced by Isamu and Atsuko.

2

Isamu first came to Saipan at the end of 1938 without Atsuko. They had been married for several years by then, but he didn't want to risk bringing her along without first knowing the conditions they would confront. If things did not turn out as he expected, it would be easier for him to return to Okinawa rather than both of them having to admit defeat to family and friends. He had heard from several old friends already on Saipan and Tinian who shared their working and living experiences. Frankly, the work sounded grueling—out in the hot sun all day clearing land, working sugar cane fields and having production quotas to meet. But prospects for gainful employment and getting ahead on Okinawa were bleak to say the least, and in the end, this offered some chance of building a future. He hoped to earn enough money working as a tenant farmer so he and Atsuko could eventually open a small business of their own catering to the large population of Okinawan workers on Saipan—and maybe even expand onto neighboring Tinian, which also had a sizeable number of Okinawans and was separated from Saipan only by a narrow five mile wide channel. As he thought about the possibilities of a future in Micronesia, Isamu never entertained any real notion of returning home; he was just glad to be gone. He was not certain of Atsuko's feelings on the matter, but she seemed excited about beginning life anew on Saipan. She finally joined him in summer of the following year traveling on the *SS Saipan-maru,* one of the Japan Mail Steamship Company's two newer ships put into service on routes between Japan and Micronesia.

Coming to the Mariana Islands wasn't nearly as simple as it had been in the earlier days. In fact, the only reason Isamu was accepted by Nan'yō Kōhatsu and received permission to come was because of his farming experience and the fact that two of his close friends, Kanashiro Takashi and Uehara Yoshiro, remained on good terms with the management of the operation on Saipan. They, also working as tenant farmers, were among some of the Okinawans the company management still trusted and they had put in a good word for Isamu, extolling his work ethic and reliability. Besides, he had also volunteered to pay his own passage to get there, a sum of seventy yen, money he cobbled together from his and Atsuko's meager savings and contributions from relatives and friends on Okinawa. So in the end, it cost the company very little to get him to Saipan and it stood to profit from his labor. While Isamu was not keen to go asking for money hat in hand from others, he saw this as an investment in his and Atsuko's future. In any case, he planned to repay any money he borrowed.

Okinawans had fallen into ill favor with Nan'yō Kōhatsu officials as a result of labor disputes, the most notable having been those in 1927 and 1932, involving four thousand and six thousand laborers, respectively, and for which officials held Okinawans accountable as instigators. The bone of contention among many Okinawan farmers and workers was the poor pay they received. Additionally, a growing number of them had also begun breaking their labor contracts in favor of taking up less physically demanding jobs; and moonlighting on second jobs became yet another new trend of the times. The genesis of such economic activity among Okinawans rested not only with the onerous field work, but with the continued discrimination they suffered at the hands of Japanese officials and citizens: pay scales were discriminatory—Japanese received higher wages than Okinawans for doing similar work; Okinawans, along with the growing Korean population on the islands, were still largely disparaged by the Japanese; and worse yet, the local population of Micronesians understood the lower social status of Okinawans vis à vis the Japanese and many looked upon them with equal disdain. On whole, colonial society in Micronesia was a curious mix of classes. Conceptually, Japanese colonial masters occupied the upper tier of society, followed by Okinawans, then Koreans and finally the locals—the Chamorro and Kanaka. (The Kanaka were held in lesser regard than the Chamorro because of their darker skin color.) In practice, however, excepting that Japanese mainlanders occupied the upper rung of colonial society, official distinctions between and among the other groups were not well delineated.

Not that the Okinawan community in Micronesia did not take steps to try to better its lot. The community understood, along with Okinawan communities throughout Japan's empire—on Taiwan, Osaka and even Okinawa—that its members were regarded as the uneducated and culturally bereft of Japan whose lifestyle was in need of reform in order to "advance" to Japan's higher culture. This belief was so pervasive in Micronesia that Okinawans were derogatorily referred to as the Kanaka of Japan. Consequently, as it did in other areas of the empire during the 1930s, a movement took root in Micronesia, the Lifestyle Reform Movement, which at its core sought to supplant Okinawan culture with the broader culture of Japan, but by now at the urging of Okinawans themselves.

As the couple saw it, life on Saipan offered little hope of relief from the rigidly maintained class distinctions between Japanese and Okinawans. Although they considered their life as less than idyllic, it was peaceful and generally uneventful. They contented themselves with the thought that for the time being, this was home and they had to make the best of it, all the while dreaming of the day they would own their own business. All this changed the morning of February 22, 1944.

3

Atsuko and Isamu were sitting down to their usual simple breakfast of rice gruel, locally caught fish and some sort of native fruit—this morning it was guava—preparing for yet another long day of work in the sugar cane field, theirs but one of hundreds patch-working Saipan's landscape. They worked their land, roughly eleven acres located some four kilometers southeast of Garapan, along with two Korean women they had hired to help in the fields and transport harvested cane to the Nan'yō Kōhatsu Company. Hiring Koreans was not typical. Okinawans usually hired other Okinawans and they were sometimes chided by their neighbors as a result. But as Atsuko and Isamu saw it, Koreans shared a fate similar to their own on Saipan and helping each other was the only proper thing to do. They were steady workers—reliable, hard-working and showed up to work on time. What else could they ask? Besides, they did not have to worry much about the women as hired hands, unlike men who frequented the *ryori-ya* (J: restaurants) in town, drinking and taking up with the women employed there to entertain male customers.

Garapan, the island's largest town, served as its administrative center and where most mainland Japanese lived. It was located along Saipan's western coastline about halfway up its nineteen kilometer length. Garapan, as they saw it, was a cocoon for many of its Japanese residents, filled with various Japanese shops and restaurants and where its inhabitants frequented Japanese-style clubs and movies, many adorned in Japanese-style clothing. As Isamu and Atsuko often observed, it was as if Garapan's residents wanted to avoid sullying themselves by too much contact with locals or other colonial inhabitants, namely Okinawans and Koreans. And most of the town's residents, unwilling to advantage themselves with the plentiful food the island had to offer—fruits, vegetables, and fish—imported much of their foodstuff from Japan. "Little Ginza" is what Isamu derisively called it.

There were, of course, other areas of Garapan frequented by Okinawans, but as was typical throughout Micronesia, these were generally less developed, a bit dirtier and, on whole, more unsightly. To relieve the monotony of field work, however, Garapan did offer such pastimes as the Minami Theater, which often put on Okinawan plays. For others, the ryori-ya provided needed diversions. Such was the distinction between colonial master and indentured worker.

That day, not unlike many they had spent on Saipan, appeared it would dawn sunny, hot and humid. The couple found it slightly monotonous, but not onerously so. It was just before dawn, but work in the fields started early so they were quickly finishing their meal. They usually met Sae Kyung and Hae Rin, their field hands, at the field to begin the day's chores.

"By the way, when do you plan on writing to your family again? It's been quite a while," Isamu asked to break their silence.

Atsuko could muster little more than "hmm" in affirmation. After working all day in the fields and tending to their small, but surprisingly plentiful little vegetable garden, she had neither the energy nor interest in sitting down to write. As much as she wanted to hear from her family, the realities of daily life trumped such activities. On top of that, the company had been pushing farmers to boost production in support of Japan's war effort. There were no free moments.

Isamu, judging by Atsuko's response that there would be little else to this conversation, finished the last of his breakfast and prepared to leave their small wooden hut. This was the type of dwelling in which most tenant farmers lived. The company provided them funds to build small wooden huts covered with corrugated zinc roofing. While not lavish by any means, and certainly not the quality of home most Japanese lived in, it protected them from most of the elements.

Hearing a strange rumbling in the distance Isamu asked, "Thunder?" as much to himself as to Atsuko. But as he peered outside there was not a cloud in the sky.

"Did you hear that?" he asked his wife.

Again, Atsuko was oblivious to much around her, and did not

respond. Then there were several more "booms" in succession. This finally roused Atsuko from her daze. Her brow now furrowed by curiosity, she looked at Isamu. As the sounds increased in intensity and frequency, they heard the voices of agitated neighbors through the tiny window.

Suddenly there was banging on their door; it was Sae Kyung and Hae Rin, both of them wide-eyed and out of breath having run up from the sugar cane field. They were frantically yelling, "It's an attack! We're under attack!" Atsuko and Isamu rushed outside.

Neighbors had already begun gathering along the narrow dirt road that served as the tiny no-name hamlet's only street. Not that there were that many to begin with. Twenty-two Okinawans comprised the place, most of whom were tenant farmers, others who worked the sugar mill and most from the same small Okinawan town of Kina. The couple looked at each other in disbelief as they heard the sound of more explosions and the whining of aircraft engines in the distance.

"What's going on? What is this?" Atsuko asked aloud, addressing no one in particular.

"The Americans must be attacking us," offered Hae Rin, her unusually round eyes even more so as she stared in the direction from which the sounds were coming.

"That's nonsense," replied the farmer Higa in an agitated voice. "Japan is winning its war against America. We hear reports all the time. No way the Americans even try something like this—must be a military drill."

Indeed, belief in Japan's invincibility is what had given Isamu and Atsuko hope of a better future for all these years. Yet something was clearly awry, much like Higa's assessment.

Scanning the skies, the small group realized there were actually several groups of airborne attackers—one flying around Tanapag Harbor north of their hamlet, another at Charan-Kanoa Airfield several kilometers to their south and yet another toward the southern end of the island where, they presumed, Aslito Airfield was being attacked. It was obvious that these were not planes of the Japanese military, which often flew so low over the island you could barely hold a conversation with someone standing next to you. These were US planes and this was no drill—the enemy *was* attacking. Accentuating the scene before them was the sound of Japanese anti-aircraft fire as the island's defenders tried to fend off the enemy, but to little avail. The sky was dotted with puffs of black smoke, but the attack was not slowed. Not knowing what to expect, families closed up their huts and hurriedly ran toward the heavily wooded eastern hills to take cover.

A total of forty-eight aircraft carrier-based planes comprising Task Group 58.2 attacked airfields and shipping on Saipan and Guam the morning of February 22; another group, Task Group 58.3, attacked Tinian and Rota. In total, Japanese forces lost 101 aircraft on the ground and another sixty-seven were shot down; the Americans lost six aircraft in the attack. The Mariana Islands, which until then had served as little more than a logistics and staging area for the military, had no combat units assigned to any of the islands. The day's attack, however, would open the pages of a different narrative for the islands and its residents. Japan's military planners now understood that the momentum of the war had swung toward the US and its allies and the priority would be to construct strong defensive lines across the Pacific to attrite US forces and protect Japan's home islands. The Marianas, along with other Pacific island groups, would become the outer line of defense and thus efforts to fortify the islands against further attack would be undertaken in earnest.

They could still hear the sounds of war from their hiding place within the jungle thicket. Isamu and Atsuko silently sat crouched, his arm around her shoulder.

Atsuko finally asked Isamu in a hushed voice, "Where did Sae Kyung and Hae Rin go? Weren't they right behind us?"

Pointing to his left he said, "Yes, but they went off in that direction once we reached the jungle."

She supposed they must have been trying to make it back to their families. The two of them remained in hiding, frightened and confused. They, as did many of their friends, had always regarded the presence of Japan's military in the Pacific islands as a guarantor of peace; never did they consider the idea that its presence would invite attack. Yet the war that had seemed so distant and from which they all felt disconnected, had now arrived on Saipan. It was several hours before they felt safe enough to come out from hiding and return home.

They emerged from the jungle and immediately began surveying the landscape. Black smoke billowed high into the sky here and there, at once telling a story of success for the enemy and bewilderment for island residents. Airfields were damaged and aircraft destroyed; transport shipping sunk or rendered unusable; and even the island's sugar refinery at Chalankanda was laid waste. The two quickly hurried back to their hut and once inside its relative safety, a certain calm returned to them both. Isamu, running his fingers through his hair, tried to gather his thoughts; Atsuko sat with her hand braced against her forehead casting a forlorn look at Isamu. Inexplicably, her thoughts turned to the old fisherman Aragaki and his wife with whom she'd begun doing business not long after her arrival on Saipan. Aragaki mainly fished for *katsuo* (J: bonito) and Atsuko would, once a month, go to their little place near the harbor to purchase small amounts of *katsuobushi*, katsuo that had been smoked until rock hard and then shaved and used as flavoring in soups. On occasion she even purchased the errant fresh fish Aragaki might have caught, although in reality she never actually purchased anything. Theirs was a relationship based on in-kind bartering—Atsuko brought vegetables she traded for fish; it was a mutually beneficial arrangement. She and Isamu had no talent for fishing; the Aragaki family had little time to tend a garden. As she would later learn, the family survived the attack, but with increasing numbers of enemy submarines operating in the area it would become too dangerous to venture out to sea. From then on, the Aragakis had to content themselves with subsistence fishing, netting what they could from shore.

Isamu was the first to break the silence. "I should go to the company to see if I can get any information. Somebody should know something."

Atsuko, nodding her head in agreement, added, "And I'll go visit members of the Okinawan Prefectural Association to see if anyone's heard anything."

"Good idea—let's meet back here in a few hours," Isamu replied. He suggested Atsuko ride the family bicycle as she made her rounds of Association households; he would walk to the company administration buildings. With that they left the hut in search of any information they could find.

4

The grounds surrounding Nan'yō Kōhatsu's administrative building had become a gathering place for the many confused and frightened workers who came seeking information from company authorities. An apprehensive buzz enveloped the growing crowd, which only increased as more workers gathered and time passed. Isamu looked for his friends, Takashi and Yoshiro, but it was nearly impossible to locate them with all the people. Four Okinawan workers standing near him were involved in an animated discussion.

One of them looked in Kazuo's direction saying, "Hey, did you hear about the sugar mill going up in smoke? Looks like Japan's chickens may be coming home to roost. I'll bet they're in touch with the higher ups trying to figure out what to do next."

Isamu looked at the man blankly without responding. *The sugar refinery?* he thought. He understood that sugar was not only integral to his and Atsuko's future, but that it was the lifeblood of the island's economy: tenant farmers worked the fields; others worked in the sugar refinery; the island's railroad was there to move sugar from the mill to the ships waiting in Tanapag Harbor to transport finished products to the mainland; and the many shopkeepers depended on the local population to sustain their businesses. Without the refinery, there was no sugar industry and nothing else could flourish. *If this is true, we're in real trouble,* he thought to himself.

It took company officials more than three hours to finally address the restless crowd, but rather than providing useful information, they merely offered a stream of platitudes that could be summed up in one line—"These are trying times and the emperor needs his loyal subjects to persevere to ensure Japan's ultimate victory."

"Hogwash!" retorted the man who had earlier spoken to Isamu.

Others around him picked up the sentiment of his message, if not its exact wording, and challenged officials for more information. "What about the sugar refinery?"

"What do the attacks mean for us?"

"Will the company stay in business?"

These were the answers those gathered on the grounds of the Nan'yō Kōhatsu Company's administrative offices sought, but there was little officials could provide. While they confirmed damage to the refinery, they had little else to offer. They beseeched the workers to return home, promising updates as soon as they learned more. Disgruntled, but understanding little more was to be learned at the moment, the crowd slowly began disbanding. And as the crowd thinned, Isamu caught sight of his friend Takashi.

"Takashi!" he yelled.

His friend turned to greet him. "Ah, Isamu. What did you think about what we heard?" he asked.

"With the refinery gone and military airfields being attacked by the enemy, this may be the end."

Isamu added that in overhearing others talk while he was waiting for official announcements, he learned that most of the military's aircraft may never even have made it off the ground. Isamu shook his head and said rather stoically, "You may be right. We could be in real trouble."

The two walked for a while sharing the rumors each had heard, trying to piece together a mosaic of disparate information in hopes of creating a clearer picture. Their efforts yielded only frustration. In the end, Isamu decided to return home to hear what Atsuko might have learned.

5

There never were any answers to the questions raised during the meeting after the attack, but official actions spoke volumes and their worst fears came to pass. Workers and farmers learned that the refinery would not be rebuilt. Instead, they were reassigned to dig protective shelters and defensive positions. Beginning the following month transport ships, once laden with the fruits of farmers' labor, carried women, children and the elderly back to Japan in a more concerted effort to evacuate noncombatants off the Mariana Islands and other parts of Micronesia, a process begun as early as 1943. One of these ships, the *Amerika-maru,* carrying some 1,700 passengers, mostly family members of Nan'yō Kōhatsu Company officials, was sunk three days out of port, killing 599 on board. Although another 5,000 noncombatants would be successfully evacuated before the start of hostilities in June 1944, roughly 16,000 would remain on the Mariana Islands to endure the ferocious fighting to follow.

The mood across the island was Cimmerian, leaving in its residents a general sense of malaise. While she still tended the vegetable garden and took care of their small number of livestock—one cow and several chickens—without the sugar cane field to work Atsuko too felt a bit listless and worried about the future. Isamu was off each day helping to dig shelters and doing other work to fortify the island's defenses against enemy attack. He, along with other farmers and workers, also received rudimentary military training, learning how to use bamboo spears and throw hand grenades, something he curiously seemed to relish. Atsuko cringed at the thought of such training. *If the island's safety had come down to a bunch of farmers with bamboo spears, we're all doomed,* she would sometimes think to herself. She never shared these worries with Isamu.

As she stood hunched over the sweet potato patch, she recalled their conversation of the evening before.

Isamu had begun, saying, "I heard today that one of the transport ships going back to Japan was sunk. What a pity for those women and children."

"This is ridiculous!" she exclaimed in response. "If ships can't make it back to Japan safely..." Her voice trailed off.

"Atsuko," he continued, "this may be the end. I don't know how this will all end for us if we stay, but I don't want to risk losing you by sending you back to Japan. The waters are too dangerous to travel safely. I know it's selfish, but please stay here on the island."

It had been years since Atsuko felt genuine emotion, particularly with regard to her marriage. Not that she did not love Isamu, but their relationship had evolved, or perhaps devolved, to one of efficiency, devoid of any real passion. But that night his words struck something deep within her, reigniting a connection that had first brought them together. There was no need for words at that moment; she hugged him deeply and the two spent the night together as husband and wife for the first time in a very long time.

Chapter VII

The End: Operation Forager

By late May 1944 the face of the Mariana Islands had undergone significant change. Schools were no longer holding classes; sugar cane fields were left untended; and the once-vibrant sugar industry now lay dormant. Several large military units moved onto Saipan, including the 31st Army headquarters, which had assigned units scattered throughout the Marianas and the rest of Micronesia and was commanded by Lieutenant General Ōbata Hideyoshi; the 43rd Division commanded by Lieutenant General Saito Yoshitsugu; the 47th Independent Mixed Brigade; and several other smaller battalion-sized units. A new fighter airstrip was also being hurriedly constructed on the northern end of the island near Marpi Point, mostly through the labor of locals and Koreans.

Convoys bringing troop units into the Marianas, however, increasingly fell victim to US naval submarine forces and aircraft carrier-based planes, impacting the effective combat power of Saito's forces through loss of troops, equipment and weapons, a circumstance that would weigh heavily in the coming weeks. Survivors of these attacks, many injured or bedraggled, were like silent prognosticators of the devastation about to visit the island. Further exacerbating the military's circumstances was the fact that, unknown to the military command, units would have fewer than thirty days to prepare the island against assault in part because future US plans had been incorrectly assessed. The Palau Islands were where Japan's military command anticipated the enemy attack and had thus prioritized, not Saipan. In the end, a force of 31,629 troops was mustered to defend Saipan, a number that would prove inadequate to the task of repelling an American invasion force over four times that size.

June 11, 1944 would end much as it had begun that awful morning in February. Isamu was off as usual working in support of the army's efforts to build up island defenses, so he wouldn't be back until late. Atsuko, along with other wives of their hamlet, was tasked with making bandages for the local medical aid station. While she still felt uneasy about what all these preparations portended, Atsuko had resigned herself to their predicament. There was nowhere else to go and no means to get anywhere—they were stuck, so they had to make the most of it. *There's nothing to be done,* she often thought to herself. The group of women worked on throughout the morning and into the afternoon, creating diversions for themselves through easy banter and light laughter, even taking a break for lunch in the shade of several large nearby trees.

The afternoon's serenity was rocked, suddenly and violently, at 2:30pm by an attack of US aircraft on the island, the opening salvo of Operation Forager to take the Mariana Islands. Unlike their earlier experience in February, this attack would serve as a prelude to continued unrelenting and merciless bombardment of Saipan, measured in days rather than hours. In total, 216 US aircraft attacked Saipan, Rota, Guam and Tinian, 208 fighters and eight torpedo planes, destroying 100-150 aircraft on the ground and shooting down another eighty-nine. Air supremacy now belonged to the enemy. As the attack began, each member of Atsuko's group instinctively, almost as though they were automata, quickly sought safety within the jungle thicket much as many had done earlier. Two of their number, Etsuko and Fumiko, realizing they were about to leave behind a day's worth of work, bundled up the bandages the group had finished and rushed them to the first aid station. Atsuko didn't think about it at the time, but she was never sure if they actually made it as far as the aid station or not. It was the last time she ever saw either of them.

When it was all over, the women in Atsuko's small group

rushed back to their homes. Isamu was already there, kneeling on the floor, busily packing a few things away into a makeshift bag made from an old piece of large cloth—rations, some water, and a few other sundries. He looked up at Atsuko as she came in. While clearly relieved to see her, Atsuko noticed a look in his eyes unfamiliar to her, a look of genuine fear.

"Atsuko, help me gather a few things. There is no telling when the enemy will come back."

She looked at him, not certain of what to do next. Isamu, stopped momentarily, and putting his hands gently on each of Atsuko's shoulders pulled her to the ground in a sitting position. His voice was not panicked, but had in it an unmistakable urgency.

He looked squarely at her and said softly, "I think this may be the end. Most of the military's planes never even made it off the ground. They are not as strong as we've been told. If there is another attack, head straight for the jungle and try to find a cave. And be sure to take this with you," he said, pointing to the bag. "If you're careful, it should last you for a few days."

Looking at him she asked, "But what about you?"

"Don't worry about that now. Look, we'll probably leave together, but just in case we're separated..." He stopped and looked at the bag.

She nodded slowly. Although the rest of the night was quiet, both slept in fits and starts.

They were greeted the following dawn by yet more enemy aircraft attacking the island; only this time with no Japanese aircraft to oppose them, they focused on ships and fishing vessels in the harbor area and land-based targets. Sampans also fell victim to attacks as US military planners believed they were being used to ferry Japanese troops between islands. The couple again, quickly and stealthily, made their way through the cane fields and into the jungle to wait out the attack; and so ended the day of June 12, 1944. They returned home to endure yet another sleepless night.

Just as islanders were growing accustomed to the rhythm of the air attacks, albeit frightened and weary, a new element was added—naval gunfire. The islanders endured pre-invasion gunfire delivered by enemy battleships, destroyers and cruisers on June 13 and 14, this time Garapan serving as one of the major targets. Luckily, Isamu had had the foresight to pack a few things, because once the ships began their barrage, there was little time to dally and they could not return. This would be the last the couple ever saw of their small home as anything other than smoldering lumber strewn about the landscape; and with it, their dreams.

The sounds were deafening and the massive concussive effects of exploding shells rocked residents until their insides began feeling like gelatin, an experience for which mere words could do little justice. Atsuko described the sensation as "feeling like your body was coming apart from the inside." Every resident of Saipan—Japanese, Okinawan, Korean or local—wondered if his previous breath would be his last. Respected men cowered, strong men cried and yet there was no shame as every person—man and woman alike—feared the reality of their own finality. This was the battle of Saipan.

2

As Isamu peered through the brush from his elevated position he could see Garapan awash in flames—there was little left of it. He wondered to himself how many people had been lost. A lull in the attack had given him this opportunity to find higher ground so he could see what was happening. All he could repeat to himself as he looked toward Saipan's western coast was, "It's over."

The jungle was filled with people trying to escape the earlier bombardment, some finding a measure of safety in caves on the hills behind Garapan, but there were only so many. Atsuko and Isamu shared theirs with ten others making things very cramped, but no one complained. Those unable to find shelter in caves looked for areas of particularly thick foliage that at least provided cover, but little protection. In the jungle hills these displaced civilians not only had to contend with poisonous snakes and lizards, but they also had to be certain that any place they chose to hide was behind Japanese lines or else they would likely be cut to shreds in a hail of bullets, caught between the enemy and the island's defenders. Indeed, before locating their current spot, they were forced to move from several other locations by soldiers that had turned out to be in the line of fire of planned defensive positions.

Enemy ships began firing again early the next morning. From their vantage point they could see a thirty-foot tower nestled in the hills behind Garapan, but had no idea as to what its significance might have been. What they did not know was that Vice Admiral Nagumo Chūichi, the officer who led the attack against the Americans at Pearl Harbor, and titular commander of all military forces in Micronesia, stood there watching enemy landing craft offloading assault forces onto Saipan's shores at the small town of Chalan Kanoa. While their group could not see the landing craft from where they were, Isamu, Atsuko and the others reasoned what was happening—the naval gunfire had been replaced by the sounds of fierce ground fighting—field artillery, machine guns and tanks—and it was getting too close for comfort. A soldier happened by and confirmed their suspicions—the enemy was landing. Fighting over the next several days was savage and went on night and day. The night of June 16 was particularly bad as Japanese forces launched a failed counterattack against the enemy. From their caves they could see muzzle flashes and tracers light up the night's darkness. By morning's light they could also see Japanese defenders taking up new positions closer to their own location, which Isamu correctly surmised, meant the enemy was gaining ground.

Looking at Atsuko, but speaking loud enough for the others to hear, Isamu said, "The enemy is slowly coming and the fighting is getting closer. They landed south of Garapan, which means we can't go toward Aslito—we have to move north." He then more quietly said to her, "Our food and water is just about gone. We have to move."

She simply looked at him and nodded.

Early on the morning of June 17 they left the relative safety of the cave heading further north, followed by several others. Little did they realize that during their journey north, a decisive battle was to take place—the Battle of the Philippine Sea (June 18-19, 1944), involving Japan's First Mobile Fleet under the command of Vice Admiral Ozawa Jisaburō and US Task Force 58, commanded by Vice Admiral Marc Mitscher. Japanese aviators, at this point in the war, were poorly trained and inexperienced in aerial combat, and no match for seasoned American aviators. As a result, most of the air power of the First Mobile Fleet was destroyed in what is colloquially known as the "Great Marianas Turkey Shoot." Japanese efforts were further hampered by the lack of air support from ground-based aircraft, destroyed in earlier raids on Saipan and other bases in the Mariana Islands. In the end, the First Mobile Fleet lost 480 aircraft and three aircraft carriers, decimating Japan's naval combat power.

Isamu, Atsuko and others pressed ahead across several ridges, and with this added distance, the war strangely felt an eternity away, but they knew better. They came across a large group of civilians waiting in line for food and water at a military aid station. The available food was meager—only *kanpan* (J), but it would at least stave off hunger for a while. Besides, the ration of water they received made the crackers expand in their stomachs helping them to feel full. They continued further north and by dark reached the foothills of Mount Donnay where an army field hospital was located. Their spirits momentarily lifted—an army hospital, finally some relief. Nothing could have been further from the truth. As the group drew closer, the morbid sights that assailed them defied description. The putrid air of death and suffering hung pervasively about the place like low-hanging fog along a shoreline, a situation made all the worse by inadequate staffing and medical supplies. There was no anesthesia and medical staff busily ran from patient to patient, clearly working beyond their capacity. Of those soldiers still alive, most were a bloody mess—missing limbs, deep gashing wounds and bleeding profusely. The most disturbing thing to Atsuko, however, were the cries for help, the screaming pleas for death to stop the pain amid the wretched smell. She cringed, all the while wanting to help those suffering, but she was in no position to do so.

This was the face of war, devoid of the glory, honor and medals bestowed upon the few. Here she stood, here they all stood, witness to the raw truth of the cruelty that mankind is capable of visiting upon himself—inglorious, painful and a travesty to the preciousness of human life. She had once felt some amount of pride in the Japanese military for its rousing victory at Pearl Harbor. She was by no means one of those ultra-nationalists, but she had bought into the notion that the Japanese, along with other Asians, were looked down upon by Westerners and being held back.

Held back? From what? From this? she now thought to herself. What she had experienced over the past several weeks was causing her to think differently, perhaps to think for the first time. Their own nation had brought this tragedy upon them, but now they were bearing the cost. It was not only soldiers at this hospital, there were civilians among the piles of dead as well. And what about the parents of these young men, some crying for their mothers in a far off land they would never leave? Had they had a hand in initiating this war? She was consumed by fury, but as much as she wanted to lash out, there was no one upon whom to vent her anger.

Atsuko could take no more. She pulled at Isamu's shirt sleeve, he being transfixed by what he was seeing. They hurried through the hospital grounds finding a place to rest for the evening that was out of earshot of the agonizing cries that would haunt her for months to come. Sleep did not come easily to either Isamu or Atsuko, but fatigue wracked their bodies and despite their best efforts both fell fast asleep.

By June 19 Mount Tapotchau, Saipan's highest point, was in the hands of the Americans, followed by the fall of Mount Donnay. Atsuko wondered whatever became of the wounded there. As she discovered later, the ambulatory among the patients evacuated northward. Those unable to be moved received hand grenades to take their own lives in order to avoid capture by the enemy.

They continued on, keeping the fighting to their backs; there was no time for recrimination or regrets. Slowly, Japanese military forces and Saipan's civilian inhabitants were forced further north, but their room for maneuver was running short as they approached the end of the island at Mount Marpi. They found themselves in close quarters with each other. On July 6 General Saito drafted a final message to his remaining troops extolling their efforts and exhorting them to undertake a final charge against the enemy. In turn, an army officer assembled the males among the civilians. In patriotic language he told them that this was the end, but to die in the service of their emperor would be their greatest honor. He concluded by reading General Saito's message, which began, "Whether we attack or whether we stay where we are there is only death. But realizing that in death there is life, let us take this opportunity to exalt Japanese manhood..." Neither General Saito nor Vice Admiral Nagumo was involved in a final charge against the enemy, both, however, committed suicide with gunshots to the head.

General Saito's words continued to echo in Isamu's ears as he thought about his and Atsuko's past life on Okinawa…their time together on Saipan…their travails to get to where they were now. Nothing had panned out the way he had planned. Swayed by what he heard, he wondered if this would not be his only chance at adding some sort of meaning to his life, whether he was meant to find success in death rather than life.

He found his wife and pulled her aside. Haltingly, he began a speech that he had mentally rehearsed several times, only when it came time to deliver it to Atsuko, he stumbled.

"Atsuko," he began, "life gives us only one chance to prove ourselves worthy and my time has come. There is little else for me to do but sacrifice myself for the greater good of Japan. I must join the soldiers in a final battle, much like the samurai of old."

Atsuko, dumbfounded, could not speak. Tears welled in her eyes as she vigorously shook her head in denial. "No, no, no…" was all she could say.

Isamu, now resigned to his own fate, held her by the shoulders, and saying nothing, looked deep into her eyes, she returning his gaze.

Isamu continued, saying, "Atsuko, you have been my whole life and I will always love you. Please, remember me." He continued looking at her, both crying.

Suddenly they heard a rash, almost disembodied voice saying, "You men, let's go. There's no time to waste. We must prepare." It was the army officer.

At that moment Atsuko felt she could strangle him, although she personally bore him no malice. But he was taking from her the only thing she cared about in this world. Isamu was no failure. Although life had not turned out as they planned, he was a good and loving husband who deserved to live. This, she realized, was her final chance to convince him.

She questioned why in death he would be considered an equal to Japanese when in life he had never been. And what honor was there to be achieved in a futile death? Isamu listened quietly, his head lowered and still crying. Her pleas, however, fell upon deaf ears; he was determined. Atsuko felt as though a part of her own being had been ripped from her, but there was nothing she could do. Isamu somehow felt that he needed to make this sacrifice in order to be worthy, but of what, she asked herself. She could not understand. She watched him, along with most of the civilian men, follow the army officer to a staging location.

She yelled out to him, "Isamu, Isamu!" but he would not turn around. Isamu knew that if he did, he would be dissuaded from doing what he felt must, although in his heart he repeated, *Please remember me* as he disappeared over the small ridge.

At dawn on July 7, remnants of Saipan's beleaguered military force, a hearty contingent of civilians and barely walking wounded mounted what would be the final desperate attempt to defend the island. Isamu was among them armed with nothing more than the bamboo spear he had learned to use earlier. The force stood little chance against a better-armed and experienced enemy force, yet they came determined to die gloriously in service to the emperor. Of those felled by the hail of streaming bullets was Isamu, gone forever in a lost cause for a doomed empire, but dying an honorable death in his own mind. Atsuko could not see the battle, but she could hear it, and she knew her life had changed forever. She, along with many other wives, felt a supreme sense of loss, but no words were spoken. If indeed the eyes were windows to the soul, then their shared glances spoke volumes about the despair that enveloped their hearts.

She spent the next day in solitude, devoid of any feeling, finding her life suddenly empty. Her thoughts focused on Isamu, now nothing more than a memory.

Suddenly a new commotion broke Atsuko's train of thought. There was yelling and screaming coming from the direction of Marpi Point. Her curiosity getting the better of her, she ran toward the source of the sounds and was horrified by what greeted her. Women, some with babies and young children, others pregnant, and in some cases entire families, were jumping off the edge of the cliffs. One father cut the throat of his young son before throwing him over the cliff; he then following close behind. Petrified and dumbstruck, she had no idea how to respond. The first wave of "jumpers" now gone, she sat on a rocky outcrop trying to gather her thoughts. She suddenly heard a voice, perhaps through a loudspeaker, in perfect Japanese imploring potential jumpers not to end their lives through suicide and that US forces would not harm them. The speaker offered that they themselves had been treated kindly and fed. In fact it was a Japanese civilian who himself had surrendered to US forces and was asked to communicate with other Japanese on the island in an attempt to end the senseless loss of life. The message, however, had the unintended effect of motivating many others to jump—in the end, hundreds more. They had all heard the admonitions that Americans would kill babies and rape women. After all, the emperor of Japan had beseeched them to commit suicide through his imperial message and many on Marpi Point that day believed the speaker to be nothing more than an enemy spy. The fear of Japan's leadership, of course, was that if Japanese civilians learned the enemy would not kill or rape them, they would be more likely to surrender and lose their will to fight, eliminating any fleeting chance of victory the nation's leadership hoped for.

Atsuko again began approaching the cliffs at Marpi Point, albeit cautiously. It was then she realized that a torrent of people had begun jumping off again, mostly women and children, from a height, as she learned later, of about 700 feet; this would come to be known as "Suicide Cliff." Others in the distance were also jumping into a sea of rock-filled churning water and from which no one could ever expect to return—this would come to be known as "Banzai Cliff." But in the end, it all amounted to the same thing in Atsuko's mind—wasted human life. As she stood watching the morbid sights from Suicide Cliff, there was a sudden onrush of humanity—men, women and children—heading toward the cliff's edge.

Just as suddenly she caught sight of a familiar figure, Sae Kyung, their old farm hand, dragging behind her her four-year old daughter and heading for the cliff's edge along with a crowd of others. Atsuko tried bursting through the crowd, but was knocked off her feet by its sheer momentum. She crawled, on hands and knees across jagged rock toward Sae Kyung, getting kicked, stomped and cursed in the process. Finally reaching the mother and child, she looked up into Sae Kyung's eyes and saw only a blank and unresponsive stare. She also noticed, for the first time, that her stomach appeared slightly distended. Was she pregnant? How could she have been so blind and callous not to notice? Had she known she would certainly have cut back on her chores. Atsuko, grabbing her around the left ankle, attempted to stop her movement toward the cliff and yelled out, "Sae Kyung, Sae Kyung, don't do it! Your child..."

Still, she was unable to break her comatose-like state. Try as she might to stop her forward movement, Sae Kyung's determination was just too much, all the while dragging her screaming daughter behind her. Atsuko was being pulled along the ground and further cut by the small rocky outgrowths that filled the cliff's surface. Had she continued holding on to Sae Kyung she too would have fallen over the side to her own death. In a last ditch effort to salvage what she could, Atsuko let go of Sae Kyung's leg and at the final moment grabbed her daughter instead, pulling her free of her mother's grasp. She would not, indeed could not, allow this young girl to die a senseless death. With the young girl in her arms, Atsuko crouched and did her best to run against the tide of people, getting kicked and punched in the process. Having lost grip of her daughter, Sae Kyung seemed to regain a modicum of her senses and turned to see where she had gone, but the small crowd behind her continued its slow and inexorable movement toward the edge of the precipice. The last Atsuko saw of Sae Kyung and her unborn child was as they went over the cliff to their deaths, carried by the wave of humanity intent on its own destruction.

Atsuko clutched the crying young girl with all her might and tearfully whispered in her ear, "*Nuchiru takara, nuchiru takara*! (O: Life is precious!) You will not die. I won't let you. You're safe with me. If you die, we'll die together."

It was in that instant, for the first time in her life, that Atsuko was extending her love, indeed her being, to another human in need rather than seeking acceptance from someone else. And it would be here, after having descended into the nadir of war's despair, that she would find the verisimilitude of her own life and existence.

In the final analysis, the exact numbers of civilians who jumped to their deaths on Saipan is unknown, but they numbered in the thousands.

3

Atsuko had a decision to make, or perhaps she already had. She was not about to commit suicide and she now had a young girl in her care, to whom Sae Kyung, in addition to her Korean name, had also given a Japanese name, Harumi. Atsuko decided that she needed to get away from Marpi Point for Harumi's sake—staying any longer than they needed at the place where she witnessed her mother's death seemed cruel. Besides, their own brush with death had been uncomfortably close. She wanted to leave, but where? To their front was Suicide Cliff, to their rear the enemy. They had no provisions and both she and Harumi were becoming dehydrated, hungry and physically and mentally spent from their ordeal over the past few days. Atsuko learned from Harumi that their family had fled Garapan much in the same way she and Isamu had left their home. But she also learned that they were denied access to caves because they were Korean; and

Japanese soldiers had not given them food or water, saying, "Japanese first." They had, however, received help from a kindly old Chamarro woman who took pity on them, giving them some fruit and water. Harumi also told Atsuko that her father and brother, having left their hiding place in the jungle in search of food, had never returned. Once the fighting got closer to them, Sae Kyung had decided to leave and move further north toward Mari Point where Atsuko had met up with them. But what had driven her to suicide remained an unresolved mystery.

Atsuko asked herself, *Did she crack under the pressure of war? Had she learned something about her husband and son's fate?* They would likely never know the reasons.

Atsuko finally decided that hiding in the thickets was getting them nowhere. There was no food or water to be found here. She decided their only option was to face the enemy and hope that what she heard earlier from the Japanese civilian was not simply a ploy to get them to give themselves up. They began walking south where they encountered other civilians doing the same as they were. She decided to join with them; there were about thirty in all. She thought to herself, *At least if we die we won't be alone.* No one spoke a word. It was as if they all understood it was over and there was nothing left to say. Onward they walked, further south, when quite suddenly the group stopped. The young man walking at its head, its leader she supposed, picked up a blood stained bed sheet that had once been white. He then began looking around for something else, but she did not know what. They walked a bit further and the young man stopped again this time picking up a rifle lying next to a dead soldier. He then tied the ends of the sheet to the rifle and the group moved on through what had been the final place of battle for many on Saipan. The stench of dead bodies in the heat and humidity was overpowering. Several people began vomiting and Atsuko too began to gag. While Harumi covered her nose and mouth, she seemed physically unaffected. Atsuko kept her head straight and eyes lowered for fear of somehow coming across Isamu's remains.

Atsuko and Harumi slowly continued their march forward with the others when the young man in front suddenly raised the rifle to which his sheet was tied high above his head and waved it back and forth, but she did not know what it meant. She then heard voices saying, "Stop!" She could not make out anything else that was said, but she knew it was English. Her heart began pounding wildly as she put her arms around Harumi. She saw several American soldiers coming toward them.

My goodness they're huge, she thought.

Many in the group cowered, uncertain of what would happen next. While four of the soldiers kept their rifles trained on them, two came forward with their rifles shouldered and hands extended with something in them. Becoming ever more anxious, Atsuko tried covering Harumi, but she had already caught sight of the soldiers' hands. They gestured to the group that they could eat whatever it was they were showing them. One, in fact, broke off a piece of the brown thing and put it in his mouth and began eating. Demonstrating a lack of fear with which the young are often imbued, and perhaps driven by her hunger, Harumi broke free of Atsuko's grasp and ran up to the soldier before she could stop her. Others watched as the young girl hungrily munched away at the curious brown thing, the soldier now crouching next to her and smiling. Atsuko rushed forward grabbing Harumi and took a few steps back, but the young girl looked at her and repeatedly said, "This is delicious!" With that, the soldiers motioned to the group to move ahead with them.

After finally arriving at a staging area, they were put onto trucks and taken further south. Because no one knew them, they were considered to be mother and daughter. At another staging area, all those who had been captured were broken out into three different groups: the local population of Kanaka and Chamarro; Japanese, Okinawan and Korean civilians; and Japanese military. The locals were taken to a refugee camp at Chalan Kanoa, the civilians to Camp Susupe, and surviving military personnel were taken to yet another location to be interrogated.

Harumi, with her innocence and playful nature, soon became a favorite among some of the US military, some of whom Atsuko found scary—big, dark-skinned, with kinky hair. She'd never seen a black person before. At first she stayed away from them and tried to keep Harumi away as well, but again it was this young child who showed Atsuko that they had nothing to fear from these soldiers. They possessed a quality of kindness not unlike some of the other soldiers. In fact, one of them, "Jackson" she thought his name was, used to bring Harumi a little extra food or candy from time to time, a relationship through which Atsuko herself benefited on occasion.

Harumi had helped to blunt the pain of losing Isamu. Still, she often longed for her family on Okinawa, imaging that their fate must have turned out better than her own. During their time together at Camp Susupe, Harumi and Atsuko developed a mutual attachment that was as close to "real family" as it could have gotten. They had both lost so much, but in the end found each other. When they were finally repatriated back to Japan in July 1946, they did so together, as mother and daughter; neither would have had it any other way.

There were other events born out of the war's tragic circumstances that had happy endings as well, one of them having been the story of young Shiroma Koyu, a five-year old boy who, along with others, jumped from the cliffs of Saipan. He had lost his family earlier: he and his mother got separated from his father and two younger sisters during the battle; he never saw them again. And his pregnant mother died not long thereafter. As he jumped from the cliffs as so many did that day, miraculously his fall was broken by a tree limb and he was later rescued by the US military and sent to Camp Susupe to be later repatriated.

Fighting in the Mariana Islands was witness to several "firsts." It was the one of the first times the US Marine Corps deployed African Americans in battle. It was during the fighting on Tinian that US forces first employed napalm as a battlefield weapon. And Tinian would gain historical notoriety as having been the launch site of the aircraft *Enola Gay,* flown by Colonel Paul Tibbetts, which delivered the world's first atomic bomb over Hiroshima, Japan the following year. Atsuko's more personal "first", however, when measured against such historically significant events was much less profound, but for her, could not have been more important—it was the first time she became a mother, a role she came to relish.

Chapter VIII

Oblong Sphere of Co-Prosperity

By March 1945 the urban areas of Japan's main islands were suffering relentless attacks from US long-range B-29 Superfortress bombers, now based on Saipan and Tinian in strength after the capitulation of Japan's military forces there months earlier. Using this strategic advantage, US military forces began undertaking high altitude bombing raids originating from the Northern Mariana Islands in November 1944. In order to maximize damage and further wear down Japan's appetite for war, however, the Americans then changed their tactics from using high-altitude bombs to using incendiary bombs deployed from lower altitudes, with devastating effect. Tokyo, particularly susceptible to firebombing because of its many wooden structures, first experienced such attacks in February 1945. But it was "Operation Meetinghouse" beginning on March 9, 1945 that, in the end, proved to be the costliest. Over a two-day period, two thousand tons of bombs were dropped on the city and the resulting firestorm caused an estimated 100,000 deaths; more than another 100,000 injuries; and left countless numbers homeless, by some accounts nearly one million. The impregnability of Japan's homeland defenses had proved to be a myth and the noose was being tightened around the home islands. Okinawa too would soon be called upon to sacrifice, although not of its own volition.

By this time, Ushī's existence had descended into an abyss of mindless predictability and inhumanity. Of course, she was no longer known as Ushī, but rather Hanako. Ishida had given her a Japanese name, a fairly standard practice among comfort station proprietors throughout Asia and the Pacific—their military customers should be made to feel "at home" as much as possible. Ushī, however, found this practice personally distasteful—not only was she being forced into providing sexual favors for strangers, sometimes violently, but she was also being raped of her personage. Over the ensuing months she came to detest the name Hanako, but under fear of being beaten, she had no other recourse except to go along with Ishida's wishes. She learned very quickly that violence, whether inflicted by Ishida or the soldiers, was now part of life's daily regimen, lurking just beneath the surface of most human interaction, awaiting the slightest perceived provocation to rear its ugly head.

Because the comfort station at which Ushī worked was civilian owned and operated, it was situated outside the nearby military garrison, although not more than a few minutes' walk away. (Comfort stations operated directly by the military were typically set up within a military garrison.) Ishida also maintained a modest administrative office separate from the living quarters of his jugun ianfu located immediately adjacent to the garrison, which afforded him easier access to the local military personnel who served as both his clientele and guarantors. Not only did soldiers regularly purchase the services of "his" women, but they also provided indispensable logistical support, not least of which was the twice-daily food rations he received for himself and the women in his employ.

It had been to this rather nondescript little shack that functioned as Ishida's office where Ushī was first taken by Yoshida. The three small shacks just behind Ishida's office Ushī had seen when she first arrived was where new girls were "broken in," Ishida's euphemistic reference to the practice of providing high ranking officers with young Korean virgins. Once they had been broken in, they were made available to rank-and-file soldiers. As an Okinawan juri, Ushī had been more a novelty than a virgin, so she too spent nearly two weeks in one of those wretched little outbuildings servicing higher ranking officers. The only positive thing about the experience is that when compared to her present circumstances, she was forced to have sex with far fewer men per day.

Ishida's comfort station was the old home of a former gentry-class family. It had fallen into a state of disrepair over the decades, but the military cleaned it up and made minor repairs and Ishida now used it to house the women who worked for him. Notwithstanding these repairs, it was nothing lavish. While the home had once been fairly spacious, presently its rooms were partitioned into many smaller cubicles, having used available lumber and unserviceable military equipment to do so; each was just large enough to accommodate two adults lying down on matting and space for a small dresser in which the women kept make-up and other sundry items. In one of the room's corners was sufficient space for the two blankets and towel issued to them by Ishida. The "door" to each cubicle was little more than a piece of cloth draped from the ceiling. In all, twenty-seven women lived and worked in the comfort station: twenty Korean; three Chinese; and four Japanese, among whom Ushī now numbered. Young Korean women were prized among the soldiers because they were considered more chaste, and thus cleaner, than other women being forced into prostitution, which the military believed reduced any potential for the spread of venereal disease.

The history of Japan's military comfort stations is one sometimes shrouded in confusion and obscurity. Although 1937 represented a significant turning point in their proliferation, the concept of comfort stations had been in existence since 1932 when the Imperial Japanese Navy put several into service in the city of Shanghai, China. By April 1933, Japan's Imperial Army also began the practice of establishing brothels for the "comfort" of its troops. Their popularity was such that by 1934, fourteen were operating within the city.

Practices adopted during the 1930s were not new. The concept of providing sexual services to Japanese abroad dates back as far as the Meiji era (1868-1912), a role fulfilled by women from impoverished regions of Japan, but particularly northwestern Kyushu. By 1877, however, there was more of an unofficial "official" sanctioning of sending Japanese women abroad to service the nation's expanding cadre of colonial administrators. (This was a year after the signing of the Treaty of Kanghwa, which allowed for the posting of Japanese officials in Korea and led to an influx of businessmen, farmers and fortune seekers onto the peninsula.) These women, known as *karayuki* (J), also came to serve an indispensable role in sending foreign currency into Japan, a fact openly recognized by Fukuzawa Yukichi, an acknowledged elder statesman of Japan. Thus, karayuki made critical, albeit unconventional, contributions to Japan's efforts under its Meiji era program of "enriching the country and strengthening the military" to abrogate the unequal treaties it had been compelled to sign with more powerful Western nations. The aim was to stand on equal footing with them.

By now, Ushī was but a mere shell of the girl she had been a few short months earlier. Life had at once wizened her through the depravity of her circumstances while imbuing her with a keener sense of the human psyche—its strengths, moral failings; and vicissitudes. Still, she had trouble reconciling herself to her present fate. Up each morning at six o'clock, her days, much like those of the other jugun ianfu, were devoted exclusively to her new trade—servicing the hundreds of military personnel who frequented the station weekly. By ten o'clock each morning, the women would have bathed, washed their clothes, cleaned their rooms and changed the bedding, all in preparation for the day's clients. Ishida provided each of the women with two dresses that they were required to wash after every wearing, so the women kept them in rotation. Ushī had learned early on the sacrosanctity with which Ishida regarded this rule, indeed all his rules, as she watched him beat one poor young Korean girl who had failed to wash her clothing as directed. The clothing was nothing extravagant, mind you, but nice enough to "keep the clients coming back" as Ishida often mused.

Life within the comfort station closely mirrored the social order of Japan's Greater East Asia Co-Prosperity Sphere. The ethnicity of each jugun ianfu determined her social status within the station. Japanese women, of course, occupied the highest status, followed by Koreans and then Chinese. Any privileges accorded the women based on their ethnicity were at best miniscule, but noticeable, which at times caused some amount of friction among them. It was for this reason that Ushī felt compassion for the other women. She befriended several of the Korean women who had learned to speak some Japanese; building at least a few friendships helped make life just a little more tolerable. She was sometimes chided by the other Japanese women for doing so, since they regarded the Korean and Chinese women with some amount of contempt, but Ushī learned to simply ignore them.

Servicing soldiers was not the only task performed by the women of Ishida's comfort station. As a way to curry favor with military leadership, Ishida also made the women launder the uniforms of higher ranking officers, along with his own clothes of course, and those of his wife who kept an eye on things at the comfort station while Ishida conducted business at his office. And because the war's momentum had turned so unexpectedly and decisively against Japan, every hand was now being made to contribute in some way to the nation's security, particularly on Okinawa, now the last line of defense before the enemy reached the home islands. Some of the women began to receive rudimentary training as nurses in the event they would need to be pressed into service after fighting began. Ushī had volunteered for this duty if for no other reason than to break the monotony of the days. Each of the women was also made to serve in the Women's National Defense Society, receiving basic military training under the supervision of soldiers. As members of this organization, each woman was equipped with one pair of ill-fitting black baggy pants, a cap and an armband signifying her membership.

While Ushī found the general conditions under which she and the other jugun ianfu were forced to live distasteful, the act of actually servicing soldiers defied human description in her mind—none of the words she could think of adequately captured the agonizing depravity and violence she and the other women were forced to endure. Each morning at about a quarter past nine o'clock, soldiers began forming into a long queue outside the comfort station's doors. Ishida promptly opened for business at ten o'clock every day, seven days a week and closed twelve hours later. Soldiers also had the option of spending the night with one of the women if they paid an additional fee, so for some there was even less respite. In the beginning, most of the women serviced only about ten soldiers each day, but as the number of soldiers assigned to the island grew, so too did the demands on their services until by March 1945, each was servicing about twenty to thirty men a day on weekdays, and sometimes more on weekends.

Although the men lined up in a single file outside the building, their conduct was anything but orderly. Some removed their pants while waiting in line; others even their underwear in an attempt to maximize their twenty minute time limit with the women. Ushī often heard waiting soldiers yelling, *hayaku! hayaku!* (J: hurry up!), as the women serviced their clientele. Once inside, the demands of soldiers were as varied as their number. Some wanted the women to wash them after sex. Others demanded they perform fellatio. Still others violently raped the women. At the other end of the spectrum, there were those patrons who treated them with kindness, bringing small gifts or money, and with whom some of the women developed friendships.

There were rules of conduct governing the operation of comfort stations and establishing behavioral norms for their patrons. Some, established by central military authorities, and others locally derived, all suffered from the same shortcoming—lack of adequate oversight and enforcement. There was, however, one rule that was strictly enforced: women could not leave the comfort station with patrons. Other than that, the rules assumed distinct flexibility. The requirement for patrons to use condoms was a case in point. Many soldiers used them willingly, some even bringing their own. A good number of others, however, adamantly refused to use them and beat the women if they tried to refuse them service. Although the military provided ample stocks of condoms so they could be used for their designed purpose—a single use and then discarded—Ishida and the many proprietors like him required women to use condoms multiple times, washing them after each use. The prohibition against women providing sex during periods of menstruation was another poorly enforced rule. At some comfort stations this rule was observed. At others, particularly where large numbers of soldiers were serviced, women were forced to stuff strips of cotton rags inside themselves and continue having sex with patrons.

Ushī bore witness to what happened to jugun ianfu as a result of their prolonged sexual subjugation under the extreme conditions of the Imperial Army's comfort system, an experience that carved profoundly indelible memories in her and rendered her to pray that the same fate would not befall her. The arbitrary use of condoms by patrons had a deleterious effect on the health of many jugun ianfu. And the longer the fighting raged throughout Asia and the Pacific, the less concerned soldiers became with contracting venereal disease; most had planned to die in battle in any case. Of course, such attitudes showed little regard for the welfare of the women who would suffer the ravages of disease. As a consequence, incidents of venereal disease were not uncommon, requiring those who contracted it be injected with the dreaded "Number 606" medicine; it left a terrible aftertaste in the mouth and it was believed that once injected the patient couldn't touch water for a week.

Venereal disease was not the only hazard jugun ianfu confronted. Women also suffered from extreme swelling and bleeding of the vaginal area; and cases of infection causing their sexual organs to fill with pus were not unheard of. Ushī also knew of women who had become pregnant and heard stories about others. The fetuses were usually aborted and the women put back to work in due course. In some cases, however, women took up with the fathers of their babies and lived in tents with them on military garrisons, a phenomenon that usually occurred in areas of active fighting. War swings with both edges of its sword, and while it destroys far more lives than it creates, there were those comparatively few occasions when it bestowed life. Ushī was always befuddled by this and regarded life as randomly spontaneous. "How would all this end for her? Indeed would it ever end?"

She spent most of her days looking for mental escape from her surroundings, desperately meandering the recesses of her mind and memories, but to little avail because nothing brought with it the comfort of closure. Everything remained uncertain. She thought of her family and friends; her earlier life in Itoman; and her days at the Matsuda-ya, which had become "home" to her and the women with whom she worked, her family. She had pretty much concluded long ago that Nakagusuku Fumiko and the juri who had accompanied her downtown that fateful morning last year were all dead, but she still was not certain. More and more she found herself reminiscing of her times with Munekazu. She wondered if he ever thought of her. In her heart she cared for him deeply, but had done her best to avoid revealing those feelings to him. He was, after all, married and nothing good could have come from complicating their lives; such an affair would have led to scandal. She had watched over time as Munekazu's feelings for her seemed to intensify. There were several times in fact she simply wanted to throw caution to the wind and give up her heart to him, but restrained herself, contented with being physically close, but emotionally distant. Her present circumstances, however, somehow amplified her feelings for him and she could no longer hide them from herself. She felt his absence like the weight of a rock in her chest; that feeling of palpable pain when love goes awry. *Where was he now?* Did she still occupy the same place in his heart or was she now but a mere memory among many others that filled the tapestry of his past? And even more importantly, would he ever see her in the same way after her experiences at the comfort station?

2

The wind blowing off the Pacific Ocean along the island's eastern shores seemed colder than usual this year, made all the more so by the dark heavy clouds that hovered low above the island and the despair that permeated the air around her. Nakagusuku Fumiko sat motionless, but full of thought and emotion, in the home of her younger sister, Umeko. Her wounds had just about fully healed—she suffered several injuries to her right leg and hip during the attack last year. For the rest of her life she would walk with a noticeable limp because of the improper care she had received at one of the makeshift hospitals quickly thrown together after the attack destroyed Naha's main hospital. In fact, calling it a hospital at all might have been stretching the facts; it had been little more than a rickety medical aid station in the days immediately following the attack.

Whenever she began feeling bitter about her leg, she recalled the fates of the young women who had been with her, all of whom were now dead. She was sometimes chastised by her friends in the Tsuji district, who too were proprietors of establishments employing juri, that she treated the women who worked for her less like employees and more like daughters.

They're probably right, but what was wrong with that? she would sometimes think to herself. *Treating people with kindness is no moral failing. It's the one thing that makes us human and not just a bunch of animals driven by lust.* She was perceptive enough to understand that dire economic straits had driven women into the juri profession, not necessarily any love for it, and if she could improve their circumstances—even just a bit—she was prepared to do so. Still, she wondered at times if her indulgence of the women had not contributed in some small measure to their deaths. Had she been a sterner employer, would they have tried to run off to safety that morning after she implored them to stay where they were? She watched them all die as the scene played itself out before her, almost in slow motion, each of their bodies falling in a hail of bullets as they tried to make it up the street.

Ironically, her own injury was not a direct result of the attack. Rather, once the attacking planes had cleared the immediate area, she ran to the girls' aid and found two of them, Namī and Nabī, still alive, although barely so. In a frenzy, she had run off to find assistance. Her eyes filled with tears, she was unable to see the road ahead clearly and it was then that she tripped and fell on debris strewn about the street, landing in a ditch, and injuring her hip and knee. Because hers were not life-threatening injuries, she was not immediately tended to although the pain was excruciating. The worst result of the situation was that when help did finally reach Namī and Nabī, it was too late.

She convalesced at the home of a family friend. Nakagusuku Fumiko was fortunate that they had enough room and were willing to put her up because she would have had nowhere else to go. Her home, indeed her life, had been the Matsuda-ya—she had nothing else. Even so, it was several weeks before she was well enough to return to where the Matsuda-ya once stood. When she saw what was left of the building that held so many memories for her, she wept uncontrollably. There was little else she could do.

Then her thoughts turned to those who had been inside. *What had become of Ushī and the others?* she asked herself. There was no sign of them and no one could offer any concrete information as to what might have happened that morning, so she assumed they too had died. Poor Kenjiro, he did not deserve such an end to his life. All he ever really wanted was to help out around the Matsuda-ya and he had taken such pride when she agreed to give him a job—what a pity.

Her present source of melancholy was the realization that everything she had worked for and everyone she cared about had been taken from her in the blink of an eye. It was her current state of mind that finally drove her back to her ancestral village of Yonabaru near the Chinen peninsula on Okinawa's south-eastern coast. She needed the warmth of familiarity to heal those wounds not visible to the naked eye.

Nakagusuku Fumiko had always been particularly fond of Ushī. Partly because she had come to the Matsuda-ya at such a young age and partly because she was so different from the other girls, Nakagusuku Fumiko had been protective of Ushī: she was prepared to intercede for her with sometimes disgruntled patrons at a moment's notice and would not permit the other girls to tease her too much. Perhaps she saw in Ushī the daughter she had always dreamed of having, but never would. But she too was now gone, replaced by an inconsolably cold, dark, bottomless void.

Nakagusuku Fumiko was no stranger to unexpected loss. She lost her first and only child through stillbirth. Her own husband, a laborer, died years before, clearing land for a craftsman who was among those who built the hillside tombs dotting the island's landscape. He had happened upon a habu nest and was bitten multiple times; his death was at least quick. Left without much money, she was forced to find her own way through life. This is how she had come to own the Matsuda-ya. Nakagusuku Fumiko had not even had enough money at the time to cobble together the down payment. She relied on the help of family and friends to raise even the insufficient amount she was successful in raising. Finally, through the largesse of a family friend who owned a popular restaurant in the Tsuji district and who was willing to act as a loan guarantor, she was able to open the business, which until its destruction, she ran with at least marginal profitability. She had never much been interested in expanding the Matsuda-ya. It was enough for her that it generated sufficient income to take care of her and her employees.

Nakagusuku Fumiko was an old-fashioned Okinawan woman. Born in 1888, the year of the rat on the Chinese lunar calendar, her family had done its best to instill traditional values in all the children. In fact, despite its prohibition, her hands had been adorned with hajichi when she and her husband were married. As a result, she tried to run the Matsuda-ya establishment embracing the traditions of Okinawa as much as possible, which included giving each of her employees an Okinawan name. Of course, she had to remain mindful not to run afoul of Japanese authorities, so she had given the establishment a Japanese name—Matsuda—in order to avoid attracting too much undue attention. But now everything was gone and she was back in Yonabaru trying to make sense of her life at age fifty-six. There was little hope that the Tsuji district would be rebuilt any time soon she surmised, so she was left with the lingering question, "What do I do now?"

3

"Hayaku! Hayaku!" came the familiarly shrill voice of Ishida's wife as she pushed the jugun ianfu in her charge to hurry their preparations for the day's business. She marched up and down the halls of the comfort station with all the command presence of a military drill instructor; very little escaped her keen eye.

"Kumiko! *Bakayarō*! (J: idiot)," she shrieked. "You have enough make-up slathered on to be in a Kabuki play with Ichikawa Danjūrō—Wipe some of that off and put the lipstick on more neatly. You Koreans will be the death of me yet! —Aiko, help Kumiko pull herself together!"

Ushī felt particularly sorry for "Kumiko," whose given Korean name was Mi-hyun. Mi-hyun was young, inexperienced and more than the others, was having difficulty in adjusting to her new circumstances. Like so many other women, she wound up working at a comfort station through guile and deceit. Her Japanese teacher in Korea had been instructed to select several of his most well-developed female students, who under the ruse of having been chosen to work in a factory to assist in Japan's war effort, were brought to the headquarters of an army unit located on the outskirts of Seoul. Mi-hyun, along with all the other students, was brought to Okinawa. But for Japan's ill fortunes of war, the girls, all of them in their mid-teens, would have likely been sent off to more distant locations like Palau or Rabaul. By this time, however, Japan had either lost these territories to allied forces, as in the case of Palau, or had relinquished control of important surrounding shipping lanes, as in the case of New Guinea, Rabaul having been transformed into a major Imperial Army fortification on the island by 1943 with over 100,000 troops assigned.

Mi-hyun and ten other girls were brought to Okinawa in early January 1945. Mi-hyun and two others were brought to Ishida's comfort station where they spent the first several weeks "reserved" for officers since they were virgins, after which they entered the regular rotation servicing rank-and-file soldiers. Five of the eight remaining women wound up at comfort stations in central and southern Okinawa; three were dispatched to the Motobu Peninsula further north.

Mi-hyun struck Ushī as being far too sensitive for this type of work and she worried about her well-being. She tried befriending her, but it was difficult since Mi-hyun spoke no Japanese and Ushī knew very little Korean. Still, she tried to help her as much as she could and some of the Korean women seemed to watch over her as well, all of them sensing the gossamer-like consistency of her young spirit. While Ushī had not known Mi-hyun before her arrival at the station, she believed that her experiences while servicing the officers had broken her spiritually and psychologically—yet another casualty of the war that would go unrecorded.

Ushī was finishing up the last of her sweeping chores. As she pushed the dirt outside the front door she saw the usual growing line of waiting patrons who began to jeer when they saw her, some waving their pants above their heads. The first soldier in line just looked at her with a big grin. *Yuck,* she thought to herself. *Another day of lying on my back for the satisfaction of these…these…* But her thoughts trailed off. *At least there is a breeze today,* she observed, quickly trying to think of something other than the men who stood before her. On those windless days, the air inside the comfort station became unbearably putrid. Hundreds of sweaty bodies having sex all day left the place mired in an indescribable stench. Most of the women seemed to have grown accustomed to it; she never would and the odors sometimes left her gagging.

Having finished the sweeping, she absent-mindedly glanced up at the "rules board" posted outside the station's front door.

"Military Only" and "Officers, three yen; Non-commissioned Officers (NCO), two and one half yen; Privates, two yen." Where was all this money going? Neither she nor any of the other women ever received a *sen* of payment. (1 sen=1/100th of a yen). The standard refrain was that Ishida would make a lump sum payment to the women at the war's end, deducting for their meals, clothes and cosmetics, of course. Neither he nor his wife ever shared how much any of that cost, and in any case, there was a general worry among the women that they would never see any money; Ishida and his wife were real penny-pinchers.

She continued reading: "Hours of Operation: 12:00pm-5pm: Privates; 5pm-8pm: NCOs; and 8pm-10:00pm: Officers." The longer the war dragged on, the less these rules were observed. The women were already being forced to start two hours earlier than the times posted; this had been by request of the military. Although they were supposed to close at ten o'clock each evening, if patrons paid extra to spend the night with a woman, she was obliged to remain with them and rejoin the regular rotation the next morning.

"Hanako, finish up out there and get to your room. We have work to do today you know."

Ushī took a deep breath, closed her eyes and tried to gird herself for the day ahead as she turned to go back to her room.

4

Ushī stood waiting in her room for the station's doors to open for business; she could hear the men outside getting impatient. She had pushed aside the door to her own room, such as it was, and wrapped it behind a nail in the wall provided for this purpose. She was ensconced in thought about what the day would bring, because while there was a certain rhythmic predictability to life in a comfort station, the personalities of soldiers they were forced to serve could be as different as night was from day. Some could be gentle and would want to be pampered. In fact, some of the men might even profess their love for certain women, visiting them time and again, entertaining hopes of marriage. The character of others, however, was cursed with irreconcilable violent streaks and they tended to treat the women like chattel, something to have their way with in any form desired, which usually wound up with the women either being beaten or savaged in some way. This dichotomy amongst the soldiers played itself out with two of her own usual patrons: Colonel

Yamashita and Sergeant Nakamura. They occupied opposite ends of a spectrum with regard to their characters and senses of humanity.

She cringed at the thought of a visit from Colonel Yamashita, secretly praying his unit would be moved to another part of the island so she would not have to spend time with him—he often paid to spend the night. He was from the southernmost prefecture of Japan's main island of Kyushu, Kagoshima. He was not a particularly bright man; in fact, she and some of the other women found him to be somewhat dim-witted, although he spared no opportunity to regale others with what he regarded as his own profound views on life. Most of the women contemptuously referred to him as "Confucius," the great Chinese sage, when he was not around. Boisterous and coarse, Colonel Yamashita perhaps used his ill temper to compensate for his intellectual shortcomings. Sometimes soldiers in his unit would mock him when they came to visit. Because he often flailed his arms about while in one of his many uncontrolled tirades, the soldiers' simian references to Yamashita's behavior was an easy, albeit unflattering, one.

While usually avoiding any discussion having to do with his commander, on the infrequent occasions that he did, Sergeant Nakamura's description of Colonel Yamashita took a slightly softer tone, but was much more insightful. He certainly agreed that as a commander he was inept; he sometimes mused aloud about how a man of such deficient character and ability could have risen to the level he had. But Sergeant Nakamura believed Yamashita's success was the result of his family's connections—he was a distant relative of General Yamashita Tomoyuki, who had quickly conquered the British on Singapore and Malaya at the start of hostilities in the Pacific. Because of this, he believed that Yamashita had suffered retarded development as an officer, becoming a vacuous commander who never really understood the nuanced art of leadership; he cared very little for the well-being of soldiers under his charge; and was driven by unbridled narcissism.

"Everyone exists for his satisfaction in some way. He must try to achieve through fear and intimidation what others have the brains to do." This was how Sergeant Nakamura sometimes summarized his thoughts.

Ushī really did not care about the underlying reasons for his behavior; her only interest was how it tended to manifest itself with her. On several occasions he simply came into the room without uttering a word and proceeded to rape her. On other occasions, when she hesitated in acquiescing to one of his more depraved demands, he would spend time beating her; Ishida's wife would not intercede on her behalf, or any of the other women's for that matter. Sometimes there would be stretches of time when Yamashita would not visit at all. While she felt a certain relief for the respite, it was also psychologically debilitating as she was forced to await his inevitable return and the cycle of violence he brought with him.

If Yamashita represented her patron from hell, then Sergeant Nakamura was a saint—the cosmic balance to a world inalterably weighted toward violence. Somehow, through his gentle eyes and easy manner, Ushī had connected with him on his first visit. The war had not yet jaded him; somehow he was still able to find the good in most things. In stark contrast to Yamashita's seemingly endless need to crush all those around him, Nakamura believed in helping people and making them feel better about themselves. Ushī sometimes found it hard to believe that they both came from the same prefecture of Kagoshima, reinforcing her notions about life's randomness.

Nakamura had been with Yamashita for several years as one of his administrative aides. Yamashita commanded the 64th Infantry Brigade, a subordinate unit of the 62nd Infantry Division; this was the same unit to which Yoshida and the other soldiers were assigned. For the life of her Ushī could not understand how or why Nakamura continued working for such a man; she asked him once why he did not seek a transfer to another unit. While it would have saddened her, Nakamura's lot in life would surely improve as a result. He simply told her it was his duty, as a soldier, to serve Yamashita. Only once did he hint at another reason, something to do with an obligation his family back in Kagoshima had to Yamashita's family, but he would share no more than that. It was because of this, however, that Nakamura warned she should never divulge their friendship to Yamashita, or indeed even mention Nakamura's name to anyone for fear of word getting back to him. With such a volatile personality fuelled by petty jealousies, there was no telling how Yamashita might react if he learned of their friendship.

It was not long after their first encounter that Nakamura no longer engaged in sexual activity with her. Rather, they sat and talked—sometimes about life at the comfort station; at others about military life; and as their relationship progressed, they often discussed their earlier lives. It could never have been mistaken for any sort of romantic love, although Ushī would not have found that objectionable. It was, however, unmistakably some kind of love. Nakamura had once described it as "human love," which, on whole, he felt was lacking in the world. He would sometimes bring Ushī small gifts of food and other things. He once brought a book of poetry for her, but she had to admit to him that she was largely illiterate, understanding only the most basic of kanji characters, although she had learned a few more since coming to the comfort station she proclaimed triumphantly.

He smiled gently and said, "Well, let's put it to good use anyway." With that he opened the book and began reading to her, something he did on subsequent visits as well, until they had finally finished it. Such was her world now. A compilation of complex antitheses, which at their foundations had no real rhyme or reason; they merely existed as a string of unrelated happenstances.

As she stood there at the door to her room deeply engrossed in these thoughts, she was given a start when a soldier suddenly appeared before her saying, "Service please." It was the soldier who had been first in line, and he still wore that irritatingly mocking grin of his, holding the required "comfort ticket" in hand. As she began her work for the day, Ushī's mind slipped easily into another world, one of the past when life was easier and much less brutal.

Chapter IX

Dirge for Mi-hyun

Ushī remained motionless, lying on her back for a short time with her eyes closed trying to steal a few quiet moments before she went to wash herself. Yet another evening was over and she thought to herself, *Thank goodness. I couldn't stand to touch one more hot, sweaty, smelly body. Don't these guys ever take a bath?*

Finally gathering the strength to collect her small wash basin and towel, she stood and prepared to head out into the hallway. As she did she glanced over at the left side of the mat that served at once as her bed and place of employment, feeling a sudden stab of revulsion—the pile of used condoms she had washed throughout the day. She would spend time tomorrow morning looking them over to ensure they were still intact. Her world, little more than this cubicle and the activity that took place within it, was now shrouded in growing ambivalence: she was sick of being treated as a piece of meat, but was actually grateful for those days when the violence used against her was kept to a minimum. *This can hardly be called living,* she thought to herself.

Of course, no one could have predicted the turn of events that awaited the island of Okinawa those many years ago, but she found herself wondering more and more what her parents were thinking when they sold their only daughter into prostitution. Confucian ideals demanded of children filial piety to their parents.

"But don't parents have some obligation to their children too?" she had begun questioning. "Women are less valued than men, but could my parents have done this to me for a few yen if they had known what my fate would be?"

More disturbing to Ushī was the growing realization that even to the parents she loved so much she had been little more than an item for barter. They sold her soul for the price of a temporary meal ticket. *What then is the difference between my parents and these men who call upon me every day?* she asked herself. What had they felt when the money ran out, having traded her life for transitory relief? Such were the questions that had begun plaguing her consciousness with disturbing regularity and increasing intensity, but they afforded no answers. In the end, she could no longer discern any difference between the parents who had consigned her to this hell and the men who perpetrated it. Concomitantly, her own heart metamorphosed from that of an abandoned child longing for its parents to a palpable feeling of having been betrayed by those who she had loved most.

As Ushī, consumed by such thoughts, turned to head toward the door, her attention was drawn to a commotion up the hallway.

"*Manuke*! (J: loser) Bakayaro!" —unmistakably the voice of Ishida's wife. She could also hear the shuffling of many feet, the comfort station's other occupants, running toward the sound of the yelling. By now, the number of people at the comfort station had dwindled to a comparative handful, leaving among their number the jugun ianfu, Ishida's wife, Ishida and a small number of patrons who had paid to stay overnight. Ushī rolled her eyes, dropped her head in exasperation, and headed in the direction of the disturbance.

She was saddened, but not surprised, when she saw that a small crowd was gathered outside Mi-hyun's room. She could not see inside with all the people standing in front of her, so she had no idea as to the genesis of the commotion, but she could hear the voices and had concluded that whatever it was, it was serious. The voice of Ishida's wife carried with it an added dimension of agitation as she continued to spew a string of expletives at Mi-hyun.

What did you do this time, Mi-hyun? she asked herself.

When Ushī heard Ishida say, "Alright, let's just get her out of here and clean the place up," her heart sank and a new and unfamiliar darkness enveloped her.

As the small crowd parted she was able to peer between the bodies in front of her and saw what she had fervently prayed she would not: Mi-hyun's limp and lifeless body, which was now being carried out of her room by four of the Korean jugun ianfu who had been closest to her. Her head was bandaged to stop the free flow of blood.

"Just put her out back for the time being," ordered Ishida. "Aiko, run over to the base and ask for Sergeant Komura. Ask him to send someone over to fetch the body and dispose of it."

Ushī was dumbstruck. "What?" she blurted out before she knew what she was saying. "Aren't we going to make some kind of funeral arrangements for Mi-hyun?"

One of the other Korean women standing next to Ushī surreptitiously tugged at her sleeve and in a hushed voice urged her to be quiet. "Let's not make a scene here. It will only cause trouble for us all. We'll get together later and pray for a safe journey for Mi-hyun's soul into the next world."

Ishida simply ignored Ushī's outburst; not so for his wife, who by nature was much more emotive. She immediately pounced on Ushī, slapping her twice across the face.

"What do you expect us to do? This isn't our fault—she killed herself. We can't be held responsible for her weakness." Regaining at least a modicum of her composure, Ishida's wife slumped to the floor, and as if to herself she said in a breathless monotone, "These Koreans are just too much. I can't take much more of them." Ushī doubted anyone but she had heard what Ishida's wife said.

Despite her travails of the past few months, Ushī was woefully inexperienced with death—she had never personally known anyone who had died. Despite what she believed might have happened to the women of the Matsuda-ya, she still was not certain of their fate, and in any case, she had not seen them die.

The trauma of Mi-hyun's death was heightened by the crying and wailing of the Korean women; none of the others, however, seemed much affected. They just stood there looking on with an unbothered and disconnected air about them, two of whom leisurely smoked cigarettes. Her heart pounding wildly, Ushī broke out in a cold sweat and was barely able to swallow. She suddenly became aware of every movement her body made—breathing, blinking, and swallowing—each function taking on an exaggerated importance. The slaps she received at the hands of Ishida's wife had not bothered her at all. What had left her disconcerted, however, was the callousness with which Mi-hyun's remains were being treated.

Can't we even be treated as people when we die? Will we remain nothing more than fodder for the great Japanese war machine? she asked herself derisively. As these thoughts filled her mind, tears welled up in her eyes. She suddenly felt helpless and at the mercy of everyone around her. Slumping to the floor, she wept inconsolably, but no one came to her assistance.

Through the blurred vision of her tears, she saw with new clarity the scene laid out before her in Mi-hyun's room. There was blood everywhere, but it was pooled in front of her small dresser on top of which there stood a blood-soaked broken sake bottle—again despite the rules, a patron had been permitted to bring liquor onto the premises. It was quickly apparent to Ushī what had happened. Mi-hyun had committed suicide. She had broken the sake bottle almost in half and having placed the bottom half on the dresser, impaled the side of her head countless times while holding the implement steady with her hand. Ushī, at first perplexed by Mi-hyun's motives in committing such an act, finally came to understand what she believed had driven her to kill herself—the death of one of her friends, Ji-yung, with whom she had traveled to Okinawa. The actual truth, however, about what plagued Mi-hyun's soul was far more complex and bizarre and Ushī would never realize her own innocent complicity in the loss of Mi-hyun.

Ji-yung had been almost a mirror image of Mi-hyun. She perceived life through the eyes of a child, seeing only the good in people. She had lived a sheltered life in Korea and was thoroughly un-indoctrinated in the ways of the world or the depravity that man can so readily heap upon his fellow man. Although small in stature, Ji-yung was physically mature for her age. Her constitution, however, had been weak and she suffered almost immediately from the extreme demands of work at a comfort station. She contracted several infections and bled profusely, requiring extended hospitalization, the expenses for which Ishida was forced to bear. On her most recent trip to the hospital several weeks earlier, she simply never returned and no mention was made of her. Of course, the jugun ianfu were never told what happened, but they all suspected that in the end Ishida had determined Ji-yung was a bad investment, costing him more than she was bringing in, and he had simply cut his losses. Ji-yung's disappearance had a noticeable impact on Mi-hyun. Ushī surmised that Mi-hyun's grief had become too much for her to bear, causing her to take her own life.

Mi-hyun had indeed been both distraught and despondent over the loss of her friend, becoming visibly disconnected from her surroundings. She had, however, come to befriend one of the young Japanese soldiers who visited her regularly; he had become her one salvation in this haven of iniquity. Sometimes catching glimpses of the two together, one could easily have mistaken them as children at play. Ushī found it curiously innocent, but somehow refreshing. The young soldier was probably using every yen he earned to come visit Mi-hyun and she looked forward to his visits with great anticipation. Then one day he stopped coming with no word or explanation. Ushī could see Mi-hyun was becoming increasingly agitated at his absence, but could do little for her. Then two days earlier she casually asked Nakamura if he knew anything of the soldier's whereabouts, whose name was Nakayama. Nakamura responded that while he did not know the soldier personally, he was aware that several units had been transferred to other parts of the island. Hoping to assuage Mi-hyun's grief, Ushī shared this information with her with the idea of making Mi-hyun feel better.

"Don't be so sad Mi-hyun, you'll see. Nakayama will be back to visit as soon as he can."

In fact, the news had had the unintended effect of sending Mi-hyun into a deep depression from which she would find no road back. The one remaining bright spot in her life was now gone; she had already lost Ji-yung and the loss of Nakayama was too much to bear. The only coping mechanism at Mi-hyun's disposal had been death.

The day following Mi-hyun's death, as Ushī was sweeping the outer area of the comfort station, she looked up and happened to see the young, eager and innocent face of Nakayama. She felt her heart nearly burst from her chest at the same time she lost her breath. Looking over her shoulder to ensure Ishida's wife was nowhere in the area, she rushed over to Nakayama and grabbed his elbow, pulling him out of line. The soldier in line behind Nakayama quickly quipped, "You'll have to go to the end of the line now. You've lost your place." Ushī simply glared at the soldier who, feeling the full strength of her silent rebuke, merely lowered his head.

"Where have you been? Mi-hyun was worried sick about you. We thought you had been transferred," Ushī pressed emphatically.

Nakayama, a little taken aback, scratched his head in quizzical fashion and explained that he had not been transferred, but rather that his money had run out for the month and he needed to get paid before he could come back. He further explained that he had asked one of his friends to pass a message along to Mi-hyun, but it was now obvious that he had not, most likely consumed by his need to satisfy his own carnal lust. He apologized for any trouble he might have caused, but promised he would somehow make it up to Mi-hyun.

As he spoke a strange chill ran down her spine. *There is little chance of that,* Ushī thought to herself. *What good will it do to tell him now, in front of all these people? Let him enjoy the last few minutes of happiness he will have for a long time. He'll learn the truth soon enough and then there will be plenty of time for grief.* It seemed to her that pain and grief was now all any of them had left, indeed the only remaining bridge to the human love Nakamura spoke of; the world had become a cold, desolate and wholly unfamiliar place.

She led Nakayama back to his spot in line, smiled weakly at him and merely said, "Take care of yourself." With that, she turned to go inside to take her usual place at the door to her cubicle, understanding that the fog of war had claimed yet another two innocent victims—one whose life had been lost and another left behind to bear the pain of that loss.

Chapter X

Painful Truths and Other Realities

A soft late March afternoon sunlight shone against the wall as Munekazu sat cramped in the surroundings of the room Jiro had transformed into his small library. Piles of books and papers were stacked in nearly every conceivable space. He had had to help Jiro move books here and there just to accommodate the three of them—himself, Jiro, and Shimabukuro, another school colleague, now all sitting together discussing various issues of the day. If one watched carefully, small bits of dust could be seen floating lazily about the room in the dwindling light, having been dislodged from the many books they once called home. The awamori bottle had been placed on a small stack of books in the room's center and each of the three friends had before him a slightly smaller stack that served as a table and held his drinking cup. Munekazu had long stopped believing the room to be suitable for any reasonable human occupancy, but since the city's destruction several months earlier, public drinking establishments were few in number and those that did exist tended to be raucous in ambiance and their patrons equally unpleasant.

None of the friends complained about the tightness of the quarters, however; they at least had a quiet place to gather and finally a short respite to enjoy it—they had been given time off from school and the war preparations that now consumed life on Okinawa—the day was theirs. As teachers, they enjoyed respected positions within their communities. Consequently, select teachers from schools throughout the city, along with other community members of importance, were chosen to perform duties as local leaders in the National Defense Home Unit auxiliaries (civil defense units) in addition to their responsibilities at their respective schools. A system newly instituted by the military island-wide only the month before, this was yet another effort to ramp up the island's defenses against impending attack.

Local military leaders, pleased with the work of the three friends in organizing neighborhood civil defense activities, rewarded them with a day off, but recognition of their efforts was undertaken in such a way as to scold others who the military felt were performing laggardly. Thus, Munekazu, Jiro, Shimabukuro and three others were extolled for their work in a show of public munificence before all the teachers at Naha National School, an exhibition that carried with it an unmistakable air of noblesse oblige that somehow left Munekazu and his friends feeling uneasy. Despite the bittersweet taste of their reward, however, the three decided to make the most of the day. Added to this measure of their good fortune, they found that Naha's awamori dealers had proved to be a resilient breed of islander, having weathered the attack quite well; they were back in business in rather short order and the three now heartily enjoyed the fruits of their labor.

"This has become such a wretched place to live: poverty, disease, starvation and now war. What other pestilence awaits its turn to visit us?" asked Shimabukuro, his face already crimson from the warming effect of the awamori he drank with little thought of moderation. Shimabukuro's reference to war extended beyond last October's attack. Enemy planes had again attacked the island on several occasions since. War was now on Okinawa's doorstep, but no one could fathom precisely what that would mean.

Munekazu responded, saying, "Yes, what *will* become of us? No one could ever have imagined Okinawa as a military target. We have so little and are of no consequence in the larger war effort."

Jiro, also fortified by the awamori, waved his right arm in a broad sweeping motion in front of himself, saying, "Gentlemen, I agree with your points, but you forget one thing. The mere fact that we have the Imperial Army on the island makes Okinawa inviting to the enemy. Why go where the Imperial Army isn't? And because we are part of Japan, perhaps the idea is to somehow get closer to the main islands for some sort of attack."

Shimabukuro thought for a moment, digesting Jiro's comment, and then offered, "What will become of us? I'll tell you. Our destiny is like the old Korean proverb, a shrimp between fighting whales is crushed, or something like that. We, gentlemen, are the shrimp."

Jiro, buoyed by both the turn their discussion was taking and another sip of libation, continued, "Yes, that's right. And Okinawa's fate is tied to Japan by an unbreakable rope, only I am beginning to feel we are more of a shield protecting Japan's fate rather than a partner."

Then, almost as if to himself, Shimabukuro asked a question that gave both Munekazu and Jiro pause. "What if...what if Japan is defeated by the Americans? What will happen to the shrimp then?"

Munekazu simply nodded absent-mindedly in agreement without saying a word, unwilling to openly entertain such a notion. He thought of the sacrifices already made by the 60,000 islanders uprooted from their homes and ways of life to be evacuated further north on the island and out of the way of potential fighting. What would become of them in Shimabukuro's scenario? Indeed what would become of any of them?

As he took another sip of his drink, Munekazu's attention was temporarily drawn to the headlines of the many newspapers strewn about the room. The *Okinawa Shimpō* was the island's daily publication and in its present form represented consolidation with several earlier publications. Quickly glancing over the front page of one paper, he, as were the publication's many other readers, was reminded that it had first been established in 1893. Originally published under the moniker of the *Ryukyu*

Shimpō, the paper would not reclaim that name until the post-war period.

"We still are not permitted to freely send our men to join the ranks of the Imperial Army. We are good enough to serve as its laborers, but very few of us can join as soldiers. Setting physical entrance standards just above the characteristics of the ordinary Okinawan man was no accident. Such rules create rifts between us and the main islands. It is as if we are not trusted by the military. What does the Greater East Asia Co-prosperity Sphere actually mean then?" Munekazu mused aloud. He then got a glint in his eyes and shouted, "Ahh! And what of the 'Five Heroes of Hisamatsu' and their great deeds during the war with Russia? It was only through their patriotism and quick thinking that the Imperial Navy learned of Russian fleet movements and was able to destroy the enemy in the Battle of Tsushima Straits." (May 1905)

"During these trying times Japan must accept its Okinawan brother on equal terms and Okinawa must answer the call of the empire. This is the meaning of 'co-prosperity'," Munekazu concluded, lapsing into silence.

Jiro, smiling wryly, just looked at his friend for a moment and finally said in a hushed tone, "Kaze-kun, your ideas have matured a bit, haven't they? At one time there was little anyone could say against Japan that did not evoke a sharp rebuke from you. Now you yourself begin to question the wisdom of some of the nation's policies. That's good. Remember, authority that places itself above question soon becomes tyranny."

The group sat pensively for a while, each lost in thought: Munekazu experiencing that nagging and ever-increasing consternation at the apparent dual standard the Japan he loved so much applied against the island prefecture; Jiro firmly believing that Japan was leading Okinawa into war for which there could be no happy ending; and Shimabukuro convinced that the island and its people would likely be crushed if war ever did come.

When someone did finally speak it was Shimabukuro, who offered more of a random musing than anything in the way of insight into their earlier discussion.

"I wonder what's happened to the thousands who left Okinawa? Living in places like Osaka, Kobe, Taiwan, and Japan's Pacific Islands, their lives must be better than what we are suffering here at home. They are the lucky ones."

With Shimabukuro's observation, Munekazu immediately began thinking of his own family and realized he had not heard from either Atsuko or Seiho in well over a year. But given their strong characters, he assumed both were doing well. They had harbored hopes of starting up their own businesses as they left Okinawa and he believed they were well on their way to doing just that. *Any day now we'll get word that Atsuko and Seiho have struck it rich,* he thought to himself, smiling as he did. Then, without warning or presage, a strange darkness settled over him, and a name from the past suddenly took form in his consciousness—Miyazato Takahiro, a young boy from the Takahashi-chō neighborhood. With Takahiro's image emblazed in his mind's eye, Shimabukuro's idealization of those who had left Okinawa as being the "lucky ones" struck a raw nerve.

Takahiro was just fifteen years old when he received word that he had been recruited as a member of the Manchuria Youth Corps; that was in March 1940. It was not that Takahiro was a sickly child, but he had always been smaller in stature than his classmates and was neither athletic nor outgoing, which made him a natural target of bullying by others. Munekazu had always felt compassion for his plight and tried to encourage him. Takahiro, polite and self-effacing almost to a fault, was at heart a good child who wanted to do nothing more than please his elders. Thus, when Munekazu learned of Takahiro's selection into the Corps, he had been delighted. He thought the experience might toughen him a bit and give him the wherewithal to begin standing up for himself in the world.

The Corps, known formally as the Youth Colonization Volunteer Corps for Manchuria-Mongolia, was conceptualized by Katō Kanji and developed as a formal government program through Japan's Ministry of Development in 1937 as a means for populating the Asian mainland with Japanese citizens and harnessing natural resources for the nation's war effort; the first recruits reached Manchuria in 1938. The government centered its efforts on teaching young recruits proper agricultural techniques and methods for raising livestock. During their three-year training obligations, youths also received training in military and academic subjects in addition to their agricultural instruction.

Katō envisioned the Corps not only cementing the nation's foothold on mainland Asia, but also imbuing Japan's youth with a moral purity and purpose through arduous work and a Spartan lifestyle. To assist in achieving this end, all camps were administered as paramilitary organizations. Male youth from across the nation, the preponderance of whom came from poor rural areas and were typically between the ages of fifteen and twenty-two, were recruited to work the fields of Manchuria and Mongolia, after which they were expected to settle the land and become farmers in the area. By commencement of hostilities with America in 1941, ninety-four such camps had been established in northern Manchuria. A small handful was categorized as "Large Training Centers" with approximately 3,000 youths assigned to each. The majority of camps, however, were "Small Training Camps" with no more than 300 boys assigned to any single camp.

The experience had been an ordeal for young Takahiro as Munekazu learned through letters he sent home to his family. To begin with, Manchuria's icy cold winters were completely foreign to Takahiro; his constitution simply did not stand up well to the climate. As a result, he took ill rather often, which made him appear weak in the eyes of the other boys and the cycle of bullying Takahiro had endured most of his life began anew. The adult cadre as well began singling Takahiro out as an underperformer. One morning he was made to recite the Emperor's Imperial Rescript on Education by himself to the other members of his platoon, which consisted of about sixty boys. Munekazu, of course, could recite the Rescript with no problem—he had learned it as a youngster and believed in its message that each Japanese citizen must be a loyal and morally superior subject of the emperor. His mind drifted a bit as he began reciting its narrative:

> Know ye, Our subjects:
>
> Our Imperial Ancestors have founded Our Empire on a basis broad and everlasting and have deeply and firmly implanted virtue; Our subjects ever united in loyalty and filial piety have from generation to generation illustrated the beauty thereof. This is the glory of the fundamental character of Our Empire, and herein also lies the source of Our education.
>
> Ye, Our subjects, be filial to your parents, affectionate to your brothers and sisters; as husbands and wives be harmonious, as friends true; bear yourselves in modesty and moderation; extend your benevolence to all; pursue learning and cultivate arts, and thereby develop intellectual faculties and perfect moral powers; furthermore advance public good and promote common interests; always respect the Constitution and observe the laws; should emergency arise, offer yourselves courageously to the State; and thus guard and maintain the prosperity of Our Imperial Throne coeval with heaven and earth.
>
> So shall ye not only be Our good and faithful subjects, but render illustrious the best traditions of your forefathers. The Way here set forth is indeed the teaching bequeathed by Our Imperial Ancestors, to be observed alike by Their

> Descendants and the subjects, infallible for all ages and true in all places. It is Our wish to lay it to heart in all reverence, in common with you, Our subjects, that we may thus attain to the same virtue.

Munekazu even recalled the date it was issued, October 30, 1890. But as he thought of Takahiro, he realized that a boy of his retiring personality would hardly have been able to recite such a document when under the menacing gaze of his peers, each perhaps eagerly awaiting his slightest misstep. That is apparently what happened. It had been like throwing more fuel on an already raging fire and the verbal taunts of his colleagues turned physical. Young Takahiro, no longer able to bear up under the torture, found suicide an easier escape to enduring the seemingly never-ending harassment his life had come to offer. One day, after signing out his rifle and ammunition for sentry duty (the boys stood guard on the border with Russia) a single crack of a bullet exploding from the end of a weapon was heard. Young Takahiro's body was found by his comrades, lifeless and bloody, as it lay on the cold Manchurian plain dusted with bits of dry blowing snow that adorned the landscape.

The life of a good young man, lost needlessly and violently, could hardly be considered service to the emperor. Takahiro had been a loyal subject of the empire and his recompense was daily torture. Munekazu was wracked with guilt each time he thought of Takahiro. He had been so excited for him, so encouraging to him and his parents. The Corps was an important way for young men to serve the nation in its greatest time of need, Munekazu had told them. In the end, he thought, all he had really accomplished was to have a hand in the boy's death and there was no way to reconcile that with his own conscience—his soul would remain marred for life. *Damn that cadre. They were the adults—the teachers—they should have worked harder to save that boy and not make him a sacrificial lamb. He deserved more than that. Takahiro, please forgive me—I failed you,* he thought to himself angrily. Takahiro had had no one like this in life, but ironically in death he now had Munekazu as his soul mate.

The three friends, nursing their second bottle of awamori that Kiyomi set out for them, had abandoned all pretenses at conversation. Each laid quietly across the floor in whatever position the surrounding books allowed him to. Munekazu slowly drifted off, his arms outstretched over several volumes, longing for the peace of sleep to keep visions of young Takahiro at bay.

2

Munekazu awoke where he had laid his head the night before, in Jiro's small library. He tried focusing his eyes, but the blurred vision that accompanies a sound sleep and the thick-headedness of a hangover made this difficult. He finally gave up and let the back of his head hit the floor with a soft thud, surrendering himself to his lethargy. Gazing quietly at the ceiling, he listened to the sound of his friends softly snoring in the background. He had not made it home last night—that was obvious. He was not too concerned though as this was not the first time he had failed to return home after drinking too much and in any case, Yoshiko knew where he was and had likely concluded he was safe at his friend's home.

His thoughts returned to the conversation he had had with Jiro and Shimabukuro the evening before. Munekazu quite enjoyed their free exchange of ideas and how each could share his most intimate thoughts with the others without fear of personal reprisal, or worse yet, being reported to authorities. Free speech had become a luxury since the war, the result of Japan's continued militarization and its civilian government leaders being reduced to little more than political eunuchs. Teachers particularly fell under the watchful eye of authorities, especially since the arrest of ten educators in Yaeyama for improper thought.

Try as he might though, Munekazu was unable to restrain his thoughts as they again and again revisited Jiro's observation of his own thinking. He had never allowed himself to articulate these feelings of his, but Jiro had summed it up quite neatly and he now realized that it was this change in himself that had become the source of his nagging uneasiness over the past few months. For years Munekazu had believed in the inviolability of Okinawa's ties to Japan and espoused the importance of the prefecture's role and sacrifice in the nation's future—a united Japan with room and equal opportunity for all imperial subjects. The problem was that he no longer believed in the benevolence of the Japanese government, particularly the military, which were now one and the same. To him, the most damning evidence was the imperial military's continued fortification of Okinawa against the enemy by using local civilians, conscripting them for various military duties, which in effect potentially sacrificed the island's human treasure for the sake of Japan's mainland. He had finally come to realize that Okinawans were expendable in the greater cause to safeguard the homeland. *In short,* he thought to himself, *the island could be considered like so much cannon fodder.*

Rolling over on his side and propping his head against the palm of his hand, Munekazu glimpsed the headlines of several old newspapers—*did Jiro ever discard anything?*—these were now several months old. The first one referenced the early January 1945 attack on the island. As he continued leafing through the papers he realized that his friend had them ordered by date. He continued. The next headline that caught his attention was the January 22nd attack; then the one that had occurred on March 1st. Indeed, while the attack on January 22nd had not been as large as last year's, it was devastating nonetheless, lasting all day from 0600 until 1800. He recalled how unnerved islanders were; he and his family spent another day in that dark and dank cave, but at least they now knew where to flee for safety. Then there were the regular enemy flights over the island. These, however, were not attacks. The flights consisted of only one or two larger planes (bombers) that did little more than fly overhead. They had become so commonplace in fact that the military stopped sounding air raid alarms when they arrived, and did nothing to try to destroy them. Munekazu and others recalled similar events preceding the October 1944 attack and regarded the planes as a foreboding omen. What did all this mean? Were they simply to be bombed into oblivion while imperial forces sat by idly?

3

There were seemingly insurmountable operational issues the 32nd Army was suddenly forced to confront that would, at least for a short time, remain transparent to Munekazu and other islanders; January 1945 had opened the pages of a new chapter on the island. Under orders from Imperial General Headquarters in Tokyo, the 32nd Army was unexpectedly required to dispatch its premiere fighting unit, the 9th Division comprising twenty-five thousand soldiers, to the Philippine Islands in order to bolster units there in the fight against US forces. In the 32nd Army's planned defense of Okinawa, however, the 9th Division formed its core strength against anticipated enemy landings. As a result, the Army's leadership now had insufficient manpower on the island to the task of its defense, which in turn impacted military and civilians alike in two major ways. First, it required development of a new operational defense plan: instead of opposing enemy landings on the western beaches of Okinawa, enemy units would be permitted to land largely unopposed. The northern two-thirds of the island, lightly defended with fewer and smaller units, would deliver harassing fire against the enemy. The bulk of the island's defenses, however, would be concentrated in depth, in its southern third and most heavily populated area.

Okinawa's civilian population would also contribute to the island's defenses in the face of the comparative last minute changes and dearth in manpower that now plagued the 32nd Army. Lieutenant General Ushijima Mitsuru, commander of the 32nd Army, decided to augment the Army's strength through use of local civilians for purposes of manual labor, a measure first approved by Tokyo in June 1944, through creation of the Labor Corps, which at its zenith had just under 18,000 locals and Koreans—both men and women—assigned: 16,600 to army units and another 1,100 to navy units. Not trained to fight as soldiers, the primary function of the Labor Corps was to assist Army units with construction of airfields and defensive fortifications, perform general logistical labor and provide other necessary services. Additional civilian support units were also created to provide essential services, including civilians conscripted for military service. Finally, male and female students alike, ranging in age from fourteen to nineteen, were mobilized; the former being formed into the Blood and Iron Imperial Service Corps and the latter into nursing units. Munekazu's own younger sister, Kaori, was mobilized and became a member of what would come to be known as the *himeyuri corps* or the Lily Student Corps.

While Munekazu could not understand the meaning of recent events, he had come to believe that from the perspective of the military the island's inhabitants remained a potential liability. They regarded the strength of Okinawans' loyalty to the nation's cause was like that of gossamer, and thus not to be relied upon. But military leaders had little understanding of the island's centuries of history and culture. Munekazu recalled that this was not the first of Japan's clarion call to arms for Okinawans, which dated back as far as the days of Toyotomi Hideyoshi (1537-1598) when the royal court at Shuri was pressed to provide men and provisions for the planned invasion of Korea. The response, however, had remained largely unchanged over the centuries.

Islanders eschewed the show of military strength and prowess that Japanese mainlanders held in such high regard—they were a peace-loving people. The military regalia and accolades that accompanied Japan's battlefield accomplishments were both a foreign and uncomfortable concept to islanders.

We are loyal to our country, but assuming such an aggressive posture grates against our cultural foundations, Munekazu thought. He recalled that for centuries the island nation had voluntarily submitted to China as a tributary state, its raison d'être having been diplomacy. And as he saw it, asking islanders to make ever greater material sacrifices for the sake of the empire defied logic—they simply had nothing left to give. Okinawa was the poorest among the nation's prefectures, its residents having emigrated for decades in search of economic respite. They were hardly in a position to sacrifice more. His own family stood as testament to that fact. Perhaps Shimabukuro was right. Seiho, Atsuko and the thousands like them might indeed be the lucky ones, now removed from the darkness and squalor of the times that cast a pall of despair across the island he called home.

Then suddenly, as if hit by a bucket of cold water, he jumped to his feet and vigorously ran his fingers through his hair in an effort to remove any remaining fogginess from his head. Recalling the date, he realized the family would be making preparations for the special activities reserved for this occasion—the Vernal Equinox; they would be visiting the grave of his father. Quietly, without disturbing his two slumbering friends, Munekazu made his way back home. The day was Wednesday, March 21, 1945.

Chapter XI

Twilight of an Empire

The morning of Friday, March 23, 1945 dawned brightly and serenely. Despite the island's many problems the three friends had discussed among themselves so emphatically only days earlier, Munekazu felt relatively at ease; there was nothing particularly portentous in the air. As he awoke he saw that Yoshiko was already busily preparing a simple breakfast of soup, umu and even a little of last evening's pork. Muneyasu, unable to resist the smell of meat wafting through the house, got up as well to have breakfast with his father; close on his heels were his two cousins who never saw a meal they were prepared to refuse. Munekazu sometimes joked that Tomiko's sons would one day become champion sumo wrestlers, like Akinoumi Setsuo or Terukuni Manzo, so the family was obliged to keep them well fed. Hideko, Kamadū and Tomiko, however, totally unperturbed by the culinary aromas that assailed the others, remained fast asleep. After finishing breakfast, Munekazu would begin hastily making preparations to head off to school. He and several other teachers had to supervise their students in a construction project the army was undertaking, the students serving as convenient labor.

As he gulped down his meal, however, Munekazu found his thoughts continually returning to his discussion with Jiro of several days ago—he simply could not help himself. The very bedrock of his beliefs had been shaken and he could offer no meaningful contestation to the truth Jiro had exposed. To ease the discomfiture that now beset him, he began playing with Muneyasu and his young nephews as they ate, their mouths opened wide in laughter as he tickled their rib cages in turn. As he continued with his teasing, he was struck by and engrossed with his young son's youthful innocence. What would become of

Muneyasu's Okinawa?

So consumed in thought and play was Munekazu that he hardly noticed the animated voices suddenly emanating from the kitchen where Yoshiko remained busy. After a few minutes, he saw his wife, accompanied by Arashiro Chiyoko, appear in the room before him and the boys. He looked up briefly and sighed deeply to himself, not looking forward to any exchange with his wife's friend, but he was at least able to muster the requisite civility.

"Arashiro-san, how nice to see you again. How is your family?" he asked with as much genuine sincerity as he could.

But neither Yoshiko nor Arashiro Chiyoko uttered a word in response; both just continued staring at him with their mouths half agape. Feeling a little annoyed at this apparent rebuff to his concerted effort at friendliness, Munekazu furrowed his brow and returned to his breakfast.

It was Chiyoko who spoke first. "Tamashiro-san, forgive my rudeness, but you must come see for yourself." Without warning she suddenly knelt down and bowed her head to the ground, a display of deference she had never before accorded him, indeed given her character, Munekazu did not believe she had it in her. Savvy as she was, Arashiro Chiyoko was using this display to underscore the importance of her entreaty. Yoshiko looked on in silence, her eyes meeting Munekazu's; she very slightly nodded her head as in affirmation of Chiyoko's plea.

Munekazu realized that the source of Chiyoko's newly found propriety may have been the fear he saw in her eyes; clearly there was something seriously amiss. No matter what dislike he might feel toward her personally, if she was in trouble it was his responsibility as a neighbor and civil defense leader to extend a lending hand.

He stood and responding to both women simply said, "Alright, but I must get to school soon so let's hurry."

Yoshiko quickly roused her sister to watch her two sons. Then

Munekazu and Yoshiko, Muneyasu in tow complaining about leaving his breakfast behind for fear his cousins would eat it, followed Chiyoko out the door, out of Takahashi-chō and toward the nearby western shores of Naha. Silently, she pointed out toward the East China Sea in the direction of the Kerama Islands located some fifteen miles from Okinawa's shores southwest of Naha.

They were not alone—with them stood large numbers of the city's residents staring off in the same direction, looking on in silent awe. A small and quiet group of islands, the Keramas hardly attracted the attention of Okinawan mainlanders on any other day—they were merely geological outcroppings that formed part of the landscape of a hazy horizon. The Kerama Islands were comprised of twenty-two small islands, only four of which were inhabited. While only a short distance separated them from mainland Okinawa, a wide cultural chasm divided the inhabitants of the two land masses—most mainlanders considered Kerama islanders as backward, desperately holding onto bygone cultural rituals and icons as a lifeline to a past that had long since outlived its usefulness. On whole, Okinawan mainlanders treated the residents of the Kerama Islands as country bumpkins—cultural outliers. The irony of such thinking still eluded Munekazu.

Today, however, was different. As he and Yoshiko tried to take in the spectacle before them, it was difficult for the two to rationalize. The islands were being besieged not only by enemy aircraft, but for the very first time there were naval vessels in the area as well, the vanguard of an armada that would ultimately number well over 1,400 ships in the coming days.

What was the enemy up to? Was he trying to gain a foothold only a stone's throw from the prefecture's main island? Munekazu asked himself.

Even from their distance islanders could hear the attacking aircraft dropping their bombs on the small islands. He finally turned to Yoshiko and said, "You had best go wake up mother and Hideko. I need to report to school immediately."

Then looking squarely at Chiyoko, for whom he was for the first time feeling anything resembling genuine compassion, he said, "Go home to your family. If anything happens here, I'll come and let you know. But you should begin making preparations—there's no telling where this might lead."

With that she bowed deeply to Munekazu and scurried off, at least minimally reassured by his words. He then returned his gaze toward the Kerama Islands and thought to himself, *Oh my god, what does this mean?* But by now the question had a distinctly rhetorical ring to it. He surmised the military significance of the Kerama Islands, which in and of themselves held no proprietary benefit for the enemy beyond the special attack units comprising the Imperial Army's suicide speed boats, located somewhere within the small island chain. The Kerama Islands would, however, be quite valuable as a staging point for launching larger attacks against the Okinawan mainland and the Imperial Japanese Army.

It was difficult for Munekazu to pry himself away from the spot where he stood. Instinctively, he wanted to continue watching the enemy's activity, but there was little to be gained from that. He thought briefly to himself, *acha nu nēn chi ami* (O: Tomorrow is another day). It was with that thought still fresh in his mind that he heard the opening salvoes of the battle for Okinawa—US Navy aircraft were now undertaking preparatory bombardment of Okinawa itself. He turned and quickly made his way to Naha National School.

2

As dawn slowly released its final hold on darkness the following morning, Munekazu quickly made his way back to the western shores of Naha. Yoshiko, Tomiko and Kamadū, filled with anxiety the night before, had remained awake until the early morning hours, but finally surrendered to sleep, completely exhausted. The four children too rested quietly. Although he had tried to calm his family's fears, Munekazu also remained uneasy, hence his reason for being here. Despite the earliness of the hour, he was not alone among islanders wanting to watch what was happening to the small island chain so close to their shores; distance and the low light of morning, however, afforded few immediate answers.

The aircraft that had attacked Okinawa the previous day did not appear to be anywhere in sight at the moment, so Munekazu steadfastly resolved not to move from this spot until he learned more, as much for the sake of satisfying his own curiosity as for his promise to Jiro to meet him here. Wanting to make himself more comfortable as he waited, Munekazu tried sitting but quickly abandoned the idea when he realized that he could not see because of all the people standing in front of him. More enemy ships arrived that day and planes continued attacking the small islands, but the tempo of activity was increasing. Neither he nor Jiro, or any of the other islanders understood what they were seeing; they only knew the enemy was up to something. From where they stood they could clearly hear the repeated report of naval gunfire sighting the Kerama Islands. Islanders also observed, with some amount of disdain, that there were no soldiers of the Imperial Japanese Army about. There was something ominous in the air.

Then as the next few minutes passed, Munekazu and Jiro, watching in transfixed horror along with the others, saw the fury of the attack against the Kerama Islands turn toward Okinawa. Several ships of the enemy's ever-expanding naval force moved into position and began bombarding Okinawa itself, although some distance away from where they now stood. (Nearly 13,000 six-inch and sixteen-inch shells would be fired against the Okinawan mainland as part of an "area" bombing pre-invasion operation. Because US forces had scant intelligence as to the disposition of Japan's forces on the island, which by this time were well concealed in caves and hardened positions, wide bombardment of the island was undertaken. The attack achieved little in the way of destroying any 32nd Army tactical assets, but in the end, decimated civilian homes and farms.)

Turning to Jiro, Munekazu said in a solemn tone, "America and Japan...Japan and America...Okinawa's destiny lies somewhere between these two very different worlds. Our final story has not yet been written."

Jiro nodded in agreement without uttering a word, his eyes remaining glued to the scene before him. Silently, Munekazu prayed for the welfare and safety of the Kerama islanders because he now realized that their fate stood merely as a precursor to Okinawa's own. With that, the two friends rushed off, each to his own home, each to his own fate.

Despite all they had seen over the past several days, it was not until Monday morning, March 26, that mainland Okinawans had reason to allow their already high anxiety to give way to their worst fears. Munekazu had decided to return one final time to the shores of Naha to see what might be happening with the Kerama Islands. He was not altogether certain why he felt the need to come; after all, Okinawa itself was now being attacked. Still, he decided to make the trip. He had not stopped by Jiro's home to invite him along. Somehow their parting two days earlier had had an inexplicable air of permanence to it—an uncomfortable finality that any subsequent meeting would have only painfully prolonged. No words, of course, had been spoken between the two close friends, but the look in Jiro's eyes told Munekazu that he felt the same way. Their lives, once inextricably linked, would follow separate roads, at least for the foreseeable future.

Though barely visible from their vantage point, Munekazu and the dwindling number of intrepid islanders who stood with him could see what they thought were smaller vessels, perhaps a score of them, making their way toward the small island group as if preparing to land somewhere. The mountainous islands in the foreground, however, partially blocked their line of sight. What they now bore witness to would come to constitute one of the saddest chapters in the annals of Okinawa's history and would remain seared in the consciousness of islanders for generations to come. These were the initial troop landings in support of Operation Iceberg, the allies' full assault on Okinawa. The enemy was finally here; not news of their victories via radio or newspaper reports; not long range attacks through aircraft or naval gunfire; he was here in body and soul, which now evoked a strange feeling of vulnerability within Munekazu. Despite the growing number of attacks and loss of life over the past few months that characterized a new life paradigm on the island, the war had somehow still felt antiseptic to him. A war that until today had been little more than a distant thought, a topic of conversation around dinner tables and among friends across Okinawa about events from which they had been seemingly disconnected was now their reality. The hell and fury it presaged, and the devastation that would follow in its wake, not one of them could have imagined.

Munekazu recalled with some amount of bitterness the celebratory atmosphere that had filled the air around Naha in the months immediately following the attack on Pearl Harbor, scenes which now stood in stark contrast to the enemy ships at the mouth of the Kerama Islands and Hagushi Bay. The streets had nearly overflowed with citizens—young and old; rich and poor; students and teachers—in frenzied jubilation carrying lighted lanterns with the *hi no maru* (J: rising sun) symbol of the Japanese empire. Reports of imperial military victories had followed unabated over the years, yet here was the enemy with Okinawa as its target. The sense of betrayal he now felt left him empty and cold, almost like a stranger in his own home.

Then without warning, Shimabukuro's words suddenly flooded his consciousness, which now stood as a strange allegory for what Munekazu was witnessing. Okinawa was indeed a shrimp amongst whales. Where it would ultimately land after the thrashing of these two giants had concluded was a question only the kami could answer.

Chapter XII

War's Tortured Realities

"...when the war is over and we consider calmly this unprecedented migration of 120,000 people, we as Americans are going to regret the unavoidable injustices that we may have done."
Milton S. Eisenhower, Director, War Relocation Authority, March-June 1942

It was the afternoon of Sunday, April 1, 1945.

"Crack!"

The sound pierced Seiho's ears and echoed across the field where he now stood. He was off and running at full speed like a bullet shot from a rifle, his arms and legs pumping for all they were worth, kicking up dust as he went along and doing his best to ignore the sting of sweat running into his eyes.

Gotta keep running, he thought to himself. Seiho finally slowed to a stop and surveyed the area, thinking to himself, *safe!* He had never found the hot relentless southwestern Texas sun much to his liking; nor was he particularly keen on the area's arid climate and nondescript landscape. This place was worlds apart from the moderate climate and happy life he had enjoyed in Lima, Peru, a place that had been home to him for several years and where he had found some measure of success after years of poverty on Okinawa. He would likely never adjust to the harsh realities of existence in Crystal City, Texas; like it or not though, this was home for the time being.

But he did love baseball. He triumphantly stood at second base, with a broad smile on his face, thinking to himself, *Great! A double!* as his teammates cheered him on from the sidelines. Without conscious effort, he lifted the cap from his head, wiping his brow of the perspiration that ran down his face through invisible channels, onto his chin, and then to the ground. Standing among the small crowd of onlookers was Megumi, his wife of some five years, who was also gleefully cheering and applauding. Seiho's love of baseball was one of the few things that gave him an escape from the travails of their life at the camp, but it was Megumi's strength of character and resilience that helped him confront those travails. Without her, he likely would not have survived their ordeal of being forcibly uprooted from Lima and brought to this strange place.

As the game concluded, Seiho's success on the field proved to be the difference in his team's narrow victory. After a brief celebration with his teammates, they accounted for all the equipment and three of youngest players sped off to the sports office to return what they had borrowed. He went to sit with Megumi, awash in an air of self-satisfaction.

"Great game," she began, looking at him warmly as only she could. Five years of marriage and his insides still turned into gelatin when she looked at him as she was doing now. "But..." she added playfully, "...don't let it go to your head."

Seiho, smiling sheepishly, turned his gaze toward the ground, kicking the dirt as he did so. "C'mon, let's go get a cold drink," he suggested. "It's pretty hot out here."

No one enjoyed a cold drink on a hot afternoon more than Megumi—she had come to regard it as one of life's pleasures; nothing seemed to break her spirit, not even their current circumstances. With a big smile she nodded her head vigorously. Walking slowly from the ball field and onto the road, they passed the makeshift swimming pool. Turning left onto 12th Avenue and then right onto Airport Drive at the sumo sports area, they made their way toward the canteen, a walk that took them through the "D Section" housing area. They, on the other hand, lived in a small triplex in neighboring "Q Section" and, fortunately for them, only a short walk from the latrine. On hot windy days, however, when they found themselves downwind of the latrines, they wondered just how lucky they actually were.

Having gotten their drinks, Seiho paid using two of the red tokens the camp issued as scrip—this was how he was paid for his work at the warehouse. Red tokens were issued in denominations of one, five, and twenty-five cents and one dollar; the green token was worth five dollars. Megumi on the other hand, working the gardens of the camp, was paid with credits that could be used at the Japanese Union Store and other places of commerce on the camp. German internees had their own canteen and market, the German General Store. On those rare occasions when the couple was prepared to throw caution to the winds, they would venture over to the German bakery and pick out some pastry or bread. Admittedly, they realized this might be considered decadent, but it was one of the few luxuries they could occasionally enjoy in camp life. And it was one of the few times they had contact with Germans. Although they all lived in the same camp, Japanese, German and the few Italian internees seldom interacted with each other. (The camp's German and Italian internees, also residents of Central and South America, were deported and brought to US detention centers).

The couple stepped outside into the glaring sunlight and decided against walking back home just then, instead opting to sit in the shade of the chapel located adjacent to the canteen. As the two sat there quietly enjoying each other's company Seiho absent-mindedly noticed a blister beetle crawling over the edge of his finger, so named because of a slightly toxic liquid it released if startled that caused skin to blister. He decided to leave it alone rather than risk being bitten, and he fell deep into thought.

Life at the Crystal City camp certainly could not be considered nirvana; they were internees after all, but as Megumi often pointed out, it could be much worse than it was. She was able to look beyond the ten-foot barbed-wire fences; flood lights and guard towers; censored mail; daily headcounts; and roving perimeter patrols, in the end calmly concluding, "It can't be helped."

How on earth was he lucky enough to have happened upon her? And what had she seen in him? he sometimes mused. Clearly theirs had been anything but a typical marriage. Whether measured from an Okinawan or Japanese perspective, everything had mitigated against their union, but it was Megumi's strength that prevailed in the end.

Her family originally emigrated years earlier from the town of Hagi in Yamaguchi Prefecture, Japan, to Lima, Peru. Hagi had been part of the old Chōshū domain during the Edo period. It served as the domain's center of power and was where the Mōri, the domain's ruling clan, built their castle. Fiercely proud of their samurai heritage, the Kido family was immediately opposed to any consideration of their only daughter Megumi's marriage to an Okinawan. They had, however, proved themselves no equal to Megumi's determination. In the family's final face-off they implored her to respect the memory of her forebears.

"The name of Kido carries with it important responsibilities. You cannot disregard this obligation," her mother had insisted. Her father simply declared the matter closed to further discussion, forbidding any consideration of marriage to Seiho.

Quite boldly Megumi declared, "This is not the 19th century and the *Meiji Restoration* is over. Such traditions no longer hold true—I wasn't even born a part of them; I was born here in Lima. We are all in Peru in search of a future that Japan could not provide us—Japanese or Okinawan—we are all the same and we want to make new lives for ourselves. How can we do this if we remain chained to a past that Japan itself renounced?" She continued, "It is almost 1940, not 1840. Our hearts are the basis of our union, not outdated samurai ethics. I will marry the man I love and if you disown me, so be it."

In the end, her argument prevailed and it was then, quite ironically, that her parents learned she had inherited the fighting spirit of her samurai ancestors, only as is often the case with offspring, not in the manner they had hoped. That day, years ago, was the last time she had spoken with her family—until they arrived at Crystal City.

Strangely, US government policies that sought to forcibly remove people of Japanese descent from Latin America, with the cooperation of local governments, and into internment camps on American soil proved to be a salve for family differences that had originally torn the Kido family asunder. Megumi's parents were also netted by Peruvian authorities in the wide round-up of Japanese citizens (*issei*), as well as second and third generation Japanese, *nisei* and *sansei*, respectively. They were eventually brought to Crystal City and now lived in the D Section housing area. Seeing how happy her daughter was with her life and marriage, Megumi's mother had finally relented; her father, however, remained staunchly firm in his position and would not speak to his daughter. The fissure separating the Kido household into factions was further exacerbated by the "disappearance" of her two older brothers. No one in the family knew their precise whereabouts, because they fled with their families as authorities began closing in. Megumi suspected they were somewhere in Chile. She surmised that while Brazil would have been a more natural place for them to flee, the situation for Japanese living in Brazil had become precarious since the country declared war against Japan in August 1942.

2

The anger Americans felt in the days following the attack on Pearl Harbor on December 7, 1941 gave way to unbridled fear, the object of both being the nation's population of Japanese and US citizens of Japanese descent, Okinawans numbering substantially among them. Few distinctions were made as this group bore the brunt of America's national ire and the resultant policies aimed against them. The surprise attack with no declaration of war was considered by most Americans as the height of treachery. It likely would have made little difference even if they had known that Japan's fourteen-part message declaring its intention to break off negotiations with US officials and declare war against the nation was transmitted amid a comedy of errors and a paper-thin timeline, thus causing Japanese embassy officials to miss the scheduled delivery time. The message, wrapped once in the vernacular of diplomacy and then again in the Japanese cultural propensity for using indirect language, would likely have failed to communicate Japan's true intentions. That Japan was giving up on further negotiations was clearly evident; that it had chosen a course of war against America was hardly articulated in an unequivocal manner. So seared into the national consciousness was the devastation of the attack that nothing could likely have assuaged America's damaged psyche or the feelings of mistrust that would be directed toward its population of Japanese. Such feelings were further fueled by incidents like the "Ni'ihau Incident" after they became public knowledge.

Airman First Class Nishikaichi Shigenori's Mitsubishi Zero fighter was one among several shot down on the morning of December 7, 1941 during the attack on Pearl Harbor. Unable to make it back to the carrier, *Hiryu*, after sustaining damage to his fuel tank, he was forced to crash land on the island of Ni'ihau (nē-ē-how), located some 130 miles from his position near Oahu. Mistakenly, Japanese intelligence had reported that the island was uninhabited and thus would suitably serve as a point for downed pilots to rendezvous with an Imperial Navy submarine assigned rescue duty. Ni'ihau residents, on the other hand, unaware at the time of the attack that had taken place at Pearl Harbor, offered aid to a distressed Nishikaichi. Because his English was poor and their Japanese capability non-existent, islanders sought the assistance of several Japanese-speaking residents: Shintani Ishimatsu, born in Japan, and Harada Yoshio and his wife, Irene, both born to Japanese parents in Hawaii. Nishikaichi ultimately confided in them the true nature of his dilemma and his plans to be rescued; none of the three, however, shared this information with the other islanders.

Perhaps torn in his loyalties between Japan and America, Harada secretly armed Nishikaichi with a rifle and handgun, the result being that he shot and wounded an islander as they attempted to capture him once they learned the truth about who he was. In the end, Nishikaichi was killed by islanders; Shintani was incarcerated for the duration of the war; Harada killed himself; and his wife was taken into custody and incarcerated on Oahu until well into 1944 on the belief that she was a spy. Although the immediate problem of Nishikaichi was resolved with his death, the long-term damage was done and seeds of mistrust had been sown, the bitter fruit of which would be borne the following year. A US Navy investigation, influenced in part by the circumstances of the Ni'ihau incident, concluded that there was sufficient "likelihood that Japanese residents previously believed loyal to the United States may aid Japan."

Buttressing these fears were several other events. First, the public was unnerved by the numerous incendiary and often inaccurate reports carried in major newspapers. In the weeks following Pearl Harbor, the Los Angeles Times published such headlines as "Jap Boat Flashes Message Ashore," "Caps on Jap Tomato Plants Point to Air Base," and "Japs Plan Attack in April…". Second, adding a touch of credence to news reports were the sporadic and largely inconsequential attacks on the west coast undertaken by the Imperial Navy. On June 21, 1942, a submarine attacked an oil refinery in Santa Barbara, California causing minimal physical damage. Over the next several months three more small-scale attacks were undertaken against uninhabited areas of Oregon, and although none caused any actual damage, the psychological blow to an America still reeling from the Pearl Harbor attack was substantial. Consequently, a chain of events was set in motion that would profoundly impact the lives of Japanese and the Okinawans among them, not only in the US, but in various Latin American countries as well.

February 1942 introduced monumental change in America's social and political paradigms through two presidential executive orders and enforcement of new security measures. Executive Order (EO) 9066, issued on February 19, 1942, authorized the Secretary of War or his military commander designee, at their discretion, to designate areas as operationally and strategically imperative and thus undertake removal of "any or all persons" residing within them as they deemed necessary. Two important points should be kept in mind regarding this order. First, in neither concept nor scope, was it enforced solely against Japanese, although they were more rigorously targeted. While some 5,000 Germans and 300 Italians resident in the US were also interned, these figures were dwarfed by the 115,000-122,000 Japanese interned, seventy thousand of whom were US citizens. Second, while EO 9066 provided a framework the US government believed was necessary to help ensure national security, it was Public Law (PL) 77-503 passed by Congress on March 21, 1942 that gave it teeth. PL 77-503 made it a misdemeanor to violate the provisions of EO 9066, providing for a fine of up to $5,000 and/or imprisonment for not longer than one year for each separate violation.

President Franklin Roosevelt followed these measures by subsequently issuing another order, Executive Order 9102, on March 18, 1942, creating the War Relocation Authority within the Department for Emergency Management, that carried with it a simple and straightforward charge: "to provide for the removal from designated areas of persons whose removal is necessary in the interests of national security...."

Designating areas as militarily important and forcibly removing people was only half of the equation—finding places for evacuees to be taken was quite another matter. Consequently, the War Relocation Authority was also tasked with providing for the needs of evacuees and overseeing their activities at relocation sites it was to become responsible for building. Further impetus for internment was provided when Civilian Exclusion Order 34, issued by Lieutenant General John DeWitt, Commander, Western Command, on May 3, 1942 was executed. The order required all people of Japanese ancestry, citizens and non-citizens alike, to report for evacuation from what had been designated as Military Area No. 1, which included the western parts of California, Oregon, Washington and part of Arizona. The evacuation order was mandatory for all who could claim to be at least 1/16th Japanese. Military Area No. 2 included the remaining territory of these four states.

Original plans called for developing subsistence homesteads for evacuees in the nation's interior western states, much as the Department of the Interior was doing for America's urban poor under Roosevelt's New Deal. The logistical enormity of overseeing many small and scattered groups of evacuees across the western US, however, was beyond the military's capability, now mired in a two-theater war. Adding to the problem was pushback from state governments against having Japanese evacuees living unsupervised throughout their respective territories. Consequently, after meeting with governors of eleven western states in April 1942, Milton S. Eisenhower, director of the War Relocation Authority, concluded that the only way to garner state support for relocating evacuees and provide the supervision their governors demanded was to create large centralized internment camps subject to federal supervision and guard. Ultimately ten such camps were created in California, Arkansas, Arizona, Utah, Wyoming, Colorado, and Idaho.

3

Understanding the foundations upon which the program for

domestic internment of Japanese citizens and US citizens of Japanese descent was based provides important insight into the US government's rationale for its collaborative program with various Latin American countries to capture people of Japanese ancestry and eventually intern them on US soil. Ostensibly, the program was undertaken as a national security measure. In a more practical sense, these internees were used in prisoner exchanges with Japan to secure the release of American citizens caught in Japanese-held territory at the start of the war and detained by Japanese authorities, in effect rendering them chattel for barter. Unlike the case of domestic internees, there were no potential thorny constitutional issues attendant to US government treatment of Japanese from Latin America because they were classified as "illegal aliens."

The US government collaborated with the governments of thirteen Latin American and Caribbean nations under this internee exchange program: Peru, Guatemala, Bolivia, Costa Rica, Nicaragua, Colombia, El Salvador, Haiti, Mexico, Dominican Republic, Panama, Ecuador and Honduras. Responsibility was given to the US Department of State for deportations from Latin America and subsequent hostage exchanges with Japan. The Immigration and Naturalization Service, a part of the Department of Justice, rather than the War Relocation Authority, was responsible for operating the camps that housed these internees. Thus, the War Relocation Authority was charged with domestic internment operations while the US Justice Department handled international internment policy. In total, 2,264 people of Japanese ancestry fell victim to the program's success in Latin America and the Caribbean, the preponderant number of whom, approximately 1,800, came from Peru. Okinawans came to constitute about fifty percent of the total number of Japanese interned on US soil under this program.

In all, the Justice Department operated twenty-seven

internment camps within US borders, the largest of which was the facility at Crystal City, Texas, which housed 3,326 internees at its apex.

4

Megumi and Seiho lounged about in the shade for several hours before deciding to return home. It was hot and neither was particularly keen on sitting indoors. Only the unwelcome visit of a scorpion disrupted their otherwise peaceful afternoon. Megumi simply detested the little creatures and was prepared to give them wide berth whenever she encountered one. Having grown up on Okinawa, Seiho was more accustomed to seeing insects about him so they usually did not bother him, but even he had to admit that he was uncomfortable with the strangely dazzling array of insects and reptiles that called Texas home—scorpions, centipedes, poisonous snakes and fire ants. Of all of them, however, what bothered him the most was the tarantula. Sure, he had heard they were neither poisonous nor particularly aggressive, but his skin itched and tingled uncontrollably whenever he saw one, almost as if the thing was actually crawling on him. Just thinking about one of those large hairy spiders gave him the shivers.

Seiho sat outside their small triplex as Megumi prepared dinner. (Illustration 7) Although the sun was well past its zenith, the day remained warm even this early in the year. He skimmed the camp paper, the *Crystal City Times*, published by internees, for any stories of interest—nothing really. It reported on the success of last month's *hinamatsuri* (J: Girl's Day festival); announced a musical recital scheduled for later in the month; and reminded internees of next month's sumo tournament. The paper also listed upcoming softball league games for the next two weeks. What the paper did not list, however, were events that could be considered distinctly Okinawan—information on such activities was passed by word of mouth. Singing, dancing and even recitals by renowned *sanshin* (O) player Nakasone Katsujiro, were activities that took place in private homes rather than publicly. (Illustration 8)

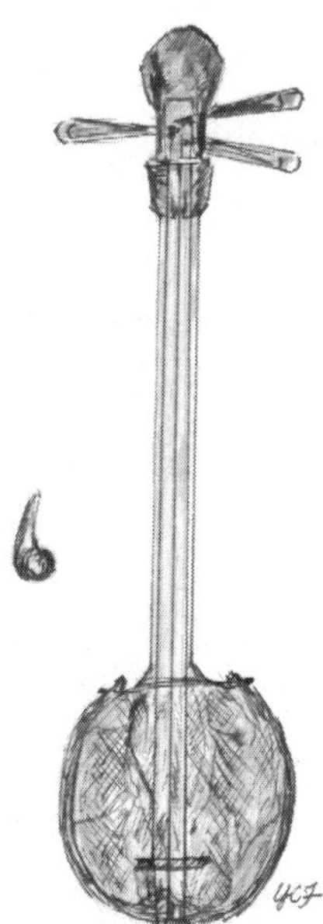

While Seiho was not at all enamored of camp life, he had to admit there was quite a lot going on for internees. The newspaper itself, although subject to censor, seemed to him anomalous to their circumstances. He would sometimes ask himself rhetorically, "Why drag us this far only to give us housing, food, and entertainment?" He, of course, knew the answer. Each of them stood a good chance of being repatriated to Japan in exchange for American detainees and treating Crystal City internees well was part of the propaganda war against Japan. Two major exchanges had already taken place, one in 1942 and another the following year, involving eight hundred of their number. He and Megumi only prayed they would not become part of the next exchange. This is what their life had become, living from day to day; planning for the future was a futile exercise.

Although Seiho had no basis for comparison, Crystal City was actually regarded as a model camp by its administrators. First, Japanese and German camp populations were segregated and their respective sections overseen by self-governing units that experienced little interference from American administrators. The camp also offered just about everything internees could ask for: sports, library, entertainment, hospital, an elementary and high school, community center, Japanese language classes, employment and a Japanese grocery store complete with rice, tofu, soy sauce, dried shrimp, fish, meat and other sundry foodstuffs. Internees even received a beer ration. Their triplex also had cold running water. Neither they nor the other Japanese internees wanted for much. If one was able to ignore the barbed-wire fence that kept them caged; the roving guards outside the fence and police details inside; and the guard towers, you could almost delude yourself into thinking this was a normal existence, but for him nothing could have been further from the truth.

Closing his eyes, he leaned his head against the outside wall of their triplex, his face tilted skyward. He felt the warmth of the sun engulf him as his mind drifted back to his and Megumi's life in Lima. He thought for a moment. *Warm, but not too hot anymore.* His copy of the *Crystal City Times* easily slipped from his hand as a slight breeze blew across his body and he entered a relaxed semi-conscious state. He recalled his early days in Lima working in the restaurant of a successful Okinawan, Nakasone Daisuke. He was a lively and energetic man, perhaps no more than fifty or so in age, who took Seiho in soon after his arrival to help him around his restaurant, *la Isla Bonita* (The Beautiful Island), washing dishes, running errands, or pretty much doing whatever was needed. Nakasone was married to a Peruvian woman, but was without children—Seiho never asked why. He had been in Lima for years as he transformed *la Isla Bonita* from a hole-in-the-wall shack into a prospering restaurant catering to the large Japanese and Japanese-Peruvian presence in the city.

A strong relationship developed between Seiho and Nakasone, one that transcended usual employer-employee ties. He had been impressed with Seiho's drive and energy and the more he grew to trust Seiho, the more responsibility he entrusted in him. It was during this time that Seiho first began running into Megumi. The Kido family owned a large grocery store from which the restaurant often purchased goods. When Seiho first began going to the grocery for supplies, Nakasone warned him that the Kido family was one of the many Japanese families that did not hold Okinawans in the highest regard. He himself had heard Mr. Kido refer derogatorily to Okinawans as *otro Japones*, the "other Japanese," a phrase their Peruvian employees quickly adopted as well. Seiho, however, almost immediately forgot the warning when he stepped inside the grocery; it was the first time he saw Megumi. She was busily helping other customers so she did not notice his surreptitious glances, or so he thought. On subsequent visits his furtive glances gave way to unabashed staring, which he did in spite of himself. He knew it was rude, but could not help it; no matter how much he looked at her, his eyes could not be satiated. But he never approached Megumi and she never seemed to return his gaze, indeed she did not seem to notice him at all.

One day as he was returning to the restaurant after another of his shopping trips, he heard a voice behind him say, "Excuse me for bothering you, but..."

He turned and found himself looking into the face of the woman who had become the secret object of his desire, but he could not get his lips to form any words—he simply stared at her.

Megumi continued, saying, "I apologize for causing you so much trouble. I've noticed you staring at me when you come into the grocery. Why do you do so?"

The question was posed straightforwardly, but without any hint of condemnation. Even with Seiho's slightly browner complexion he could feel the heat of embarrassment reddening his face. Sensing this, Megumi continued talking to put him at ease and in the end suggested that on future visits to the grocery he come to her for assistance. From the very beginning, it had been Megumi's strength of character that somehow saw him through troubling times. Their relationship grew from that point, but always under the watchful eyes of her parents.

After several years of loyal service to Nakasone, Seiho reluctantly asked if he would help sponsor him in opening a new restaurant. He would, after all, at once be quitting his job and asking for Nakasone's assistance. Far from the reaction he had anticipated, Nakasone seemed quite pleased at Seiho's industriousness. They went out almost immediately looking for a suitable place to open his business. It turned out to be a greater expense than Seiho had anticipated, however, despite his earnest saving habits and frugal lifestyle. So, in the end Nakasone volunteered to assist in underwriting part of the cost. The work was hard, but rewarding; finally, he had his own business—*la Joya Brillante* (The Sparkling Jewel). It was not long thereafter that things became much more serious with Megumi. The two of them lived a happy life despite the strong objections of her parents and recrimination of family friends. Megumi, however, seemed impervious to it all.

Japanese immigration into Latin America began as early as

1899 followed closely by Okinawan emigration to the region beginning in 1903, first into Mexico and then into Peru three years later. By 1941, Okinawans constituted approximately one-third of the Japanese population in Peru. Prior to 1899, there had been a large influx of Chinese immigrants, but they came to be regarded as generally inferior workers by Peruvians; and in any case, the availability of Chinese workers was negatively impacted by the Sino-Japanese War (1894-1895). This led Peruvian officials to encourage Japanese immigration, which they saw as a potentially more suitable arrangement.

In March 1940, however, things took an ugly turn for Japanese residents in Lima and Callaó, Peru, the genesis of which was the social and economic disparity that existed between the city's Japanese and Peruvian residents. Over the decades Japanese communities prospered, particularly in cities. On whole, Lima's Japanese community lived in comparative luxury, its members purchasing nice homes; employing Peruvian domestic servants; sending their children to Japanese schools; and interacting with the upper tiers of society. Such economic success stood in stark contrast to the lives of many Peruvians, which sowed seeds of discontent. Added to this was the fact that the Japanese community tended to isolate itself from the broader Peruvian community within which it existed, creating an unhealthy aloofness.

An incident occurred in which a Peruvian domestic worker, Marta Acosta, was killed during a factional dispute involving members of the Japanese community, which served as the spark for city-wide riots targeting Japanese: many of their homes, restaurants, and businesses were destroyed and looted. By 1940, because of the large Japanese population in Lima, keen commercial competition had erupted between and amongst various groups, the numerous barbershops being representative of such discord. In the end, the barbers, represented by two large associations, concluded that the most effective way of easing competitive tensions would be to force some shops to close, and one association enlisted the cooperation of Japan's Consulate General in affecting such closures. It was the result of this business squabble and during the retaliation of one association against the other that Acosta was killed and widespread rioting ensued.

Seiho and Megumi were fortunate. Because they treated their three Peruvian employees kindly and did their best to pay them a fair wage, the three stood guard outside *la Joya Brillante,* protecting it against the rampage that besieged the Japanese community. Nakasone's *la Isla Bonita* did not emerge from the melee in similar fashion. After ensuring the safety of their own restaurant, Seiho and Megumi rushed over to assist Nakasone, but it was too late. Broken windows and doors, flames shooting upward from the roof, and looters running down the street with Nakasone's property told of the fate that had befallen his beloved restaurant. They searched for Nakasone and his wife, Alessandra, but they were nowhere to be found. As they later learned the couple, along with many other Japanese residents, had taken refuge in one of the Japanese schools.

The riot marked a turning point from which there would be no immediate return. Many Japanese and Okinawans decided to leave Peru and return home. Nakasone, with a Peruvian wife, decided to stay, but he was never able to return the restaurant to its former prosperity. While Seiho and Megumi were able to resume their business, it was never the same either. They, as did other Okinawans and Japanese who decided to stay, fell under the watchful eyes of Peruvian authorities, who by now were anxious to rid themselves of their Japanese immigrants.

By the early months of 1942, authorities began rounding up Japanese and Peruvians of Japanese descent, seizing their businesses and other property in the process; *la Joya Brillante* was no exception, which Seiho and Megumi lost in February 1942. Japanese males were the target of these early roundups, but because Megumi was with Seiho when he was first apprehended, she had been insistent that the two of them not be separated. In the end, Peruvian authorities were so intent upon removing all Japanese that both were taken into custody. They were put aboard the US Army Transport *Cuba* in early spring 1942, where their passports, along with those of the other passengers on board, were confiscated by US authorities. Arriving in New Orleans, Louisiana fourteen days later, they were asked by US authorities for the same passports that had been earlier taken from them. Unable to produce them of course, the deportees were immediately declared illegal aliens and placed into custody. Passengers were separated for a time in New Orleans into two groups: women and children together and men segregated from them. Both groups were forced to strip naked and doused with what deportees presumed was a delousing concoction. They then spent two days on a train along with armed guards, shades drawn and no idea as to their destination.

They finally arrived in the southwest Texas town of Crystal City, the self-proclaimed spinach capital of the world, where they boarded trucks for the internment camp. One of the first things Seiho and Megumi saw after getting off the train was a strange statue of a cartoon-like character with a misshapen face that was dressed like a sailor. "P-O-P-E-Y-E." Megumi was able to spell out the letters in English, but had no idea how to pronounce the word or what it meant. The trucks moved through the small town and along dusty isolated roads until finally arriving at their new home, the Crystal City internment camp. Such had been their journey here.

What a life, Seiho thought to himself lazily.

His state of semi-slumber was interrupted by a distant, and at first, unidentifiable voice. "Dinner is ready," he was finally able to discern the disembodied voice telling him.

He stood, stretching his body in a long, slow and leisurely manner and headed inside to join Megumi for dinner.

They sat quietly eating their meal. Seiho, pensively preoccupied, looked vacantly at his food as he ate. Megumi, glancing over at him from time to time, was puzzled by his uncharacteristic lack of conversation. It was only a few hours ago that he was celebrating his team's softball victory. And this was one of his favorite meals—tempura, miso soup and a few slices of sashimi.

Finally deciding to break the silence, Megumi asked, "Is there something troubling you this evening Seiho? You're not usually so quiet."

He responded quietly to her question by asking, "Megumi, do you think we'll ever be able to return to Lima? One day the war has got to end."

Megumi thought for a moment and then answered, "And what would we return to? Peru is no longer our home. We were cast out at the first opportunity. But that does leave the troubling question of what happens to us at the end of the war."

Still consumed in thought, Seiho added, "You're probably right, but I had hoped we could return some day." Continuing in a hushed tone he said, "If that's the case, then there is little left for us. What happens if America wins the war? Are we to stay in these shacks forever? And what if Japan wins? We would likely be returned to Japan."

Megumi thought again for a moment, and in part to herself and in part to Seiho, said, "I have never even been to Japan." She then offered what Seiho felt was a cold harsh truth he had not permitted himself to think about. "We are…" she started slowly, "…without a home, without a country. We have nowhere to go and nowhere to return. We have no destiny."

Chapter XIII

Of Iron and Blood, Broken Jewels and Lilies

Kaori sat crossed-legged at the front end of the cave, one of several comprising the 32nd Army's field hospital at Haebaru, she and a few of her classmates engulfed in its dark and dank stillness. They watched as another group of girls took their turn digging out the cave they had been assigned to complete. The night was pitch black and the candles they were using to illuminate their work area did little more than emit a dim and insufficient glow, hardly up to the task of providing the light required—they could barely see anything. Kaori became mesmerized by the rhythmic movement of their shovels and pickaxes silhouetted against the darkness, which fell into a strangely complementary cadence with the enemy's naval gunfire, now bombarding the island. With each explosion she felt tremors reverberate through her body while she sat still as a statue awaiting her turn to begin digging once more. All the while the girls sang a song they were learning in school, "A Song of Parting." Singing helped to alleviate, at least in part, the arduousness of the task at hand and the growing trepidation that surrounded their situation. In the darkness that surrounded them, no one could see that Kaori was not singing.

It had only been five days earlier, on March 23, that the school received word from the 32nd Army Headquarters that 222 female students of the Okinawa Women's Normal School and the First Prefectural Girls' High School, along with 18 of their teachers, were to be conscripted by the Japanese Imperial Army as nurses to assist medical personnel with wounded soldiers. (An additional seventy-nine girls from other schools on the island were also conscripted as nurses and sent to areas further north, along with three teachers.) Kaori and her classmates were assembled the following day during the early morning hours and brought immediately to Haebaru, located about five kilometers southeast of Naha; there had not even been time to notify her family of where she was being taken. One of their first assigned duties was to dig out these caves that were to be used as shelters.

In her mind's eye Kaori had somehow envisaged something quite different, perhaps even more glamorously patriotic, from what it appeared they were likely to experience. She and her classmates had begun receiving rudimentary training as nurses as early as last November; for them it was a welcomed diversion from the rigors of their regular studies. So she naturally thought they would minister the sick and wounded far from any potential battlefield areas in some gleaming white building and sterile surroundings, all while donning clean crisp nurses' uniforms and remaining untouched by the war directly. In any case, many of her classmates believed the enemy would be defeated in a matter of days and had even brought along school books and other supplies so they could study.

What naiveté, she now thought to herself. The field hospital at Haebaru was little more than a collection of caves dug out from a grass-covered hillside and she and her classmates had quickly been reduced to manual laborers, now covered in dirt and grime. Still, she was grateful to their teachers who worked hard to keep the girls' spirits high. They even planned a special ceremony for the next day for those students who were scheduled to graduate. And she had heard rumors the principal planned to attend as well.

The girls of the Okinawa Women's Normal School and the First Prefectural Girls' High School, who ranged in age from fifteen to nineteen, were mobilized by the 32nd Imperial Army and would come to be known as the *Himeyuri Corps* in the post-war era. Although they would become the most well-known of the female students mobilized, their numbers actually comprised less than half of the 543 female students who were ultimately conscripted for various duties. Formed eight days before the main invasion of the island and only in existence for about eighty-eight days, when the student nursing corps was disbanded on June 18 while the battle stilled raged, the girls and their teachers were summarily dismissed, made to evacuate the caves they occupied and forced to fend for themselves. The Himeyuri students and their teachers suffered a mortality rate of about fifty-seven percent.

Male students were also mobilized, some of whom became members of the Blood and Iron Imperial Service Corps. Ranging in age from fourteen to nineteen, the students were drawn from the Men's Okinawa Normal School, various middle schools, prefectural technical schools (fishery, agricultural and forestry, etc.), and private schools.

Students of the Blood and Iron Imperial Service Corps were divided into upper and lower levels depending upon their ages. Younger students were formed into the signal corps and assigned responsibilities for delivering dispatches and repairing cables for communication equipment. Older students were given more physically demanding tasks—bridge repair work, transporting war materiel and supplies and similar duties. In total, approximately 1,300 male students were mobilized to assist in the defense of Okinawa.

2

As the family gathered in the kitchen and began discussing what they should do—would it be better to remain in their home or seek shelter elsewhere—Munekazu recalled his promise to Arashiro Chiyoko to keep her apprised of any developments in the situation. He suspected she already knew—it would be difficult to miss the sound of the enemy's naval gunfire and the resultant tremors it sent through the ground. *Still,* he thought to himself, *a promise is a promise.* He explained the situation as he surmised it to Tomiko and then asked her to take care of that task while he, Yoshiko, and Kamadū tried to determine what the family's next steps should be. Reluctantly, Tomiko agreed, but urged the family not to make any final decisions without her.

Munekazu was growing increasingly uneasy. The enemy's presence accounted for part of his anxiety, but only a portion of it. It was more the uncertainty of their circumstances that really unnerved him. The military had only days before begun mobilizing students, girls and boys alike, and Naha National School was no exception. Some of the teachers had also been ordered to accompany their mobilized students. Fortunately for him, none of his students had been selected for mobilization yet, nor had any of Jiro's, but he was well aware that that could change at any moment. If that were to happen, what would become of his family? For the first time in a very long time he began taking stock of what they meant to him and more than anything he wanted to ensure their safety.

Sometimes the daily routine of life lulls us to a point where we take for granted those things most important to us, he thought. *Was he a disloyal subject of the empire?* he asked himself. He had to concede that perhaps he was, but he was determined to see that no harm came to any of them—they were now his priority. *How would the loss of my family contribute to Japan's war victory?* he thought. He did not know what tomorrow would bring, but whatever it was he felt they needed to face it together. And to his way of thinking, leaving their home would be the best way to keep them all safe.

After learning the news about the students, he had rushed over to the normal school to check on Kaori at the first chance that presented itself—that had been in the late afternoon on March 24. Instead of the usual lively and vibrant school grounds filled with the voices of young girls and their activities to which he had grown accustomed, he was greeted by an eerie silence and stillness. There were no students; no teachers—nothing moved. Overwhelmed by an ever-growing sense of angst, he hurried about the school knocking on doors and searching classrooms for signs of life. He finally happened upon the school principal, who Munekazu had known since his own days at the men's normal school. He was a short, rotund and jovial man with a balding head who usually had a good word for everyone—Munekazu had always liked him.

Upon seeing Munekazu in such an uncharacteristic state of distress, the principal took extra pains to calm him.

"The girls are all safe," he reassured Munekazu. They had been transported to the Army's field hospital in Haebaru around midnight and were being well cared for. In fact, he would be leaving for Haebaru himself in the next few days to conduct the school's graduation ceremony for those students who had completed their studies. "So, you see there really is nothing to worry about," he had calmly added. "The girls are far removed from any danger, but will be doing a great national service for Japan's empire. Ah, I do envy them," he concluded.

When Munekazu asked if it might be possible to briefly see Kaori, he was met by the principal's friendly rebuke. "Kaze-kun, that would simply be inappropriate. We all have our responsibilities in service to the emperor—this is Kaori-chan's. We really shouldn't pester her with other matters right now. And the school has dispatched over two hundred students—what if every family made the same request. We'd have a mess on our hands. She will be fine, you'll see." With that, Munekazu had no choice but to leave, but somehow the principal's words rang hollow in his ears. Far from assuaging his fears, his concerns only increased. For the time being, however, there was little he could do.

This exchange with the principal, however, proved seminal to the birth of a new perspective into which his soul had been trying to breathe life for months, but which he had resisted at every turn. He now concluded that the empire of Japan had little use for Okinawans beyond their value as cheap labor for the war effort; as human beings, however, they were expendable. By this reasoning, Kaori had also become expendable. The military's propaganda endlessly exhorting civilians to choose death over being captured by the enemy now began to strike him as particularly ludicrous. How could there be glory in dying for the emperor when they were not even respected in life? The Americans may indeed be the demons portrayed by Japanese authorities, prepared to rape their women and kill babies and men. But the expectation that Okinawans should mindlessly accept such stories as unassailable truths and willingly choose to become *gyokusai* (J: broken jewels) in an effort to die honorably, in his opinion, reduced Okinawans to little more than cannon fodder for the empire. (One of the first instances of gyokusai occurring in Okinawa prefecture occurred during the US military assault on the Kerama Islands.)

As the family discussed its situation, Munekazu gradually came to realize their choices were rather limited. The island, which in the past had always felt so large to him, now seemed miniscule, almost infinitesimal in the face of the growing number of enemy ships anchored off the western shores of their home. In his estimation, they could not travel to the northern part of the island; such a trek would take them through the Army's defensive positions and right past the bulk of the enemy's ships now in Hagushi Bay (Yomitan) and where much of the shelling was concentrated. Besides, there was no telling when enemy troops might storm Okinawa as they had the Kerama Islands. And they could not go east. That would take them toward the towns of Yonabaru and Nishihara and the Pacific Ocean. By this reasoning, they concluded that the only option, should they decided to leave, was to head south, toward Itoman. This would at least provide an opportunity to maneuver out of harm's way should it come to that. But the fundamental question remained unanswered—should they leave?

Yoshiko was adamantly opposed to leaving, as was Kamadū.

Tomiko, however, was more ambivalent. His mother's rationale was both simple and straightforward—this is where she had spent most of her life and raised her family. Despite the dangers that presented themselves outside their home, she felt safest being here.

This hardly adds anything meaningful to the discussion, Munekazu thought to himself, but if he was to convince Kamadū to leave, he knew he would first need to convince Yoshiko; Kamadū listened to her.

Yoshiko's reasoning, however, was harder to assail. First, she countered, they had no idea how things were going to turn out—leaving could wind up being more dangerous than staying. Outside their home they would have to contend with both an advancing enemy and the island's imperial defenders. She also observed that despite everything that had happened to this point the children, Muneyasu, Hideko and Tomiko's sons, had been relatively calm until the family began their discussions of leaving amid the enemy's shelling—now all four children were visibly distraught.

"How can we manage such a move with four scared children?" she asked Munekazu. "I don't think we'll get very far." Putting an exclamation point on her argument, she reminded Munekazu of how well they had fared during last year's attack and the enemy's subsequent attacks earlier in the year; she remained convinced the kami would protect them this time as well.

Then, almost as if some divine being was acting on cue to strike through Yoshiko's entire argument, sounds of nearby explosions could be heard—intense and concentrated. Rushing out of their home and out into an open area that afforded a better vantage point, they could see planes attacking Naha's port followed by naval gunfire that also targeted the port and chewed up large tracts of the city's earth.

Munekazu, his eyes filled with compassion for his wife,

looked at Yoshiko and simply said, "We have no choice...we must leave immediately…for Itoman."

Having finally cleared the extensive seaborne minefields laid by the island's defenders, US battleships, cruisers, and destroyers were able to maneuver into position to bring the island into range of their guns and deliver much more accurate and deadly fire. The day was March 29, 1945.

3

The sounds of war were deafening to Kiyoko's ears, the pounding having become nearly incessant. She had never heard anything like it. It was as if someone had put an iron pot over her head and was continually hitting against it with a large metal implement; and the concussive impacts of nearby exploding ordnance almost drove her insane. Although Kadena itself was not yet being targeted by the enemy, it was only a stone's throw from Yomitan, roughly ten kilometers, which now bore the brunt of the attack. Shelling, however, had occurred near Kadena village and she somehow believed that the unborn child within her could hear every blast and feel each explosion, just as she was able to.

Instinctively she wanted to run away; she wanted to return to the safety of her home in Naha and be with her family. It had been years since she and Munekazu enjoyed one of their quiet chats together, separated from all else in the world and sharing their innermost thoughts. Even after all these years she vividly recalled how she felt almost as if they were safely tucked away in a cocoon—she desperately wanted to feel that way once again. Deep inside there was a voice screaming for her to get out of Kadena and return to the Tamashiro household. She realized, of course, that while this was a natural reaction to the imminent danger they now faced, it was hardly a feeling upon which she could act. Her home was Kadena and Kazuo's family was her own.

Word reached Kadena from Yomitan village of the enemy's growing armada in Hagushi Bay and the intensifying barrage of the area. Panic had ensued among the villagers. Homes, farms and hamlets were being besieged by enemy aircraft and naval bombardment. The destruction, in the words of Yomitan residents and others living in the vicinity of the Hagushi beaches, was complete and incalculable. What had begun as a trickle was now a comparative torrent of humanity unleashed from Yomitan and its environs as villagers sought to escape with their lives by moving further inland. For those fleeing southward, Kadena served as a natural pass-through area.

As Kiyoko, Kazuo and the rest of the family gathered to watch those fleeing, they were overcome by a mixture of horror and curiosity. They also gradually realized that some of the villagers who had fled southward were now returning.

"Why on earth would they be coming back?" Kazuo asked aloud, but it was a question posed more to himself than to the others. He decided to find out why. According to two farmers he stopped, each leading an ox-drawn wagon carrying what he presumed were their worldly possessions, advance units of the 32nd Army forced them to turn back.

They explained they were told that, "Unless you islanders want to become targets for the enemy or be cut down by our bullets, turn around and head north. You're just in the way here."

The first farmer smiled slightly and scratched his head saying, "Well, that didn't sound like it would be too much fun, so we turned back. Heading up toward the Motobu peninsula might be safer at that. In any case, we'll probably be returning home in no time although there may not be much left."

Chiming in, the second farmer offered that while they had been turned back because they traveled along the road with their carts, many who were fleeing in small groups and without wagons or draft animals were able to avoid the military's detection and continue their trek southward. With that, the two were off.

Indeed, villagers from throughout the central Okinawa area of Nakagami had begun trying to get out of harm's way as quickly as possible, including residents of Kadena. To Kiyoko, they each conveyed their own tale of desperation and desire to survive. Yet each was plagued by a disturbingly similar crestfallen air that clung to them like a stench. She noted the sullenness of their eyes and gauntness of their faces. They moved almost without any real spirit; there was little life in them. Many, however, like the two farmers Kazuo had stopped, left with the expectation of returning home in a few days' time. To them, the enemy's attack was but one more hardship to endure in a long line of many—drought, starvation, poverty and now war.

By this time Kazuo had seen enough. He finally gathered his thoughts and hastily urged his family back home—they too needed to flee, but he still had no idea where they should go. Kazuo had suspected something when the sugar company suddenly closed its operations only a few days earlier. It was then, purely as a precautionary measure, that he had Kiyoko and his sisters begin laying out provisions in the event they needed to leave their home. Food was prepared; water jugs filled; and tools carefully laid aside that might prove essential during any protracted journey. Of course, how their livestock would be tended to during any absence remained an unanswered question. He did not want to come back to dead pigs and chickens, but taking them along was out of the question. And the spring planting season would soon be upon them. He worried that they might not be back in time to take advantage of it.

As Kiyoko hurriedly began assembling the items earlier laid aside, Kazuo's mother decided that she and her two daughters should make a final run to gather fresh vegetables or whatever else they could find for the trip.

"We don't know when we'll be able to return," she added.

Kazuo really saw no need for this, but put up no argument; it was better to appease than oppose at a time like this. He simply said, "Please don't be too long, mother. We'll need to leave in the next few hours. And please be careful." With everything he had seen and heard that day, Kazuo finally decided it would be best to flee northward, keeping the enemy to their backs, trying to avoid any potentially major fighting between the 32nd Army's defenders and the invaders.

The 32nd Army, forced to abandon its initial plan of defending the Hagushi beaches against enemy landings after units critical to this effort were transferred from Okinawa, had already largely given up the Yomitan and Kadena areas in favor of building a defense in depth further southward beginning in the Chatan-Toguchi area; the Kadena and Yontan airfields were likewise abandoned. Consequently, Kazuo's mother and sisters were able to search for food far beyond the boundaries of their own small farm unbothered by Imperial Army units. The three found that most of the places they foraged in the Kadena area, however, had already been picked clean by others with the same idea. Undaunted, they headed further northward determined to come back with enough food to sustain them, no matter how long the fighting might take. Having suffered through several periods of famine during her lifetime, Kazuo's mother was one who believed you could never have enough food stored away. After much searching, they finally found an area that had not been totally picked clean and that yielded a goodly number of umu.

Kazuo's mother urged her daughters to pick more quickly—they had lost track of time and she now realized they had been out longer than planned. Just as they decided they were finished and preparing to head home, the field in which they had been foraging suddenly came under blistering attack from naval gunfire, laying waste to everything. In a matter of seconds, their three lives were changed forever. Kazuo's mother tried desperately to gather her wits—her head was spinning, ears ringing and vision blurred, but still the shells rained down. She looked in the direction she had last seen her two daughters and tried calling out their names, but only a barely audible whisper crossed her lips. As she regained some amount of focus in her vision, she saw only small remnants of the basājin one of her daughters had been wearing—nothing remained of the other. As she tried to grasp the reality of what she saw, to her horror, she realized that she could neither move nor feel her legs. Looking down she was aghast to see only two bloodied stumps where her legs had once been, the result of shrapnel slicing through them. As sensation returned to her legs, the pain she experienced became unbearably excruciating, but fortunately, her consciousness was brief. In those few seconds she had remaining, she prayed for the souls of her two daughters, and her son's safety.

Chapter XIV

When Worlds Collide: Operation Iceberg

Nakagusuku Fumiko awoke with a start. Looking around in the darkness, she felt enveloped by an inexplicable sense of nothingness—an incomprehensible blackness where nothing moved; nothing stirred. And then it dawned on her—the sudden silence was unsettling. As strange as it sounded, for days she and other islanders had accustomed themselves to the constant distant barrage of enemy shelling and suddenly there was not a sound to be heard, not even a rustle in the air. Roused by a growing sense of foreboding, she got up and for a few minutes wandered aimlessly about the small house in Yonabaru, cane in hand, slowly moving from one room to the next. To her way of thinking, however, remaining inside would hardly satiate her curiosity. She peered outside, but as she expected, there was nothing to see. She decided against waking Umeko since her husband Kenshin was sleeping in the same room with her. Finally girding herself to any potential dangers outside, Nakagusuku Fumiko mustered her courage to venture beyond their home.

Stepping out into the small yard, she found she could still see nothing. The night was cool and the sky ink-black and clear. A large moon, surrounded by tiny glistening specks of celestial life, shone brightly and illuminated the landscape in its lunar glow. Moving slowly from the front entrance of the courtyard and into the street, she decided that having a look at the Pacific Ocean coastline might be worth the effort of the walk it would take to get there. In her younger days such a trip would have taken much less time, but in her current condition the trek would be more onerous and time-consuming. It was about 4:00am, April 1, 1945.

At that time of morning the roads would have been deserted in any case, but there was an unusual stillness about the small neighborhood. She was not certain how many of their neighbors might have left the area, but a good number of them and others in Yonabaru were evacuated by the military and moved further north. She, Umeko and Kenshin had decided not to be evacuated; they felt safer staying within the familiar surroundings of the town. Not that the Army was necessarily giving them a choice in the matter, but the town's residents had an informal network that kept them abreast of the activities of local military units, so most Yonabaru residents who had been evacuated north had actually preferred to do so. Those who wanted to remain, however, quickly absented themselves from their homes and the area until the evacuation was over, much as the three of them had done. She sometimes congratulated herself that theirs had been the right decision; after all, most of the enemy's activity was taking place further to the north and away from Yonabaru.

Slowly making her way over the uneven road and craggy landscape, and trying her best to avoid the military units in the area, she finally reached her destination—a hilltop overlooking the surrounding area. Looking out over the vast expanse of the Pacific Ocean, she noticed unusual activity to the southeast of where she presently stood. Large ships and smaller vessels were maneuvering in the water.

Was this the enemy or Japan's imperial military? she asked herself. She could not tell in the dark; she was about seven kilometers away. *Were they coming ashore?* To her it looked as though they were in the vicinity of Minatoga. Not wanting to make a fool of herself by appearing to be a panicky old woman, she tried making sense of what she saw. She sat down on a nearby rock for a short time, head in hand. As she sat, the predawn stillness was violently and suddenly rocked by what would be the largest naval pre-landing preparatory fire ever conducted—nearly 45,000 naval gun shells, 33,000 rockets and over 22,000 mortars—much of it concentrated on the eight miles of Hagushi landing beaches some twenty miles away.

Nakagusuku Fumiko could not have known, of course, but she was witnessing a well-choreographed assault on the island as part of Operation Iceberg. What she saw were units of the US Marine Corps 2nd Division creating a diversionary attack, an operational feint, to draw Imperial Army forces toward the area of the Chinen Peninsula and away from the actual landing site on the Hagushi beaches in Yomitan. Once the din of the attack filled her ears, Nakagusuku Fumiko's confidence returned—she knew that what she was seeing were not imperial military forces. With that, she began making her way back home as quickly as she could.

She walked along carefully trying to avoid the hard coral outgrowths that filled the area, but was startled out of her wits when out of nowhere she heard a loud disembodied voice rebuke her saying, "Hey, *obāsan* (J: grandmother), what are you doing out here? Get home where you belong. This is a military area."

Unnerved, Nakagusuku Fumiko tried to hurry along while simultaneously taking her eyes off the ground in front of her to look about to see where the voice had come from, but the uneven ground caught her cane at an odd angle causing her to lose her balance and fall face forward. Then out of the darkness came a hand, helping her up.

In an unusually kind voice, she heard someone say, "Obāsan, this is no place for you to be; it's dangerous. Please go home to your family—you'll be safer with them. And if you can, try to make it north; that would be best for all of you."

As she was lifted up, she found herself looking into the face of a Japanese soldier who was smiling compassionately at her. He continued. "Here, let me help you back over to the road." Once she was back on the dirt road, she hastened home.

She was met by a frantic Umeko along the roadway a short

distance from their home.

"Where on earth have you been? We have been worried out of our minds. Kenshin is out looking for you too," she said breathlessly.

Returning to the house to await Kenshin's return, she explained to Umeko everything she had seen. Kenshin soon made his way back to the house and was visibly relieved to see Nakagusuku Fumiko there. She explained again for Kenshin's sake everything she had seen, after which a palpable minatory consternation overtook the three. The intense and incessant bombing that provided the backdrop for the scene unfolding in the house only added to the dark ambiance. Where should they go and what should they do? None of the three had any clear answers, but if the enemy was coming ashore near the Chinen peninsula, they surmised they really had only two choices—head due west toward Naha or further north closer to Imperial Japanese Army units, which might afford them more protection. In the end they decided to split the difference and make their way toward Shuri, roughly half-way between Yonabaru and Naha and slightly closer to the military units. From there they might better be able to assess their predicament.

2

Kiyoko had tried to be as compassionate as she could. She knew Kazuo was unwilling to accept the fact that his mother and two sisters had in all likelihood been killed during the bombing. They waited hours for the three to return. When that failed, Kazuo had gone out in search of them, but this too was to no avail. The ferocity of the early morning attack on April 1, however, caused Kiyoko to lose patience, yet she still tried to be as gentle as possible.

"Kazuo, your mother and sisters might have decided to go ahead without us. If we leave now, there is a chance we'll meet up with them somewhere along the way."

Kazuo retorted sharply, "They would never do such a thing. We agreed to all leave together. No, the best thing to do is wait for them to return."

Finally exasperated beyond control, Kiyoko said, "Listen to that!" and she pointed outside. "Should we wait for a bomb to come crashing through the roof before we decide to leave? And what about *our* unborn child…are you willing sacrifice its life as well while you wait?" She continued. "I pray for the safety of your sisters and mother, but we can't sit here any longer. If they are alive, they will be fleeing and most likely head north as we decided, while we sit here inviting our own deaths."

Allowing Kiyoko's scolding words to settle in for a few minutes, Kazuo finally responded in a soft, almost distant voice. "I suppose you're right. I'm sure they are fine. Let's pull some things together and go."

Kiyoko breathed a sigh of relief and the two began sorting through the items they thought they could manage. Because they planned to travel on foot they were limited with what they could carry—and besides, they now had three fewer people to assist in bringing along necessary items. Kazuo's mother and sisters had taken their carrying implements when they went out in search of food—a long pole with two baskets at either end that was carried across the back of the shoulders. Now Kiyoko and Kazuo had to improvise. Wrapping their provision in several large furoshiki, Kiyoko passed the packages to Kazuo who then slid them down the handle of a hoe, which he then slung over his shoulder. It was not ideal, but it worked.

At 8:00am, as suddenly as the intense bombardment had begun, it stopped. Having packed provisions enough for four days, the couple left the house in order to take advantage of a lull in the enemy's attack. Staying as far away from the coastline as possible, the two hurried northward as quickly as they were able, given Kiyoko's advanced condition. Along the way they ran into others with the same idea. If nothing else, Kiyoko found comfort in knowing she and Kazuo were not the only ones running for their lives. They wound up traveling with two other small groups, their number now totaling twelve people in all. They commiserated and shared stories they had heard. Kiyoko and Kazuo believed much of what they were hearing was merely rumor and did not place much stock in what was being said—the tales seemed to grow more fantastical with each passing kilometer. Despite this, they remained grateful for the company. The group pushed ahead. Their first destination would be Yomitan, which they would keep off to their left. The idea was then to head toward Nakadomari; and then on to Onna. They did their best to remain as close as possible to nearby sugar cane fields, which would afford sufficient cover in the event they needed to hide themselves.

Their final destination was Nago, and perhaps points even further north, although there was very little beyond Nago except wilderness. Given their circumstances, however, this might be the ideal place to hide. Ordinarily, neither Kiyoko nor Kazuo traveled much beyond the village of Kadena; the furthest north they had ever been was Onna, and then only on one occasion to visit distant relatives of Kazuo's family. Neither had ever been to Nago. As Kazuo thought about the distance they were to travel, he blanched. The provisions they were carrying would hardly sustain them. So he cautioned Kiyoko to look for anything edible along the way that they might be able to use to replenish their supplies.

By about 10:15am, April 1, Kiyoko, Kazuo and their small group reached a point where they were parallel to the village of Yomitan, only further inland, which unknowingly placed them only hours ahead of advancing US military units; trying to move with stealth as a group slowed their progress as did Kiyoko's pregnancy. As they moved through the area they came across small units of the Imperial Japanese Army, part of the 1st

Specially Established Regiment, there to function as a harassing and delaying force. They could not stop the enemy, but could impede his advance for a time. One of the soldiers, who appeared to be in charge of a few others, beckoned the group over. Speaking to no one in particular, he asked them where they were headed. One of the group's number explained their plan to reach Nago.

"That's a good idea," Sergeant Matsumoto replied. "This is no place for civilians." Studying the group for a moment, he rubbed his chin with his left hand and continued, "You have women in your group. You know what will happen if the enemy catches up to you, don't you? Your women will be raped and the men and children killed. That would be a terrible end." Then singling out Kiyoko with a quick jut of his chin, he remarked, "Not sure what they'll do with her. Better take some precautions." Kiyoko felt her entire body cringe.

Then motioning to several of the other soldiers standing near him to bring over a wooden box, he continued. "Here, take these hand grenades and if you are about to be captured pull the pin and die an honorable death in the name of the Emperor. Three people for each grenade should do the trick." With that, one of the soldiers handed them four grenades and demonstrated how the pin should be pulled. Sergeant Matsumoto smiled briefly and then barked a few commands to the soldiers, which sent them scurrying off. As he turned to leave he looked over his shoulder and simply said, "Good luck."

The Hagushi beach area was bisected by the Bishi River (present-day Hija River) and the US military attack plan called for US Marine Corps units (1st and 6th Divisions) to land north of the river and advance northward; US Army units (7th and 96th Infantry Divisions) to land south of the river and advance southward. Because of the fateful and untimely decisions made days earlier, Kazuo and Kiyoko, along with the others in their group, would close with and meet the enemy long before many of Japan's imperial defenders on the island did; an encounter that would leave each of them bewildered and wondering exactly who the enemy really was.

3

Ushī found it difficult to imagine how life might torment her any more than it already had, having first been sold into prostitution by her family; then forced to become a jugun ianfu; and now trapped in the middle of a war. Despite her young age, she had come to believe that there was nothing precious about life; there was only heartache and despair. At times she wondered if death might have been a more suitable companion for her current state of mind rather than enduring life's tribulations. She sometimes likened her short life to the large placards that once hung outside kabuki theaters in old Edo that announced current performances and featured actors—she had never actually seen one, but Sergeant Nakamura had once described them to her. Only in her case, inhumanity seemed to be the perennial performance with depravity and scorn as its main characters. When she fell into such moods of morosity, however, her mind would quickly recount the scene in Mi-hyun's room after she committed suicide and how her corpse had been treated with utter disregard by those who should have cared something about her. This recollection was enough to make Ushī realize that in reality death was hardly an option. Strangely, it was Mi-hyun, unable to fend for herself in life, whose spirit now guided Ushī from her afterlife.

Because Ishida's comfort station had been located in such close proximity to the 32nd Army Headquarters in Shuri, Ushī and the other women at the station experienced the war from early on. Seeing the widespread destruction of Shuri and the homes of its residents had had little impact on her. Having seen all that she had, there was now a new callousness about her being, which inured her to the ever growing list of war's horrors.

Curiously, however, what had affected her was seeing the bombardment of Shuri Castle. Despite the difficulty of life on the island, to Ushī the castle remained a symbol of the Okinawan people. She knew little of the history attendant to the Sho Dynasty, the details of its demise, or Okinawa's past dual suzerainty to Japan and China—she had neither the formal schooling nor genuine interest to make any of that meaningful to her. Rather, to her way of thinking the castle's importance lay in its symbolism of Okinawan culture; it was what little remained of islanders' heritage that had not been cast aside by Japan's own culture or destroyed in the current fighting. Its ability to endure the enemy's constant bombing and not be left as a pile of rubble gave her hope that the Okinawan people could endure as well and emerge victorious over both the Japanese military and the enemy.

By now Ushī was prepared to grasp hope from just about any quarter she could and seeing the castle withstand constant enemy bombardment was now her lifeline. *Shurei no mon*, one of the castle's main gates, and *Kokugaku no mon*, the gate through which the king and his family had passed for the last time in 1879 when forced to abdicate the throne, had been destroyed long ago during the initial attacks. She sometimes wondered why the military had chosen Shuri Castle as the final location for the 32nd Army's headquarters, which would at the very least make it an inviting target for attack. Perhaps the soldiers too believed in its indestructibility. Then as if to reassure herself she would at times think, *All else may be destroyed, but not our Shuri Castle....not the Okinawan people.*

By this time remaining above ground was nearly impossible—the shelling was too intense—so Ishida, his wife and the jugun ianfu took shelter underground along with the soldiers. While the ground quaked and the sound of endlessly exploding ordnance was maddening, they were comparatively safe. And, despite the inconveniences the war presented, there were some unexpected kernels of mirth and light-heartedness in their new subterranean dwellings. For better or worse, responsibility for the jugun ianfu now fell to the military as Ishida's services were no longer required. So he was put to work hauling supplies back and forth; his wife worked in food preparation—every hand was needed in the fight against the enemy. The women of the old comfort station sneered at them both, the Ishidas having been reduced to their level. A few of the girls even took time to dole out their own form of battlefield justice on Ishida's wife, rendering a swift kick to her rear as she bent over to do her chores or directing a well-placed slap across the back of her head when she least expected it. Ushī chose not to involve herself in such antics, but she had to admit to feeling a certain satisfaction at seeing Ishida's wife getting a taste of her medicine. But she realized that in the end any transitory satisfaction attendant to such acts of retribution did little to improve their situation.

Beyond these fleeting moments of relief, their new circumstances provided little to be thankful for. By this point, most of the soldiers had reconciled themselves to their own deaths, and as a result, cared little about the welfare of the jugun ianfu. They recognized only lust and violence, neither of which was constrained by any boundaries of propriety. Their lives—the women and soldiers alike—had sunk to such a level that Ushī often felt they were little better than animals being driven solely by their base needs and desires. There were, of course, soldiers assigned to keep guard over jugun ianfu, but they too sought to take full advantage of the situation.

The dirt, grime and dampness of their surroundings soon rendered the sanitary conditions within their underground sanctuary unbearable. Food was rationed. The cordialities of daily life were quickly cast aside. There was no water with which to wash—this was no place for such luxuries, so soon lice abounded.

It makes little difference, Ushī thought to herself consolingly, *we are all in the same boat and it is unavoidable.* At least she had had the foresight to bring along as many condoms as she could carry. Some of the women who had not brought any were having unprotected sex all day, every day. While Ushī was usually prepared to share and help others, she realized that she first needed to watch out for her own welfare, so she kept her stash of condoms for her own use. Under such vile conditions, of course, the women suffered infections, a few of the cases becoming severe. Despite all this, they were required to perform their services for the soldiers. It was wretched—disease, stench, and parasites.

The depravity of war has surely descended to a new nadir. Is this how human beings were meant to live? Ushī asked herself.

4

Kaori struggled to regain her grasp on reality. Not unlike trying to grip a handful of sand that easily sifts through one's fingers, so too did her hold on sanity seem increasingly evanescent. She realized that the years of fantasy and mock bravado about discharging her duties to the empire were simply that—this was real and she was scared. She and her classmates could hear quite clearly, in the distance, the enemy's advancing attack and the associated pounding of exploding ordnance. Despite her growing anxieties, she could not, of course, reveal her true emotions; none of the girls could, but most of them feared the worst and longed for the warmth and comfort of their old classrooms.

It seemed as though the wounded had begun pouring into the field hospital at Haebaru almost immediately and the students were expected to perform as they had been trained. While Kaori excelled in her mock nursing drills, the sight of real human blood and gore left her cold. The bodies piled up, hour after hour, day after day, some gushing blood from every anatomical orifice;

others mangled almost beyond recognition; still others without limbs. At the outset, the students' duties had been divided based upon their school classification. The older girls assisted with surgical operations while the younger ones brought what little food and water was available to suffering patients and handled bed pans; the latter set of duties had occupied Kaori for a time. As the number of wounded mounted geometrically, however, their small number became overwhelmed and each girl was required to assist where most needed. With only a handful of medical doctors and military personnel to assist, the students played an integral role in rendering medical care.

Kaori had been going about her duties that morning when one of the army surgeons barked at her to give him a hand with a soldier whose arm was bleeding profusely. It was clear even to her untrained eyes that, given the severity of his wounds, the soldier would likely never be able to use his arm again. Kaori approached reluctantly. The surgeon then barked at her again.

"What are you doing? Get over here and give me some help." Startled, Kaori complied. "Alright, I need you to sit on his chest and hold his arm still while I cut through it."

Cut through it? she thought to herself. "Shall I get the anesthesia?" she asked haltingly, recalling the training she had earlier received.

"Damn it, we need to conserve that for the really serious cases. Now sit down on this man's chest so I can get this done!" the surgeon ordered loudly.

Kaori looked at the surgeon and then again at the patient and just shook her head in a manner that conveyed "no", she could not do what she was being told. Visibly exasperated, the surgeon pushed her aside and bellowed for another student who quickly complied with his order. Kaori watched until the moment the blade of the saw made its first grinding cut into the patient's bone and he screamed in agony. Kaori ran out of the cave to catch her breath, but not before she left what little breakfast she had eaten on the cave floor, her ears pulsating to the sound of the surgeon's invectives.

Conditions only worsened as the fighting continued, but at least Kaori was gradually able to gird herself against the brutal realities of life in a wartime operating room. It was the unspeakable suffering of convalescing patients to which she would never become acclimated. With food and water running short, there was an insufficient amount to dispense. They screamed and yelled for water, for food, but there was so little. The worst of them, losing control of their mental faculties, had to be sequestered and physically restrained in a dark separate area of the cave. There was blood and infection everywhere she turned—the stench made her wrench inside and gag. Her skin crawled with lice. She felt they were no longer human.

Is this the glory I've so often been told about? Is this what the honor of dying for the Emperor looks like? she asked herself. Kaori wanted to run away and hide. But where would she go? Here there was suffering and pain; out there the enemy was coming ever closer bringing with him certain death. She recalled the many admonitions about the American enemy—their soldiers would rape and kill Japanese women. Visions of hordes of American soldiers raping her filled her head. Looking about, she felt the world closing in on her. Kaori did the only thing she felt she was able to do. Finding a dark and relatively quiet corner, she curled up into a ball and cried.

Chapter XV

No Fire Like Passion, No Snare Like Folly

Fighting raged on Okinawa throughout April and May 1945, but by early June the issue was no longer in doubt. Major units comprising the 32nd Imperial Army were being decimated by a relentless barrage of naval and field artillery gunfire, aerial attacks, and advancing US ground forces. In fact, support troops were being used to fight alongside first-line combat troops in order to replenish the depleted ranks of 32nd Army's fighting units. Major fighting continued on the Oroku peninsula just south of Naha and in other areas, but Imperial Army units had retreated further south to establish new defensive lines, occupying an ever-decreasing area of the island in the process; by May 31, Japan's beleaguered army units had withdrawn to an area just south of Itoman. This turn of events had an even greater pernicious impact on the local population. Confined to a relatively small corner of the island, Japanese soldiers and islanders now occupied essentially the same territory, and having become interspersed, placed defenseless civilians between two combating militaries.

* * *

Munekazu sat in a crouched position, hiding among the thickets of a pandanus grove, peering at the outside world. He was so deep in thought, however, that he saw little of the landscape before him. He was taking a break from entertaining the children with old Okinawan ghost tales—it was one of the few diversions they had. Although Hideko would sometimes get scared, Muneyasu and Tomiko's two sons never seemed to tire of them. Today he recited one of Muneyasu's favorites—the young wife of

Matsugawa who had died years before for want of a rickshaw while she was ill. And, so the story goes, on the anniversary of the night of her death, she would sometimes hail an unsuspecting rickshaw driver to take her home to Matsugawa from Sogenji where she died. Muneyasu often liberally embellished these stories, his young listeners hanging on his every word. Today was no different despite the boys' illness. In fact, the stories seemed to calm them a little.

His life had changed dramatically and irrevocably in the past weeks. He looked over his shoulder without thinking and began counting the family members with him to reassure himself they were all safe—Yoshiko and the children, Tomiko and her two sons. He had picked up this habit ever since losing Kamadū. She now numbered among the war's growing list of casualties and he remained grief-stricken by her loss. The woman who had sacrificed her body to give him birth and nurtured him into his manhood was now gone and he realized he had taken her for granted for many years, simply assuming she would be there forever. Her end had come about so quickly and unexpectedly that he sometimes still had a hard time believing she was actually gone.

He did not consider himself to be a bad son, but he reluctantly conceded that he had not been as filial to his mother as propriety might have demanded. As Kamadū grew older and more emotionally dependent on her family, Munekazu had lost patience with her and came to rely on Yoshiko's compassion to deal with her, and as a result, their relationship had blossomed. He now found himself envying Yoshiko just a little. As he considered their present circumstances, he also came to realize that perhaps the one thing he could do to make amends for his past failures with his mother was beyond his ability to accomplish—giving her proper death rites and interring her body in the family tomb. This had become of paramount importance to Kamadū in her closing years. Indeed, if Munekazu was to give credence to traditional beliefs, Kamdū's soul would be denied an eternal resting place and she would roam the island as a malevolent spirit. If this was the case, he continued thinking, then the island would likely become filled with spirits of the damned, all of whom had been denied proper rites to enter the afterlife; death and untended corpses littered the countryside everywhere they went. He quietly promised Kamadū that the family would pray for her at the family altar when they were finally able to return home. He now found himself saying a silent prayer for the well-being of Kaori, Kiyoko, Seiho and Atsuko—wherever they might be.

Munekazu vividly recalled that day when the violence of the enemy's bombing on Naha had become so intense that he and Yoshiko decided the family simply could longer remain in their home. They began packing provisions and making arrangements to move the family southward toward the Mabuni area, which was about as far as they could go before arriving at the ocean's edge. Neither of them had ever been to Mabuni nor did they know what to expect, but that really did not matter at this point; they had go somewhere and Mabuni was as good a place as any.

As their small group moved outside the home and began their southward trek, Yoshiko yelled out to him for help; Kamadū had suddenly stopped and begun gazing forward with a weirdly blank expression. Munekazu rushed back to lend assistance. He tried speaking to Kamadū, but her speech was so hopelessly slurred and had been rendered into such an unintelligible string of gibberish that he could not understand what she was saying. She also appeared to have little control of her faculties—the right side of her face seemed to inexplicably droop and her eyes had a look that somehow conveyed she was no longer among them. He had never seen anything like it. He carried his mother piggy-back for about three miles, but her condition only worsened; in the end she was unable even to maintain her balance perched on his back. They stopped, hiding inside a small house, hoping Kamadū's condition would improve, but this had not been the case.

The longer they stayed, it seemed, the worse her condition became—she no longer even spoke. Yoshiko had implored him to take the children; she was prepared to remain behind with Kamadū and nurse her, but Munekazu refused to hear of such a thing. Kamadū was no longer capable of walking on her own, being carried or taking care of herself. Feeling the increasing weight of his responsibility to safeguard two generations of the family amid the ever-growing ferocity of the battle, Munekazu was finally compelled to make a fateful and painful decision—they would need to leave Kamadū behind. Munekazu had remained behind for a few minutes making his tearful good-byes to the only mother he had ever known. He doubted, however, that she understood anything he was saying, but he continued nonetheless. He began feeling a burning rage inside of himself for the circumstances that had brought him and his family to this point. The glory of war, victories and Japan's territorial expansion seemed so distant and meaningless, so infinitesimal in its importance that he could no longer believe he once regarded them with the dogmatic fervor he had. They were the dreams of a lifetime ago held by a different person; he no longer labored under a cathexis for Japan's ultimate victory. When he returned to the group, Yoshiko would neither look at nor speak to him. He knew, however, that she understood he had done what needed to be done.

Munekazu was not certain of their precise location, but his best guess was that they had traveled to a point somewhere in the vicinity of Gushikami near the island's southeastern coast. Once he found his bearings, they would then follow the contours of the hillsides along the shoreline toward Mabuni located on the island's southeastern-most tip. While the plan seemed sound enough, he was troubled by a number of things. First, it seemed to him that an increasing number of people were moving southward—the further they went, the more islanders there seemed to be. Second, the fighting also seemed to be following them, which even to his own mind untrained in military tactics portended disaster. Finally, although the thunderous pounding of large shells continued, the sound of small arms fire was becoming increasingly interspersed with it—the enemy was coming closer with each passing day. Even if they reached Mabuni successfully, at some point they would have nowhere to run.

The family was exhausted; no one was able to sleep with the constant explosions and sound of gunfire. As Munekazu looked back at them over his shoulder, he realized they had become a haggard looking group—he hardly recognized any of them. It was only then that he realized they cut a similar figure to others who saw them. He had at first been appalled upon seeing groups of islanders filthy, lice-laden and clawing for food out of a barren earth, but he came to understand surviving during war left no room for needless decorum.

We are all one now, he thought. *There are no more social distinctions because of jobs, money or some other contrived pretense of prestige. We are all hungry, dirty and scared in the same way.*

Their provisions had run out long ago, so they too were now reduced to scavenging for their existence. "What a fall from grace," Munekazu often lamented. They spent their days in hiding anywhere they could find—an old cave, among the rubble of destroyed homes, or a pandanus grove—to avoid detection and quite possibly being killed. They traveled by night, looking for any water or food along the way. Tomiko's two sons and Muneyasu, overcome by thirst, had disregarded admonishments not to drink any standing water they found. There were puddles of water and mud everywhere, the result of the heavy rains that had fallen over the last ten days of May. Consequently, all three were now violently ill, afflicted with diarrhea accompanied by bouts of vomiting. When Yoshiko had gone to check the source of the water the boys had drunk, she quickly understood the problem. Lying only feet away from the small pool of water were two dead bodies, one of which had been bleeding profusely. She suspected blood and bacteria had seeped into the water. Understanding the problem, however, did little to remedy it. What was already an arduous trip was now further complicated by the children's illness. They had barely made any headway over the past two days and the sounds of war crept ever closer.

Yoshiko and Tomiko moved forward toward Munekazu where he continued surveying the landscape. They both impressed upon him the importance of finding fresh water for the children. Even if they had been healthy they would have needed drinking water; they could not endure the early June heat and humidity without it. The earthen vessels they were using to catch rain water were far from sufficient to sustain seven people. But the boys were now dangerously dehydrated as well as a result of their sickness. Munekazu understood their concerns, but hesitated. The steady sound of gunfire nearby gave him pause, although it was difficult to determine the direction from which it was coming. He wondered if it would not be better to continue on to Mabuni carrying the children, but the two sisters vehemently disagreed, pointing out that moving the children would only worsen their condition. Yoshiko also pointed out that there was no telling when they might find another suitable resting place and in any case there was still too much daylight to consider leaving. Munekazu reluctantly agreed and set out carefully in search of water. He asked a few islanders he met along the way if they had come across any potable water. Only one person indicated having seen any, but the source was about three miles in the direction of Naha as Munekazu could best estimate, which would be impossible to reach given all the fighting along the way.

"*Otō-san! Otō-san!*" (J: father), he heard someone yelling breathlessly from behind. He turned to see Yoshiko running toward him. "It may be best for two people to carry water since there are so many mouths," she offered.

He smiled gently at her and nodded and the two headed off to continue their search. Within minutes, however, the area was besieged with artillery fire—they quickly found shelter in the ruins of an old home, Munekazu using his body to shield Yoshiko as best he could. Luckily the attack did not last too long and Munekazu prepared to resume their search for water. Yoshiko, however, had become suddenly quite uneasy, and wanted to return to their hiding place—she never explained why. Munekazu relented and they both hurried back to the pandanus grove.

To their horror, they found it had been reduced to a smoldering heap of vegetation from the attack minutes earlier.

Yoshiko yelled out frantically, "Muneyasu! Hideko! Where are you?"

Munekazu yelled equally loud for Tomiko and her sons. There was only silence. Then he stumbled across a sight he had ardently been praying he would not see—the bloody and lifeless remains of their family. They had been reduced to a primordial pool in the blink of an eye. There was nothing left. Munekazu, standing motionless and silent, found himself gasping for air. He tried calling out to Yoshiko, but no sounds crossed his lips. Yoshiko finally glimpsed Munekazu standing transfixed and rushed over to him. She was not prepared for the sight that greeted her eyes. She fell to the ground pounding the earth and wailing inconsolably.

"Why? Why?" she kept repeating. "They were all so innocent. They had so much life left to experience…sadness, happiness…" Her voice trailed off. Then, with a heat and passion Munekazu had never before witnessed in his wife, she stood up and turned to him, alternately pounding on his chest and slapping his face, saying, "This is your war. This is the glory you spoke of for so long. Was it worth the lives of your children? Our family? What new world order will give them back to us?"

Munekazu, the life energy drained from his being at seeing his dead children did nothing to fend off Yoshiko's rage; he stood there meekly, hot tears rolling endlessly down his cheeks.

Yoshiko, now breathless and fatigued, slumped to the ground as if she had been defeated. Then looking off into the distance, she said to Munekazu, "We have lost everything that was dear to us. Only memories of Hideko and Muneyasu will now fill the void in our hearts. Children cannot be born into such a world…I cannot bring this child I am now carrying into such violence and hatred."

Munekazu, taken aback, fell to the ground with his mouth agape; he had not known that Yoshiko was pregnant with their third child.

2

Kiyoko had to stop and rest; she simply could not take another step. She found that she was tiring more quickly as they made their way further northward. In fact, she had to rest so often that the majority of their group decided to continue on ahead of them, concerned their progress was being impeded by the frequent stops. There were now only five of them traveling together. Kazuo remained by Kiyoko's side trying to provide as much comfort as he could.

"We'll be just fine. The others are like rabbits—they must get to where they are going quickly only to have to wait once they get there."

"Where do you suppose we are?" Kiyoko asked.

Looking around, Kazuo could only respond, "I'm not really sure."

It was Kanashiro-san, one of their remaining number, who offered that they were somewhere between Nakadomari and Onna. Kiyoko sighed in slight exasperation. At best they had traveled a distance of about ten miles—they still had a long way to go. The group rested for a few minutes more and then decided it would be more prudent to continue on; there was no way of knowing where the enemy was. As they walked, Kiyoko could not help but recount, over and over, the warnings of the Japanese soldiers they had encountered earlier.

What would happen to them if the enemy caught them? she asked herself. These kinds of questions inevitably led her to think about the hand grenades they had been given, two of which they still carried with them.

As they continued along their way, parallel to the main road, but off of it, in order to avoid attracting undue attention, Uehara-san came running back down the road. She and her husband were among those who had left Kiyoko, Kazuo and the others earlier in order travel more quickly.

"Uehara-san," Kazuo shouted. "Where are you going?"

Spotting the group in the tree line, she ran over to them and sat down to catch her breath. Once she had recovered, she looked at each of them with a strange anxiousness. "We were just stopped by the Japanese military a few miles up the road. They conscripted the three men in our group. They said they were organizing locals into units to conduct guerilla attacks on the approaching enemy. Anyway, they didn't really much care about what we women did, so I came back to warn you."

While grateful for the information Uehara-san provided, it left Kazuo and Kanashiro, the only other adult male in their group, in a precarious situation.

Kazuo summed it up succinctly. "If we continue northward, we are bound to run into Japanese soldiers. If we turn back, we'll likely run into the enemy." They decided to stay where they were and seek cover in the dense vegetation of the hills in the area. They would wait for a while and assess their situation as circumstances unfolded—there was little else they could do.

By late afternoon on April 4, Kiyoko, Kazuo and the others, still hiding within the thickets along the base of the hillside, heard voices in the distance, but could not make out what was being said—"Japanese units looking for more conscripts," Kazuo immediately concluded. They waited for a few minutes, nervously lying prone and trying to watch for any activity along the road. As the approaching voices became more distinct, they looked at each other, realizing that no one could understand what was being said by the soldiers—they were speaking English. Kiyoko closed her eyes tightly, held her breath and grabbed Kazuo's hand, clutching it firmly. This was the one trouble she had hoped would not befall them.

Most of the soldiers traveled along the road, some walking and others in tanks, but a few walked through the trees and bushes. Kazuo thought they might be looking for Japanese soldiers. In any case, they all feared that at this rate, they would soon be discovered. In retrospect, Kazuo wondered if it would not have been better to have joined the Japanese unit; that way Kiyoko might have escaped northward. Kazuo and Kanashiro nervously and animatedly conferred with each other as to what they should do; they had the hand grenades, after all. This would save them from being captured and an uncertain future. In reality, however, none of them had even the slightest interest in dying. If they remained in hiding and were discovered, they might be mistaken for soldiers and killed. Fleeing was out of the question of course—Kiyoko could not manage that in her condition.

It was Kazuo who then hit upon a plan. The others would remain in hiding while he surrendered. The enemy might believe he was the only one hiding out, thus leaving the others alone and giving them a chance to flee to safety when the opportunity arose. Besides, Kazuo offered, there was a slight chance that everything they had been told about the enemy by the Japanese military was wrong. He reminded Kiyoko of the thousands of leaflets and copies of *Ryukyu Shuho* pamphlets that the enemy airdropped onto the island. Kazuo understood that much of it was wartime propaganda, but one fact had remained with him since he read the first of these missives—the enemy made a distinction between Japanese soldiers and Okinawan civilians. "You are not the enemy," were the words he clearly recalled having read.

Kiyoko begged him not to go, not to leave her alone. She looked into his eyes tearfully and longingly. He returned her gaze, offering the wisdom of an old Okinawan proverb, "*Mii ya tin niru aru.*" (Our fates are as registered by heaven.)

Somehow finding strength in Kazuo's words, she looked back at him, no longer crying, and said, "*Miitundaa duu tichi.*" (O: Man and wife are one flesh.) Kiyoko then continued, saying,"If you go, then I will go too."

The others implored Kiyoko to think of her unborn child and remain with them. Kazuo was at once in awe of his young wife, but worried for her safety and also begged her to remain behind. But Kiyoko's mind was made up. She looked back at their new friends and thanked them for their concern, but prepared to depart by saying, "If we die as a family, there is no loss."

She then looked at Kazuo and he looked at her, each firmly holding the other's hand. They waited a few minutes to allow their friends time to leave the immediate area. With that, they both stood with their hands in the air and began walking toward the enemy. The advancing US Marines quickly spotted them once they were out in the open and assumed defensive positions.

They yelled out to Kazuo and Kiyoko, "Stop and keep your hands in the air!" Of course, neither understood what was being said to them. The couple continued to move cautiously forward, arms raised, to the unintelligible speech of the enemy ordering them to halt. It was then that the sound of two gunshots pierced the air.

3

Okinawa was the first place US military forces encountered a significant civilian population while fighting in the Pacific theater. US intelligence indicated there were hundreds of thousands of civilians on the island, many of whom were thought to be loyal to the government of Japan. Consequently, additional measures were instituted to address these new and unfamiliar circumstances. In addition to the thousands of leaflets dropped by the US military informing islanders that they were not regarded as enemy combatants, a humanitarian-derived concept was also designed that sought to remove civilians from the battlefield and place them in safer refugee camps in US rear areas away from the fighting. In a practical sense, however, the US military was ill-equipped to handle such a task, a shortcoming that was ultimately demonstrated by the poor conditions that emerged within the camps: poor sanitation; lice and flea infestations; and parasitic diseases. Tropical diseases, such as dengue fever, were also rampant; and tuberculosis afflicted nearly 35 percent of refugees. In many of these instances, there was little the US military could do because the conditions that gave rise to disease and parasites existed long before its arrival. Poor camp conditions, however, contributed to their exacerbation. One case in point was the widespread instance of filariasis, a tropical parasitic disease (roundworms) passed from one host to another via the bite of mosquitoes or flies. The close quarters in which refugees were confined made this illness very difficult to combat. Inadequate supplies of food and shelter were yet other endemic problems, made worse by the heavy rains of the season.

Poor camp conditions found their genesis in three problems. First, contrary to US military expectations, there was virtually no civil government on Okinawa through which civilians could be controlled. Second, the numbers of civilians removed from the battlefield and falling under military control quickly became staggering. By the end of April 1945, the number was just under 127,000; by the beginning of June the number had risen to approximately 144,000; and by June's end approximately 196,000 civilians were under the control of the US military. In the end, US forces were unprepared to directly and adequately minister such a large number of civilians. Finally, despite the swelling ranks of civilians to which it now provided assistance, US military mission priorities remained the defeat of Japan's 32nd Army. Consequently, battlefield expediency sometimes demanded moving civilians from camp to camp, which added to the transitory atmosphere within them and worked against improving their facilities.

From its earliest landings on the island, the US military deployed "military government field teams" with the designations of "A," "B" and "C," which respectively were comprised of 15, 27 and 36 members. A-teams gathered and removed civilians from active combat areas; B-teams provided additional assistance; and C-teams were charged with operating refugee camps. C-teams were woefully understaffed and under-supplied relative to the civilian populations they were required to support. (Another group with the designation of D-teams also existed, which had the capacity to support 60,000-100,000 civilians. The first of these units, however, was not deployed until the end of April 1945.) Additionally, 25-bed US Navy medical dispensaries were dispatched along with the A and B teams.

Because the heaviest fighting was taking place in southern Okinawa, most early refugee camps were established in northern Okinawa—Ginoza and Kin along the northeastern coast and Taira and Ōgimi on the northwest coast numbering among them. As US forces advanced further south, additional camps were established to their rear in areas like Shimabukuro and Koza.

4

Ushī now found herself wandering aimlessly about the landscape of southern Okinawa—hungry, thirsty and fatigued, the fleas that ravaged her body only added to her misery. She had long since given up trying to remove them; with the thousands of human hosts available in this small corner of the island, the effort would have been useless. She had, however, inadvertently discovered a means of providing temporary relief from their voracious appetites through liberal application of mud to her skin. While it alleviated the discomfort for a while, it also had the effect of rendering her with the aura of "other worldliness." With her hair unkempt and caked with mud, covered in dirt from head to toe, and her kimono in tatters, she more resembled a spirit from the afterlife than a living being.

She was now somewhere near Komesu, well south of Itoman. This was the first time she had been anywhere near her old home in years so she naturally found herself looking for members of her family. *Would she even recognize them if she saw them?* she asked herself. Her parents would have aged quite a bit, so she watched the older people she saw along her way with particular scrutiny, although she fully knew how futile this effort was—there were just too many people. In fact, most people were in hiding as the battle seemed to inch ever closer. She realized how vulnerable she was remaining in the open; she needed to find shelter of some kind.

Crossing over the undulating landscape of Komesu, through some foliage and then on through one of the few remaining sugar cane plots, she emerged from the field and nearly stumbled over the bodies of two dead Japanese soldiers. Though she hated doing so, she rummaged through their clothing and equipment in search of anything she might be able to use. She found no food, but did find a canteen half filled with water. Opening it, she thirstily drank it contents, feeling it gently travel down her parched throat, almost as if it was some magical elixir. She suddenly felt something hit her squarely and forcefully in the center of her back that sent her rolling head over heels. When she looked up she saw two Japanese soldiers glaringly standing over her.

"Get away from there. Don't touch the bodies of soldiers who have died valiantly in battle. Go on, beat it!"

Ushī had no choice but to leave. She did, however, have the presence of mind to hide the canteen and so took that with her. It was not much, but she was grateful.

Ushī continued along, the fighting raging around her. She finally happened upon a small coral escarpment that had two very small entrances leading into tiny caves, each perhaps large enough to hold three or four people, and both of which were full of others seeking shelter. As she looked around trying to find another place of safety, a kindly older woman stuck her head out of the cave and beckoned Ushī to come over. Another voice, disembodied and scolding in its tone, chastised the older woman, telling her she jeopardized the safety of everyone; too many people would attract attention. Disregarding the admonishment, the older woman made her way toward the cave's opening and urged Ushī to scoot inside as far as she could. Ushī found that the woman, with her warm eyes and disarming smile, allayed her initial anxiousness about taking refuge in the cave. The woman and her family, all of whom now occupied the two caves, were from the Komesu area. They had never expected the fighting to last this long; they had fully anticipated that the island's Japanese defenders would quickly repel the enemy. It had only been at her insistence that her husband and brother scouted out these two caves—in the event they were wrong about the battle's outcome. The two shared stories, Ushī of the family she had not seen in years and the woman about the two daughters she had lost to illness—neither had seen their tenth birthday.

Then in a hushed voice she leaned over to Ushī and said,

"Remember, we women have more to worry about. These Americans will rape and have their way with us, especially young pretty ones like you. We must be careful. That's why you shouldn't wander around alone."

The word stuck in Ushī's head—"alone." She had not given her circumstances much thought since being cast out of the military's stronghold in Shuri, but she was indeed alone. Her mind began drifting, recalling the tumult and uncertainty of the past three weeks. It began when the 32nd Army Headquarters and other units decided to relinquish Shuri to the enemy and retreat further south—that was the first indication that things were going badly for the island's defenders. Then the women of what had been Ishida's comfort station were summarily dismissed—that was the second indication of portending disaster. The only thing they were told was to head south. *Great. That's a big help,* she thought to herself.

While she never expected the soldiers to shower the women with sympathy and compassion, she never expected to be turned out with such heartless disregard either. The problem confronting the women was that none of them knew where to go. Ushī and the others quickly found a place of relative safety and tried to decide what to do next. One of the Chinese women, renamed Konami by Ishida, came up with the best idea. If they stayed a little ahead of the retreating soldiers, but kept them in sight, they would be sure to go in the right direction and minimize their chances of getting shot while moving through Japanese Army lines. So they decided to wait until the larger units of the Japanese 32nd Army began heading south. The soldiers of several units passed them before the women decided to leave as well. As they prepared to leave she heard a familiar voice in the distance call out "Ushī." It was Sergeant Nakamura—he was the only person now who called her by that name. It had been weeks since she had last seen him and she had given up all hope of ever meeting him again.

"I heard the news that you and the other women were dismissed. That's not so good at a time like this." He instructed her to walk as they talked in order to attract less attention.

He asked about her plans and winced slightly as she explained. "Ushī, that's not such a good idea. The enemy will likely be tracking our movements, which puts you in greater danger. Put some distance between yourself and the military and head down the east coast."

Just then they both heard the all too familiar bellow of Colonel Yamashita calling for Nakamura.

"Nakamura, get over here. No time for that kind of stuff right now. We have a war to fight."

Nakamura rolled his eyes a bit and said, "Ah, our paper shogun summons me. He will bellow, howl and strut about like a proud peacock until it's time for him to take responsibility for his actions. Then he will look for others to blame for his own mistakes." Looking at Ushī he said, "Go quickly and stay along the east coast if you can. We may not see each other again, but I will never forget you." And with that, he was off. There was no time for sentimentality.

Ushī shared with the others what Nakamura had suggested to her. Most, however, decided their best chance was to stick as closely as possible to military units. Besides, most had never been on their own since arriving on Okinawa, so had little idea of where to go or what to do. Ushī decided to part ways with them and made her way southward alone. One of her last recollections of Shuri was the distant sight of the castle coming under withering enemy fire delivered by the battleship *USS Mississippi*. She somehow knew in her heart that the island's final cultural icon was about to fall and with it her hope for a brighter future.

Her daydreaming was abruptly interrupted by the approach of three Japanese soldiers—they first stopped at the other cave about fifty meters away. To Ushī they hardly resembled soldiers any longer, but looked more like tatterdemalion rogues with their unshaven faces and ragged uniforms.

"Hey, you in there! What are you doing hiding out like mice? Come out here immediately—that's an order from the imperial army."

Slowly, the two small groups began to emerge from their respective hiding places, but as Ushī was about to leave the cave the older woman purposely blocked her way and pushed her aside so she fell back into the cave, now hidden from immediate view by the family standing outside. It was the first time Ushī noticed they were all much older than she was, perhaps in their forties, fifties and sixties; there were no children among them. She crouched as far back in the cave as she could, overcome by apprehension.

The soldier continued his diatribe. He explained that the Japanese Army had failed to defeat the enemy and that they would likely be overrun in the near future.

"Dying for the emperor is not an honor many have the opportunity to experience. Become a gyokusai and earn an exalted place in the afterlife. Being captured is the only sin you can commit."

The family protested, but the soldiers turned a deaf ear and explained that one way or another they would all die that day—either honorably and voluntarily or "by a bullet," as he held up his rifle.

Having had his say, the soldiers fished out three hand grenades and formed the islanders and themselves into three smaller groups. Ushī, huddling in the corner of the cave, could see only the feet of the others outside. Suddenly she heard three explosions in quick succession and felt the concussive impacts of the grenades detonating. She sat motionless; she heard nothing. She tried to venture out slowly, but immediately at the cave's entrance were the bloodied and mangled remains of the others. She recoiled in horror at the sight and rushed back inside. For her young mind, which had experienced so much human degradation and depravity in her short lifetime, this was the final straw. This moment was tantamount to jumping from a psychological precipice into a maelstrom of insanity and horror. In that instant, she lost her final grip on reality and would never find her way back.

Chapter XVI

Destiny Unbound

Kiyoko lay resting quietly in an American military field hospital, where she had been for the past several days. She was moved from a much smaller one so she could receive adequate care during and after the birth of her daughter. She had not named the baby yet—she was waiting for Kazuo's visit to do that, although she was particularly partial to the name "Hatsumi"—the beginning of beauty.

"You are certainly the start of a new beginning for this family," Kiyoko said softly as she looked down tenderly at her daughter who she now held in her arms. She did not know when Kazuo would come; neither of them fully understood what it meant to be in the custody of the enemy nor what their circumstances portended. She did, however, now know that the stories they had been told over the years about the Americans had not turned out to be true. They had not been killed and Kiyoko had not been raped. Instead the Americans helped her with the birth of her baby daughter. That notwithstanding, she remained bemused by the circumstances that brought them to this point.

She recalled the events that preceded their arrival at the first refugee camp, replaying over and over in her mind that day she and Kazuo had given themselves up. She recalled hearing two gunshots, but had to piece together the rest from her own memory and Kazuo's recollections. The first shot came from behind them—she heard the bullet speed past her head, making almost a hissing sound as it cut through the air. So the couple concluded they must have been shot at by the Japanese military because they were facing the Americans. The second gunshot came from an American Marine who returned the shooter's fire, felling him in the process. The couple was then ordered to the ground as the Marine unit moved forward to engage the Japanese soldiers. Two other Marines rushed forward, and after checking to ensure Kiyoko and Kazuo had no weapons hidden anywhere on them, quickly led them away to safety. Kiyoko still could not reconcile the experience of being targeted by a Japanese soldier.

Kiyoko was awash in feelings of ambivalence as she tried to sort through her thoughts and emotions. The Americans had come to the island for only one reason—to destroy the 32nd Army; and the 32nd Army had but one mission: to fight a major delaying action with the enemy to give the mainland more time to prepare its defenses. It did not matter that there were thousands of innocent civilians living on the island who had no immediate stake in the war's outcome. Death had preceded the enemy's landing in unthinkable numbers, Kazuo's family among the dead; and the fighting continued to rage and so too, she imagined, did the dying. *But then,* she thought to herself, *what about these hospitals?* They cared for the wounded among the Okinawans. And here at the refugee camp in Ishikawa a school had even been established for the children. Perhaps they were not bad people, these Americans, but they were still destroying her home and killing many of its residents. Her mother and father had taught the children that "hating" was wrong and a greater stain on the character of the hater than the object of scorn, so she tried desperately to separate the "people," Americans and Japanese alike, from the acts of their militaries.

As she continued, she thought about the Japanese military, for which she reserved the lion's share of her anger. *Why were Okinawans being made the sacrificial lamb for Japan? Is this the only value Okinawa had to Japan?* she asked herself. They had always been treated as outsiders by mainland Japanese, but she still could not convince herself that Japanese civilians could so easily condemn them to such an end. She concluded that mainland Japanese must be suffering as they were. *No,* she thought to herself, *this is the fault of militaries. It makes no difference whether they are Japanese or American, they exist only for the purpose of fighting and Okinawa has become their battlefield. This is not a world we are familiar with; Okinawans have lived in peace for centuries. Will a new beginning emerge from all this destruction?*

Kiyoko, Kazuo and Hatsumi, as did tens of thousands of Okinawans, continued living in refugee camps well beyond the war's conclusion; destruction on the island was simply too extensive, and in any case, there was nowhere else to go. They believed nonetheless that they had been saved that day in April 1945 through the intervention of their ancestors for the purpose of raising Hatsumi and her future siblings—at the range the Japanese soldier fired his weapon at her, he should not have missed Kiyoko. While the family would never be considered wealthy, they would live a good life by Okinawan standards. Kiyoko later worked as a maid for an American military family while Kazuo worked as a guard at a warehouse on a US military facility.

2

Kaori and three other students had been wandering about the battlefield for days, remaining hidden by day and coming out only at night to rummage for food. They also continued looking for places to hide that would afford ever greater safety from the fighting, now much more concentrated in this corner of Okinawa. The situation around them had become violently confused. There really appeared to be no front line for the Japanese military; civilians and soldiers were intermingled, which meant they had all essentially become targets for the enemy.

The students were now located somewhere between the towns of Sashiki and Tamagusuku at the head of the Chinen peninsula, much worse for wear. They had not eaten in days and water was equally scarce. There really was no opportunity to sleep; each feared the next explosion would kill them all and none of them wanted to die. They sometimes comforted each other as they cried for home and their parents. At other times they cursed the enemy for what he was doing to their island—and to them. But as each morning dawned, they were grateful to have survived yet one more night.

Their teacher, Mr. Teruya, was killed soon after the student nursing corps had been disbanded by the 32nd Army on June 18 and told its members needed to fend for themselves. He had been caught in the open between Japanese and American forces as they were fighting. Kaori did not like thinking about it. Mr. Teruya had been one of her favorite teachers at school, and despite all the carnage they witnessed at the field hospital, he was always ready to share an encouraging word with the girls. The soldiers often yelled at them because they knew so little, but Mr. Teruya would quickly follow and whisper something positive, making things a little more bearable—"you've really put yourself into your work" or "that's the way to hang in there." But now he was gone, lost in a hail of bullets and there had been little else the girls could do but look on helplessly. One of his last warnings to them was to be careful not to get captured because of all they had been told by the soldiers about what the enemy would do to them. So one of the first things the students did was to smear their faces and hair with mud in order to make themselves less attractive.

If Kaori had not been so exhausted she likely would have appreciated the view they had of Nakagusuku Bay against a backdrop of green rolling mountains.

How can such a beautiful place be turned into such a hell? she asked herself remorsefully. That night the students decided to head further south toward Kiyan, the island's southernmost tip. They moved lethargically, however—with little sleep and even less food and water, they had no energy. They found themselves stopping frequently. It was then that Kaori first heard someone speaking in Japanese over a loud speaker—it was coming from a small boat close to shore. The speaker's Japanese was not perfect, but good enough to be understood. He was telling the islanders and soldiers to give up, that no harm would come to them—it was the enemy. While their bodies were tempted by the offer, they pressed ahead for fear of what might happen to them in captivity.

Continuing their journey, they came across four Japanese military stragglers who looked as scared and disheveled as they did. The soldiers told them that the battle was lost; it was only a matter of time before they would all be captured and killed, but the girls would first be raped by hordes of Americans. He then pulled out a pistol and two grenades.

"There may be too many of us for two grenades to do the job. Whoever is left should shoot the survivors and then kill themselves."

Is this what it has come to for us? I don't want to die—and for what purpose? Have we all gone insane? Kaori asked herself. Their small group was then happened upon by two other soldiers who were also retreating southward. These two looked a lot more like soldiers than the other four. They were certainly dirty, but somehow they exuded a military bearing the other four lacked. One was tall and, to Kaori's thinking, very handsome. She immediately chided herself for thinking such things at a time like this. The other one had a very intelligent face and spoke quite softly, but with an unmistakable air of confidence.

As the two soldiers listened intently to what the others were saying to the girls, the tall soldier's face reddened and he jumped to his feet.

"Bakayarō!" he shouted. "Why do you say such irresponsible things to these young girls? They are civilians. They have families who worry for them and they have futures to live for. It will be on the strength of their work that Okinawa and Japan will be rebuilt. We will be defeated, and as soldiers, we will likely die; that is our fate. But not these girls. Japan has no use for gyokusai now—it needs survivors."

With that, he kicked one of the other soldiers and glared menacingly at the rest. They did nothing, only sitting quietly. Then turning to the girls, his expression softened. "Listen, we have heard stories about civilians being treated humanely by the Americans. They feed the hungry and hospitalize the sick and injured. If I were not a soldier I would give up myself. You are not soldiers—you have no duty to die, but you do have a duty to live…for the sake of your parents…and Japan."

His friend, who had been talking quietly, but sternly, to the four soldiers, now joined them. He handed each girl one piece of hard tack and said, "It's not much, but maybe it will sustain you long enough to find help." The tall soldier then pointed out the direction the girls should go to remain as safe as possible. And with that the students continued along their way with a new-found determination to survive.

Kaori and the other girls made their way to a beach and hid among the coral outcroppings for a time. Driven by their hunger, thirst and fatigue, they finally mustered the courage to turn themselves over to US military authorities. They cut a pitiful sight as they emerged from their hiding place with their arms raised, crying and speaking of their families to each other. Each prayed that they had made the right decision. After being checked for weapons by the soldiers, they were taken to a holding area where other islanders were being held. First, they were sprayed with some strange concoction (DDT to kill lice and fleas) and then given food. The girls were quite reluctant to eat what they had been given, but were encouraged by the other islanders—they had all eaten and were still alive. It was the first food and water any of the four had tasted in days. The food was not to her liking, but Kaori found it filling. And she was glad to remove the mud from her face and hair. And with the clean, albeit ill-fitting, set of clothes she had received, she felt almost human again. They were now in the hands of the enemy and would have to await their fate. But having received food and water and seen injured Okinawans being treated medically dispelled some measure of their apprehension.

It would be nearly eighteen months before Kaori was reunited with any of her family members. She learned much later that most of the Himeyuri girls had not survived, dying either during the intense fighting or by their own hands. But she would make the most of her survival. Sometime later, Kaori finished her schooling under the new education system established by the US administration and would become a primary school teacher in Koza City.

3

Nakagusuku Fumiko squeezed herself underneath one of the few tents available in the camp. The sky was overcast and threatening rain so she wanted to secure a space. For her, and the swelling numbers of Okinawans who were filling the camp, the ordeal was over—she was in the hands of the enemy, away from the major fighting and awaiting her fate. She had not been treated badly by the Americans under the circumstances, but the conditions under which they all lived were far from ideal: the place was not particularly sanitary; there were food shortages; and disease was all around them. Many of the refugees were stricken with tuberculosis and there were even a few lepers among them for a time, but they were quickly moved. She was not sure where they had been taken, although camp scuttlebutt believed they were transported to Yagaji Shima, just off Nakijin on the Motobu peninsula. She tried not to think too much about her circumstances, but she could not help herself.

She sat crouched low at the front end of the tent all the while keeping her eyes fixed on a particular segment of fence line that kept the islanders enclosed. She absent-mindedly glanced down at her arms, barely noticing the all too large olive drab US military shirt that now covered them—clothing was yet one more shortage. She was not sure of what to make of the Americans. They did try to provide shelter, food and clothing, but at the same time she had witnessed some of them looting artifacts and other items as souvenirs—very little escaped her keen eye.

All those years running the Matsuda-ya I suppose has made me the wary sort, she thought half-laughingly to herself. Her stomach gave off a loud grumbling sound, breaking her train of thought—she was famished. The food situation had not always been this bad, but as the numbers of refugees grew, so did the shortages. At first, the refugees were organized into small groups and supervised as they harvested cabbage, sweet potatoes, and onions, which they still found in some abundance. But as their numbers grew, there were not enough US military personnel available to supervise these activities and the crops began rotting in the ground. Then the rations the Americans distributed began to dwindle. Two weeks ago they received only powdered ice cream to eat, but camp residents quickly discovered that mixing the powder with boiling water made a marginally drinkable brew. Last week they received corn meal, but nothing else—no milk or eggs. Nakagusuku Fumiko tried making a soup of it, boiled with the margarine someone else had received as a ration, but it tasted awful.

Lost in these thoughts, she vacantly looked about, again checking the fence line to ensure everything was alright. Then across the broad expanse of the camp's yard she caught sight of a familiar face—or at least she thought she had. Looking once more at the fence, she quickly made her way over to where she had seen the familiar figure. She could hardly believe it. She had not seen anyone she knew since being separated from her sister and brother-in-law several weeks earlier.

As she approached her eyes brightened into a smile and she shouted, "Tamashiro-san!" Munekazu quickly turned to see the face of the proprietress of the Matsuda-ya, once his favorite drinking establishment. They bowed deeply and smiled at one another, but each observing in the other an unmistakable loneliness, something only one who is afflicted with the same malady is likely to recognize.

Nakagusuku Fumiko asked Munekazu to join her over by the tent so they could chat and catch up. She had to maintain her vigil of the fence line after all—what else was there to do? It was her responsibility. As they approached, Munekazu noticed a lone and pitiful figure of an older woman, her hair graying and stringy, wearing a vacant expression on her face and dressed in an oversized US military uniform. *She might have been beautiful once,* he thought to himself, *but she is a wretched sight now.* As she walked back and forth with her arms crossed, he began to notice a pattern to her gait—she took no more than ten steps in any one direction and would then quickly turn in the opposite direction. She would, on occasion spit over her shoulder, and having done so, utter a few words to herself and begin her ritual anew.

Nakagusuku Fumiko watched Munekazu's expression for a moment and then broke the silence by asking him, "Don't you know who that is?"

Munekazu returned her gaze with a quizzical expression and responded, "I'm sure I've never seen that woman."

She smiled compassionately and said softly, "It is Ushī. She suffers from the madness of this war."

Nakagusuku Fumiko explained to Munekazu that she knew few of the details that comprised Ushī's life since she last had seen her in October 1944. She had always presumed Ushī died in the attack. She had, however, learned a little about her more recent ordeals from the islanders who brought her here to the camp. Apparently the family had been seeking shelter and happened upon the cave where Ushī was still in hiding. It appeared to them that she was in extreme distress because she had not left the cave in days, abandoning even the most basic human formalities of finding a suitable place to relieve herself or first removing her clothing to do so—she simply took care of those functions as she needed to without moving. The mother took great pity upon her and cleaned her up as best she could, bringing Ushī along with them as their family reported to the refugee camp.

"That is when I first saw her," explained Nakagusuku Fumiko. "Well, Ushī has always been like a daughter to me. I was heartbroken to see her in this condition, but grateful she was alive. In any case, what kind of person would I be if I abandoned her now? Besides, as it turns out, I took her best years from her. So I explained to the interpreter that she was my daughter and that I would take full responsibility for her care. I don't know where all of this will end for us, but we will travel that road together. And whatever horrors she has experienced will probably remain locked inside her...maybe it's for the best." Then turning to Munekazu she asked how he and his family were doing.

Munekazu's facial expression became forlorn and tears welled up in his eyes. He explained the tragedy of his mother and then of Tomiko and the children. But Nakagusuku Fumiko herself was moved to tears by Munekazu's explanation of what had happened to Yoshiko. Having made it as far as Mabuni, he believed they might actually survive the battle. But he also recognized a growing sadness in his wife as she withdrew ever further from him and the world around them—the loss of their children and her sister weighed upon her heavily. One evening he had gone off to try and find something for them to eat. When he returned, he caught only a brief glimpse of her as she hurled herself off the cliffs of Mabuni, along with several other women and children. He shouted her name, but could not be certain she heard him. In any event, it had not stopped her from taking her own life or that of their unborn child. The words she spoke to him at the pandanus grove would forever remain seared on his heart—"I cannot bring a child into such a world of violence and hatred."

Hundreds of islanders jumped from the cliffs of Mabuni or ones very much like them during the battle, either voluntarily or forcibly, becoming gyokusai in the process, choosing the path of a broken jewel to commemorate Japan's failed past rather than its future. Yoshiko's reasoning had been different—she had tried to save her unborn child from a future of uncertainty and pain, doing so the only way she knew how.

Munekazu's life would take a dramatic turn in the coming months and years. He never forgave himself for the deaths of his family members and because of this, chose never to remarry. After remaining in the camps for many months, he returned to teaching for a time, but he had been deeply impacted by the war and found himself increasingly more involved in peace activism on the island. He would become one of Okinawa's more prominent activists, over the years advocating removal of all military forces from the island, US and Japanese alike. He was finally reunited with family members at the beginning of 1947. He never learned what happened to his close friend, Jiro, who was killed early on in the bombing of Naha, but his absence was a void almost as cold and bottomless as the loss of his family.

Nakagusuku Fumiko did what she knew best. She was finally able to open a small bar in Naha catering to the local population—she did not want her bar to become a hang-out for US military personnel; there were plenty of places prepared to welcome them. She preferred to return to her traditional Okinawan roots. And true to her word, Ushī remained by her side; and to her way of thinking, that was just fine. Not knowing the whereabouts of her sister or her husband, Ushī was the only family she had left. While Ushī never fully recovered, she was able to help out around the bar with simple tasks. Munekazu and Nakagusuku Fumiko maintained a close relationship over the years, Ushī serving as a major bond between them.

* * *

Megumi and Seiho wound up as people without a country—her prognosis of their predicament years earlier had been eerily accurate. At the war's conclusion, Peruvian officials were unwilling to repatriate Japanese citizens or Peruvians of Japanese descent. After trying unsuccessfully for a time to remain in the United States, Seiho and Megumi found themselves among the 900 Japanese or Japanese Latin Americans repatriated to Japan and Okinawa. Working a few odd jobs in the Naha area enabled Seiho to save enough money to purchase a modest plot of land near Itoman and take up sugar cane farming, an occupation at which he was moderately successful. He was reunited with his family in mid-1947.

Megumi's parents returned to Japan, where she and her mother remained in touch. Her father, however, stubborn to the end, at first remained unwilling to speak to his daughter or to accept Seiho as a member of the family. After witnessing first-hand the widespread destruction that Japan suffered during the war, however, he underwent a Damascene Conversion, and came to appreciate Seiho's work ethic and devotion to his daughter. He jokingly referred to Seiho as an *Okinawan samurai.*

Atsuko and Harumi were repatriated to Japan during the summer of 1946 from the refugee camp on Saipan and the two returned to Okinawa by year's end. Having few skills, Atsuko worked at various odd jobs for a time until Kazuo and Kiyoko helped her find employment on a US military installation at a non-commissioned officers' club as a waitress. Harumi flourished in this environment and after completing her schooling attended the University of the Ryukyus where she would ultimately become a professor of philosophy.

* * *

The Tamashiro family, battered, beaten and torn asunder by the war mirrored the circumstances of thousands of other families on Okinawa—their story was neither more tragic nor more fortunate than the fates that befell others. War is the great equalizer, discriminating against no one—young and old; good and bad; rich and poor; victor and vanquished—all stand face-to-face with death. In the case of Okinawa, however, civilians paid an unconscionably heavy price, with a death toll ranging between 100,000-150,000, a number that constituted one-fourth to one-third of the island's population at the time.

The two militaries suffered significant losses as well. US casualties eclipsed 49,000: 12,520 killed or missing and another 36,631 wounded. The Imperial Japanese Army's casualties were approximately double those the Americans suffered: roughly 110,000 Japanese soldiers lost their lives.

Thus, the battle for Okinawa does not stand as testament to military heroism, battlefield valor or great strategic success, but rather for the enduring message it continues for provide to all mankind.

Nuchi Du Takara (O: Life is a treasure)

終わり

The End

Historical fiction that lives.

We publish fiction that captures the contrasts, the achievements, the optimism and the radicalism of ordinary and extraordinary times across the world.

We're open to all time periods and we strive to go beyond the narrow, foggy slums of Victorian London. Where are the tales of the people of fifteenth century Australasia? The stories of eighth century India? The voices from Africa, Arabia, cities and forests, deserts and towns? Our books thrill, excite, delight and inspire.

The genres will be broad but clear. Whether we're publishing romance, thrillers, crime, or something else entirely, the unifying themes are timescale and enthusiasm. These books will be a celebration of the chaotic power of the human spirit in difficult times. The reader, when they finish, will snap the book closed with a satisfied smile.